COPS LIE!

by

LEONARD LOVE MATLICK

CHAPTER 1

"You going to charge me!" NYPD officer Charley Griffin looked at the store clerk incredulously.

"YOU'RE GOING TO CHARGE- ME!" he shouted.

The female store clerk, Niela Patel, unsure, blankly looked at him, then backed away and then looked over to the store manager.

"No, No. It's okay officer" Lomash Singh said coming over. And then to the clerk.

"Cops don't pay; don't you know that idiot?" and then looking straight at PO Griffin, smiling, showing a gold front tooth,

"Officer it's okay, no problem" handing the bag containing an extra - large coffee and hard roll to him. He looked back at the clerk sternly; Indians treat women as worthless; not even human beings. As Lomash walked away, the cop took more items and put them on the counter. Four candy bars, 3 sodas, a couple of bags of nuts and a large bag of Doritos.

"Here. Put these in too. "Griffin said looking thru the clerk like he couldn't believe that she didn't know that cops don't pay-EVER!

Niela nodded sheepishly and put them into a large bag along with the other items that the cop didn't pay for.

Griffin took the bag, shook his head and said aloud to Officer Pete Ryan,

"Can you believe this? They're gonna charge us?"

"What are you gonna do?" Ryan said, "these people, they don't know any better."

The two cops walked out of the store into their precinct car numbered 4589. Ryan got behind the wheel.

Griffin spoke into the intercom to call Central Dispatch.

"five - (slowly) five – (even slower) five. 9 Charlie is on meal break at 0400 hours." The police platoons are named Adam, Bravo, Charlie, David, Eddie, etc. The 9 signifies that they are from the 9th precinct.

"10-4" came the dispatchers reply"

'"four" Griffin replied for the shortened reply to 10-4 that signified okay. Griffin elbowed Ryan and grinned.

"Are you going to do an 8 to 4 shift for OT?" he said. They were working the 12 midnight to 8AM shift.

Cops like the 12 midnight to 8AM shift because that's when the skels come out and that's when they make most of their arrests. The most violent crimes occur between 8PM to 4AM. Skels are the term cops use for criminals, not perps. That's the term writers gave. Skels are short for skeletons, that's what drug addicts look like, and the name stuck.

"No. I'm bushed already." Ryan said. They already had one arrest made. They saw this black skel, Truman Delerme, walking and pulled their car up to the man because his clothing appeared to show a dip in his waistband suggestive of carrying a handgun. It was actually a large comb, but Griffin had a throw-away gun in his pants and threw it on the street, an L380 Lorcin, as he got out of the cruiser. The L380 is one of the top five guns favored by criminals. Griffin's report (his UF61 or '61') stated that the officers witnessed the criminal throw the gun into the street as the cops pulled over to the curb. Not true, but who was the Judge going to believe, definitely not the skel.

"So do you want to go to Easy's after our shift" he said again tasting the booze that would also be free for cops. And then in an afterthought," I'll drive." Officers coming off of the 12midnight to 8AM shift like to party- a lot. And Easy's (The Easy Score) on West 52nd Street and Broadway, was still the primary meeting place for cops to not only imbibe in the free booze, but grab a "feel" from some of the dancers, and blow off steam or just to bitch about other cops. Or even have a face to face meet with other cops, rather than talk on the phone or exchange e-mails, which always left a tell-tale trail that could come back and bite you in the ass.

"Sounds good. Maybe we can get O'Donnell and McDonald to go also." Ryan stated. 'I'll give them a call."

CHAPTER 2

Detectives work only 10AM to 6PM, Monday thru Friday, are dressed in a suit and tie and hardly ever work nights or weekends. All it takes to become a Detective is to have only one year in grade, 150 arrests and the commanding officer's approval. That's what the Police Chief's office will say. However, in real life, if your family doesn't have cops in their family tree, you can forget getting a gold shield. There are special circumstances, such as if you make like 300 false arrests in one year, or shield the Mayor's daughter from getting pinched for a DUI.

Detective 2nd Grade Tony Philadelphia was approaching his desk in the 9th Precinct squad room on East 5th Street carrying his container of coffee, that he had bought from the same coffee shop as Griffin did, when Lt. Mark Murphy knocked on his office window and motioned to him to come into his office.

"Philadelphia, I just got a call from Highway 1 that a couple of ours was hit by an 18 wheeler." Highway 1 is out of Marine Park in

Brooklyn- motorcycles and patrol cars that ride the highways in the city.

"Jeez", Tony said," Anybody hurt?"

"2 dead, 1 critical and 1 is on a ventilator." Lt. Murphy stated. "You may know some of them- Griffin, Ryan, O'Donnell and McDonald."

"Who's dead and who are the ones who are still alive?" Tony asked.

"Griffin and O'Donnell are dead. Ryan, he's critical, and McDonald is on a ventilator. "Murphy said. "I want you to go see what happened, because Cap says it's our guys. It's the least that we can do. It was right outside of The Easy Score. You know where it is?"

"Loo, (or the diminutive for Lt., Lou) I know where The Easy Score is, everybody does. But, Loo, I've already got 3 grounders, plus all of my other cases. Can't somebody else go?" Tony said.

Tony is in the Homicide Squad, but it's got a fancy new title called, the Homicide Analysis Unit of the Central Investigation and Resource Division of the Detectives Bureau.

"No one is available." Murphy said.

Tony responded, "Loo, The Easy Score is by West 52nd Street and Broadway, which is Midtown North—they're going to claim it as in their own." Most police precincts have 150 officers in 3 shifts, but Midtown North and Midtown South each have 300 cops.

"True" Murphy said. "But like I said, it's our guys, and the Mayor and Commissioner are there already."

Tony thought that Murphy didn't want to hear it, and nodded respectfully. The brass probably wanted all of the sordid details. The Mayor and the Police Commissioner wanted the publicity. He never even got to drink his coffee.

As he approached the accident scene on the West Side Highway by West 52nd Street with his blue and red lights flashing, he could see the crowds. And New Yorkers always crowded around something to see, especially if cops were involved. He parked behind one of the cop cars. He started to show his gold shield to one of the female policewomen, in order to let him pass, but immediately realized that he knew her as she turned to him. He could never forget that ass.

"Detective Phil…" he started to say.

"Hi Tony, 'er, should I say Mr. Philadelphia." Megan Ryan smiled. The years had not been kind to her or for that matter most policewomen on the job for 10 years or more.

Megan Ryan was a blonde policewoman with big tits hanging close to the ground and an even bigger ass. Tony had fucked her in a police cruiser when they were on a tour together many years earlier. She still had the hots for him. At that time the then Police Commissioner in order to satisfy the women libbers, made opportunity's available for female cops. They would be paired with a male officer. Bad idea. Most female cops got laid whether they wanted to or not. That's why you now see female cops paired together.

"Hi Meg. Long time no see. How are you?"

"I'm fine." She smiled again at him.

He knew she wanted him to say something more, to get back to where they were, but 10 years makes a difference, even with ex-lovers.

"That's good". He mumbled and started to walk past her to the accident scene.

A Trade Mart tractor trailer had all but demolished a blue Honda Civic. The tractor trailer had hardly a dent, but the Civic was like tin .There was no front; all you could make out was the trunk of the car and a mangled mess of steel. What looked like parts of bodies were still in the car. He made his way to the sea of cops and plainclothes detectives mulling around talking to each other. The Mayor and Police Commissioner were already there. They made a show of face to the TV and press and then walked away.

Detective John Rossi of Midtown North, recognized Tony and started to wave him away.

"Hey Philadelphia, this is ours"

Tony had worked with Rossi in the 2-3 in East Harlem and never liked him; he was a blowhard and an A #1 asshole.

"Take it easy Rossi, these are our guys".

"It doesn't matter, it's still in our territory." Rossi bellowed to him. Cops are very territorial. Nobody from another precinct takes over. They wouldn't get credit for the collar, or the investigation otherwise.

"Do you want my Loo to talk to your Loo about this?" Tony asked.

"Like I just said, this is ours." Rossi responded.

"Hey, take it easy Rossi. Cop to cop, what happened here?"

"It seems that your guys can't hold their liquor. They were at Easy's watching all of the tits and ass's and they scoffed down who knows how many straight shots. Then they went the wrong way down the West Side Highway and hit this truck head-on" Rossi mentioned.

The Easy Score, like most tits and ass bars, give the cops free booze after their shifts end. Or sometimes before their shifts end. They know that they'll get protection from the skels and the wise guys.

PO Charles Griffin was a known drunk. A lot of cops are. But Griffin had been caught 5 times for DUI and never got suspended or anything. There is something called "the blue laws". Not the rest of the world where liquor is banned on Sunday, no, to this rule is the unwritten, unspoken rule amongst cops, prosecutors, Judges. Nobody touches a cop. EVER! Whether the cop is white, black, Asian, Hispanic – it doesn't matter. All cops are blue and above the law.

The Trade-Mart truck driver, Robert James, was shaken up, but not hurt. At 27,000 pounds this 18 wheeler was a lethal weapon when the Honda Civic hit it. It happened so fast he couldn't even hit the air brakes, and had everything in him to prevent the trailer from jackknifing all across the West Side Highway. But he was an experienced truck driver with 30 years of driving big rigs, and that's why Trade-Mart hired him. But he had been awake for 28 hours straight, without the required 6 hours rest that was mandatory by the NTSB, and that would lead to an investigation of him and the Trade Mart practices of pushing their drivers to the limit, without sleep.

Detective Sgt. Jake Grinnan from the Chief of Detectives office was sitting in his car next to the shaken up truck driver, trying to make sense of how this went down. He noticed Tony.

"Philadelphia, what are you doing here?" he said. All cops are addressed by their last name, whether they are friends or not. It is the same in the military and the police are a quasi -military organization.

"Hi Chief. This was our guys. Cap sent me here to check it out."

"That's right, it's your guys," the Chief commented, "But Rossi is wrapping it up." Then in an afterthought,

"Shit! 2 dead, 1 critical and McDonald on a ventilator. I don't think that he's going to make it either. Fucking Griffin, I should have had him taken off the force a long time ago from all those DUI's he had."

"Chief, I don't want to say anything about the dead, let him rest in peace, but every cop in the city knew about Griffin's drinking problem." Tony stated.

"But you're a little better than the rest of them, Philadelphia, why didn't you say something." Chief Grinnan asked.

"Chief, I'm not the person to talk to about that – first of all, I don't rat on a fellow cop." Tony responded.

"That's nice to hear, but I always had you down for something better, especially after the Penn Station shootout"

"That's past history Chief.' Tony stated. "I don't even know how I survived, let alone earn a commendation." Tony is going on now 12 years on the job, 8 as a detective. That famous shootout is now taught at the Police Academy like the Kobiashi Maru on Star Trek.

Tony was working the 8AM shift to 4PM shift on street patrol with Harry Brown when they were together at Midtown South. They were at the corner of West 32nd Street and 7th Avenue, right across from Penn Station, just standing around. It was mostly tourists and commuters trying to get home. Like most cops, they were trying to show a police presence, to ward off any incidents. They just want to put in their 20 years, collect a city pension, and retire as a security consultant someplace. He had never fired his gun on the job except for target practice and qualifying. He never even removed his gun from his holster unless he had to. He didn't want to. But that is the reason that most cops join the police force, is to be able to use a gun with impunity. Some cops like to show that they are big men and take their gun out at every opportunity, like Griffin, who should never have been vetted for the NYPD; but not Tony.

As a kid growing up in Brooklyn, he would always go to Coney Island to play at shooting at an arcade. He loved this stuff and whenever he had a chance he would sneak away to do this, finding some change here and there to get to an arcade. No one would have guessed that he was really a crack shot. More than even a marksman. You practice something for 20 some odd years and you get good at it. Very good at it. He would go to the NYPD outdoor range at the end of Pelham Bay Park and practice also. He was even asked if he wanted to become a shooting instructor at the police academy. Tony said no. That it was hard to teach shooting. There was the basics, letting go of your breath before you squeezed the trigger and shoot a few feet in front of a moving target (like a quarterback does with a football) so that it would hit them. Stuff like that you can't teach; it's inborn.

Just then, a skel comes out of the bank with his gun drawn and holding a bag full of money. He immediately spots the cops and yells "FUCK! COPS!!" FUCK! FUCK! FUCK!! And points the gun at Brown.

He fires point blank at Brown, who was shot in the face. Tony reacted immediately drawing his gun out by rote as if he was doing target practice, He fired his gun and hit the skel in the neck. There were 5 of them. The rest either didn't hear the first one yell," FUCK!" or "COPS!!" or see him fall, but skels are stupid, like circus clowns coming out of that tiny car, they used the revolving door to come out. As each one came out, this was target practice to Tony; one shot each to the head as the revolving door kept swinging. The last skel saw the others fall and tried to get the revolving door to go backwards, but it can't. Tony drilled him thru the glass and the skel fell.

The first one who was shot in the neck was still alive. Tony stradled him and put his gun into the mouth of the skel and said," Move and you'll never make it to the hospital."

The skel waved his arms to get the gun out of his mouth and that was it. One shot into his mouth and blood splattered all over. Tony turned to Brown who was unconscious. Tourists, commuters had fled. It looked like an empty city. Tony started to apply the CPR that he learned in 1st aid training at the police academy on Brown. His breathing was very shallow. He then tried mouth to mouth on him. A citizen nearby said,

"Can I help?"

"Push hard on his chest!" Tony yelled.

He got up and reached for his hand held com,

"10-13! Officer down! I repeat, Officer down! Need assistance."

The dispatcher called out," Who is this? Identify yourself."

"Philadelphia- MSN Badge 34726"

"What is your position?" the dispatcher said.

"Across from Penn Station!" Tony yelled annoyed.

"State your emergency?" the dispatcher again asked for details

"Do you understand that I'm trying to do CPR on a fellow officer?"

"Officer, I'm just trying to get some information." she said.

"And I'm trying to save a fellow officers life. Now get someone here now."

"I just need more information –like what is the officer's condition, who is the officer and where is your exact position"

"Honey, my exact position is straddling Officer Brown giving him mouth to mouth CPR!!"

"Officer, you don't have to get snippy with me, I'm just trying to do my job."

"Then do your job and get an ambulance here right now!" Tony yelled in-between breaths of air into Brown's mouth.

"FINE!" the dispatcher said, annoyed. "You can say this without getting snippy." She said again annoyed at the disrespect she felt that she was getting from this cop. "All units, 10-13, respond to Penn Station area, officer down, officer needs assistance."

In order to save money and put more cops on the street, the city hired civilian dispatchers, most of whom were on welfare to give them a job and an opportunity. But you can't change years of generational differences with cops and the community it polices. Too many lingering hatred of cops and vice versa occurred.

"Officer", the dispatcher again came on, "What is the Officer's condition?"

"He's been shot in the face. There's been a bank hold-up, a 10-20."

"Well, why didn't you say that officer?"

"Because I'm trying to save a fellow officers life and not answer your stupid questions!!"

The dispatcher now was getting really annoyed at this white officer, who was not giving her RESPECT. "Officer, help is on the way. I think that you should apologize for talking to me like this."

"What is your name dispatcher?"

"Tamika Torrance."

"Well dispatcher Torrance-NEVER!!"

PO Brown made it to Roosevelt Hospital and was put on a ventilator with a medically induced coma. They did a tracheotomy and put this blue braided thin tube into the trach opening. However, he died two days later and was given an inspector's funeral. He was posthumously promoted to Detective 1st Grade so his widow would collect a bigger pension. Police from all over the country came to his funeral. You can see his picture on the plaque at 1 Police Plaza.

Tony was given the NYPD's highest honor, the medal for meritorious duty, and promoted to Detective, even though his family tree did not contain any cops.

After talking to Chief Grinnan, Tony told PO Megan Ryan," Meg, I'm going to leave my car here awhile okay."She nodded. He left his car at the accident scene and walked the few blocks to The Easy Score on West 52nd Street and Broadway. At 11:45AM it was starting to fill up with cops that had gotten off from the midnight to 8AM shift, and those who were going on their lunch break in the 8AM to 4PM shift. Most of the cops were already drunk and had started to feel up the dancers, sticking dollar bills all the way up in their panties.

Tony made his way up to the bar. There was already full barstools. He moved to two empty stools that had been vacated by cops feeling up the dancers.

"Are you here?" One goofy looking PO that Tony did not recognize asked him knowing that the other cops went to feel up the dancers. In bars, leaving your drink on the bar is like a reserved spot or like a dog staking his territory with his piss. It's his.

"Yes, I'm here." Tony said sternly and looked at him annoyed and elbowed his way between him and the bar.

He waved to the barmaid, Angela, who gave him a big smile.

"Hi baby" she said, coming over to him, leaning across the bar and planting a big kiss on his cheek. "What can I get for you honey?"

"Hi Angela." Tony sheepishly blurted out as these hanger-on cops looked at him.

"I need to ask you something." Tony whispered" Come over to the end of the bar." They walked to the service area of the bar.

"It's about Griffin." he said.

"Griffin- that bastard." She said. "Tony, he's disgusting, hitting on me all of the time. I would never do it with him in a million years."

"You won't have to – he's dead." Tony mentioned.

Angela had a reputation and a face that signified that she was "easy". An easy lay. And she was. Dirty blond hair, cute round ass, petite breasts, sleepy bedroom hazel eyes, liked to party too much to have a steady beau. Tony had fucked her many times, not regularly, as she wanted him too, but she liked the way he would do it to her, in many different positions for a long time. She had told him once that he had all of the requirements to be a porn star.

He laughed," I only wish."

Usually, there was at least two barmaids on duty all of the time, especially this shift, from 12AM to 12PM.Claire was the other one. She was like Angela but thinner with dark hair. She had a body that begged to be fucked, and all the guys would say that she was built like a brick shithouse. But she was selective about who got into her pants. She had thought about doing it with Tony also, but she didn't want to steal him from Angela.

Angela kept bragging about Tony's sexual prowess,

"He's always ready", she told her girl to girl," And he wants to do it so many times that he won't get off of me!" They both giggled. "But he only wants to see me once in a while."

"So he's not your steady?" Claire asked.

"No." Angela responded.

"Then would you mind then if I saw him?" Claire asked.

"No. Not at all". Angela said.

After hearing that, Claire decided to do everything that she could to get Tony to take her out on a date and let him fuck her several times, like he did with Angela.

"Did you serve Griffin or did Claire?" Tony asked. He probably knew the answer since Griffin was always hitting on Angela. Griffin had always wanted to get into that piece of ass, since almost every cop at that bar had done it with Angela.

"I served him." Angela said." He had 7 straight shots of Jack. Not even water with it." she added.

Tony told Angela what happened. That their car had hit an 18 wheeler and Griffin was dead.

"I'm not sorry that he's dead- he was a really bad person and into a lot of bad things."

"Angela, what do you mean – bad things." Tony asked.

"I can't talk about it here, "she started looking around her, especially at that goofy looking cop, Bobby O'Mara, who had taken a sudden interest in their conversation. "There are too many ears here."

"I'm coming off duty in a few minutes." She said." Why don't you come with me back to my place and I'll tell you what I heard." And then in an afterthought, "Everybody knew." She intonated. She straightened up. "And maybe Tony, you can bring along that Great Dane of yours also. I miss seeing him." She giggled. She liked to call his big cock "The Great Dane."

She went back to check on who needed a refill. Claire waved to him also from across the bar, smiled broadly, and winked at him. Tony thought that she wanted him to fuck her. And maybe she did. Tony smiled back. Looking at her, he immediately started to get an erection.

At 12PM, after she got off of work, Tony walked with Angela back to her place, which was only a few blocks away on West 51st Street. As she opened up the door to her 1st floor apartment, he turned her around and kissed her. He wasn't going to wait for pleasantries. He knew that she wanted him to fuck her and he immediately obliged. He pushed her inside her place, kicked the door shut and leaned her against an easy chair. Then he picked up her wrap around skirt, pulled off her panties and let his "Great Dane" plunge into her from the rear.

"Oh fuck me baby" she yelled.

"How does it feel honey?" He asked plunging it in further. "Does it feel good?"

"It feels wonderful!" she screamed. Tony loved to hear her scream, because he knew that she was enjoying it.

Nobody could fuck her like Tony could, and she told him that every time that he penetrated her. Tony did it many times without coming, and he let her ride him, did it from the front and plunged it into her again from the rear.

After she had come several times, they were both lying on the bed, naked, "You're the best, baby" she said turning to him.

"So are you, honey." He said. "You turn me on all of the time." And then he got down to business.

"So what's this with Griffin? You know something or heard something?" he asked.

"You know baby, as a bartender, you hear things all of the time, especially from you cops," she mentioned. "Especially after a few drinks, you cops, your tongues are wagging non-stop."

"So what specifically did you hear?" Tony asked.

"I heard that Griffin and his crew and several other cops are into a bunch of shit."

"Such as?" Tony asked again for specifics.

"Such as like raiding drug dealers and stealing drugs and money. I heard them brag that they took part in over 300 raids." she said. "They got credit for the arrests and took their stuff. They call it 'Collars for Dollars'"

"WHAT!!" Tony said not believing what he was hearing." I can't believe what you're saying honey. This is just in my Precinct? The 9th precinct?"

"No, sweetie. All over the city. In a lot of police stations." She added. "They call themselves 'the coffin cops."

Tony laughed, "How did they get that name" he asked. "What do they work out of the morgue?"

"No. From what I understand is that they work out of a factory that used to make coffins. Crazy huh?" she mentioned. "Like I said baby, this is what I hear all of the time. Not only from Griffin and his crew, but from a lot of you cops, like Bobby O'Mara, that goofy looking one, that you ran into at the bar."

"I believe what you're telling me honey. But you didn't JUST overhear this at a bar. So where else did you hear all this shit from?"

She started to blush. "Well you know honey that if you were my steady beau, I wouldn't be this source of knowledge."

"So they blabbed in bed huh?"

"Yes. Just like we're talking. These cops like to brag that they are the badest of the bad; that they have a license to steal."

"Angela, I know that some cops are bad, but if this is true, this is really bad."

"It gets worse, Tony." She continued. "The wise guys found out about it and in order to let them continue with stealing this drug stuff, since they supply the drugs, they made them give them protection and also have them whack people that they couldn't get to."

He sat up in the bed. "I never even suspected something like this." He looked at her dumbfounded.

"It's all true babe." She stated matter of factly. "I wouldn't lie to you."

"I believe you honey." He looked straight ahead at the bedroom. He didn't know what to do with this now. Go to the Cap or Loo; go to IAD. Or just forget about it. He wasn't a rat; he didn't want to get fellow cops in trouble. He decided to think about it more.

For now, he wanted what these other cops got from her; more pussy, so he went down on Angela, and then took her again. This time he came in her.

CHAPTER 3

When he got back to his car on the West Side Highway, Meg Ryan was gone. He noticed that PO Ralph Murphy and John Mateo were doing crowd control. People were trying to get out of line and away from the accident.

"DON'T YOU PEOPLE MOVE!" Murphy yelled at the cars lined up trying to turn onto a side street.

"DO YOU HEAR ME!!" he shouted to one black woman driving a small white SUV.

Wrong thing to say. Rochelle Turner was not going to let any man, police or not, tell her what to do. She pressed down on the window release so that the driver's window went down. She leaned her head out of the window and first tried to calmly explain.

"Officer, I got to pick up my son at school, and he's special ed – I can't be late." She told him

"I don't give a fuck if he's disabled- you do not move!" Murphy gritted his teeth at her.

"Officer, you don't understand- I have to go get my son." Rochelle again started to tell him as she started to move out of the line of cars.

After she started to move, Murphy drew his gun and instructed her, "Stop! Get out of the car, NOW!"

Mateo told him," Murphy, take it easy, this woman has a special need, let her go." Murphy didn't even hear him.

"Officer, this can become an emergency for my son if I'm late. Please let me go to him. " Rochelle again pleaded.

"Maam, if you don't get out of the car, NOW, I mean business!"

"Murphy – LET HER GO!" Mateo screamed at him. But again, Murphy was in his own world and just focused on the woman.

Of course, Rochelle did not get out of the car, her son was too important for her to miss being late. The car started to move.

Officer Murphy fired one shot at her head, killing her instantly.

"SHIT!" Mateo yelled. "WHAT THE FUCK DID YOU DO?" He came over to the car window and could see that blood was splattered all over the front of the car. Heads explode when hit from close range.

"My gun went off." He said calmly, turning to Mateo. "And that's what you should say also."

Mateo shook his head.

Later on, on his '61', Murphy wrote," The suspect refused to obey a legitimate order from an officer of the law and my service revolver went off." Officer Mateo said that he also witnessed this unfortunate accident and corroborated Officer Murphy's account.

All that Tony saw was the shooting. He ran over to the scene, as did other cops.

"My gun went off accidently." Murphy stated to nobody in particular. For someone to shoot somebody at close range he was too calm; not even upset. Tony looked at him and then at the dead driver. He shook his head too and went back to his car. Like he was told, this wasn't even his precinct he thought. Let the cops and detectives from Midtown North handle this. If I say something, I'll just get my head handed to me for interfering in another's jurisdiction.

To get to the 9th precinct, which is on the East Side of Manhattan, Tony could have driven downtown on the West Side Highway and then turned uptown on the FDR Drive. But for some reason he didn't do that, probably because he was too upset over the shooting of that woman. Instead, he drove due east along 50th Street to get to the FDR drive going downtown. Passing St. Patrick's Cathedral and the Waldorf-Astoria he entered the 17th precinct territory. He came across a scene straight out of Brooklyn's Bedford-Stuyvesant section instead of the Upper East Side.

One skel, a D'Wayne Johnson, was being taken into custody. He was on his hands and knees in response to commands to get on the ground, when all of a sudden one of the police officer's, Daniel Brogan, started to kick him in the face. Then another police officer, Michael Toomey, started to kick him in the groin. The skel probably passed out unconscious from being hit in the balls. Tony pulled over to the curb and got out of his car. As he approached, two more cops started to kick him also.

Tony showed his gold shield. "HEY! Hey guys,…GUYS! – ENOUGH!"

The cops looked up at being disturbed.

"Detective, this guy was mouthing off to us." One of the cops stated. "We gave him a lawful order to get on the ground, and he was on his hands and knees- not flat on the ground."

"Yeah, but you don't kick him in the face." Tony looked at the skel who probably had a broken jaw. "Call for an ambulance, and book him for disorderly conduct. Was there any other charges pending?"

"Yes sir." PO Michael Toomey said. "We pulled him over for double parking."

"You kicked him in the balls for a traffic stop?" Tony asked incredulously."You cuff him and read him his rights."

"He was being uncooperative, detective and then he started to mouth off at us."

"I don't care; I'm not going to get involved in this" Tony said, waving his hands to signify, no way was he getting into this mess.

"So you don't want a piece of this collar?" another cop asked.

"Just get him help." he said as he turned and walked away ,not wanting yet another precincts trouble.

As Tony started to go back to his car, one more cop (total of 4) now started to kick the skel. And when Tony pulled away, the four cops continued to pound him unmercifully. No cop likes to be mouthed off at. Doesn't the world know that. The officer's '61' would read that the skel was resisting arrest and they had to subdue him.

Tony started driving again towards the FDR drive and he noticed several cops walking their beat. Cops walk like they own the place, they strut to make a presence known to everybody. And if they get up from a sitting position, like their free meal, the pull their guts up, like they're getting ready to be tough guys.

As Tony approached the ramp to the FDR, he saw like maybe, 20 cop cars, lights flashing, sirens blasting, racing after a tan late model Mercury swerving in and out of downtown lanes. He heard many shots being fired at that car, so Tony put on his flashing red and blue lights and took off also in pursuit. The Circus must be in town, Tony thought with this many crazy things happening today.

Two skels in the car, Terrence Williams and William Russell, finally pulled their car to a stop around 23rd Street, in the 13th precinct jurisdiction. Two officers, James McGinty and Peter O'Donnell got out of their cruisers, guns in hand and ran to the stopped car. McGinty jumped up on the hood of the car and took aim at the two skels,

"GET OUT NOW!!"

The two skels looked at each other and Terrence Williams, who had a black glove on, that the officer thought was a gun, gave him the "finger."

Officer McGinty, infuriated, emptied his gun thru the windshield at both of them, killing them instantly. He then re-loaded his weapon and continued to fire at them. A total of 37 shots was fired from his gun. Officer O'Donnell had to jump on the car hood, and attempt to yank the gun out of McGinty's hand.

"STOP!! THEY'RE DEAD!"

McGinty looked at him and said,"I thought that they had a gun and that they were going to kill me and you." Later on it would show that the two skels were unarmed and that their car had merely backfired, prompting one cop to say that they were being fired upon, which started this merry chase. McGinty would write on his '61' the same thing, that he thought that they were armed and that he was protecting his partner and himself. Of course Officer O'Donnell backed up his partner's story. When McGinty's commanding officer of his precinct saw him, he said, "Good job." And gave him a pat on the back. It had to be a full moon, Tony thought.

When he got back to the squad room, Tony knocked on Loo's door.

"Loo, got a second?" Tony asked.

"Sure come on in." Loo said as he motioned for Tony to come into his office.

"Loo, I just came back from the accident scene with Griffin and the others, and I found out a bunch of shit about them." Tony said.

"OK, fill me in." Loo stated.

"Well, maybe we need to get the Cap and IAD involved in this also." Tony answered.

"Tell me first and then we'll see who has to get involved." Loo mentioned.

"Here's the nitty- Griffin and maybe the rest of the officers that were in the accident were involved in a bunch of shit, like maybe stealing drugs and money from skels and much worse." Tony responded.

"Such as?" Loo asked.

"Such as working for wise guys and getting them tipped off as to raids and also being used to whack guys." Tony mentioned.

"WHAT?" Loo questioned. "And where did you hear this from?"

"There's a barmaid at Easy's that I know. You know the place near where I went earlier- The Easy Score, that overheard a lot of this shit." Tony mentioned.

"So you heard a barmaid tell you all of this about fellow cops, and you believe this?" Loo asked incredulously.

"Loo, I believe her. She slept with some of them, not Griffin, and they blabbed about how many arrests they had made, like over 300, and that they kept the loot and the drugs." Tony responded.

"And how about this wise guy stuff?" Loo asked," She also said that too?"

"From what I understand Loo, they wanted to impress her, that they were this bad ass type of cop." Tony mentioned also. "I don't know which wise guys, but she was pretty emphatic that they were on the payroll of the mob."

"Philadelphia, do you think that this is true and not some bitch trying to get back at some cops for fucking her and leaving her; you know hell hath no fury like a woman scorned." Loo said.

"Loo, I personally know this bartender, her name is Angela, and I believe her." Tony responded.

"Did you fuck her too?" Loo asked grinning.

"Well, let's just say, that I know her well." Tony sheepishly said.

"Because if this is true, then IAD is going to question her and question you and a lot more dirty linen is going to come thru the wash." Loo said.

"Loo, I'm not a rat. I'm just passing some information that I learned from a friend that needs to be looked into." Tony stated.

"Philadelphia, if what you're saying is correct, then this could be bigger than the Knapp Commission." Loo said.

"Okay, but I'm no Serpico, or anyone like that, Loo." Tony added." I'm not going to wear a wire on a fellow cop."

"OK, I'll talk to the Cap and IAD. But I want you to start checking this shit out to see if this is real or some bitch's lies. Start with Griffins place, his arrest records, stuff like that." Loo said.

"But what about all of my other cases?" Tony asked.

"You have to do those too." Loo mentioned.

"Can I get OT for this?" Tony asks.

"No." Loo stated," The city is trying to put a cap on overtime. Take Longo with you and check this out."

Tony knew that the Loo or Cap did not care if he had a hundred cases- just get it done, and also be able to do all of your other work too. Supervisors don't care, and that's why so many cases never get solved.

CHAPTER 4

Detective squads are made up of usually 12 to 24 guys. A Lieutenant (or the whip of the squad) , a Sergeant, or a 1st Grade, several 2nd grades, and a couple of 3rd grades. Most detectives are assigned their partner case by case by the Lieutenant who's affectionately called "loo" or "Lou".

Detective squad rooms always look the same. They're on the 2nd or 3rd floor of a precinct with green metal desks, back to back so that the detectives face each other. The city still hasn't gotten around to modernize the detective's computers which sit on each desk. Stacks of DD5's(or '5's) reports of homicides, line the desks in uneven stacks, so that it's hard for a detective to remember which case he's working on.

If a patrol officer made 150 arrests in 3 years, he would be interviewed for the detective bureau. So that's why each patrol officer wants to make arrests. The more you stop, the more you find. They're not interested if it's legal or not; the department keeps the numbers.

Each cop will say, I can go look for it, because I need an arrest. And the NYPD requires that you do a minimum of 2 or 3 arrests a month. If you don't do it, you get punished. You are transferred from patrol and put on the least desirable post- directing traffic.

Ed Longo is Tony's sometimes partner. Also a 2nd grade detective and trying to finish his 20 years and get his pension.

"LONGO!!" Loo yelled." Go with Philadelphia and check this shit out!" he said referring to what Tony had found out from Angela.

Longo was a big man and moved slowly. Too many free meals and free booze takes its toll on a body, especially a cop's body. Look at pictures of officers who have been on the force like 10 years or more and you can see a 9 month pregnant paunch, female cop asses as wide as a city block, and men balding from years of too tight hats, not to mention the scourge of cops –flat feet from walking 8 hour shifts and ulcers from drinking too many cups of free coffee.

Ed Longo was on the force over 18 years and looking forward to retiring with his pension at 20 years of service at half-pay. And like most civil servants, he loved to tell anyone within shouting range to ask him how much longer he had until he retired.

"One year, 7 months, 3 days, 42 minutes." He would say proudly." And do you want to know the number of seconds? Go ahead ask me?" he looked at his watch, "I'll tell you anyway-32 seconds as of right now."

NYPD has at any one time around 37,000 officers. There are 7,000 detectives, 12,000 patrol cops, 3000 traffic cops, 5,000 school safety patrol officers, plus 5,000 subway cops and 5,000 housing authority cops. Most of the 12,000 patrol cops are answering calls for service full-time. In busier precincts, like Midtown South or North, they are indentured to the radio, with no time for prevention. Although Internal Affairs would usually handle a case like this, the officer who initially "caught" the case about bad cops (Tony) is handed the case, in addition to everything else he has. If he can't solve a case (murder or robbery) within 4 days, it becomes a cold case and put on the shelf until some more information comes along.

Most of the cases that detectives solve are called "grounders" easy open and shut cases; ie. a husband shoots a wife, a bar fight where somebody has an argument and kills somebody with a gun or a knife. Cops love these because it gives them a lot of credit on arrests for their records for promotion, seniority, etc.

Longo and Tony went to Griffin's place. He lived in SoHo at 19 Mercer Street just off of Canal Street in a 5 story row house from the 1890's. There were approximately 8 apartments in this particular apartment house, mostly young, rich guys and gals who worked in the financial district or actors and actresses. The super, Ivan, wasn't going to let them in even after Tony and Longo flashed their gold shields.

"Officer Griffin was killed in a car crash and we have to look for next of kin stuff." Tony told him annoyed that a gold shield won't give him immediate entrance to any place.

Ivan took them in the elevator to the 3rd floor. Apartment 3C was Griffin's.

As soon as Tony and Longo went inside, it was very clear to them that this wasn't done on a cop's salary.

"Holy shit!" Longo exclaimed." This is NICE!."

Tony looked at the high ceilings, the baroque furniture, even the toilet fixtures were of the highest quality. They went into the kitchen with the 6 burner stove, Garland oven and two refrigerators.

"Who has two refrigerators?" Tony asked.

"Someone with money." Longo said. "But definitely not on a cops salary."

They went into the bedroom, with wall to wall TV's, entertainment units and cameras on the ceiling, and started to stare at the closets.

"Quite a clothes horse." Tony said flipping thru Griffin's suits, shoes and dress shirts.

"Hey, I didn't know he was a dandy." Longo said fingering the silk fabrics.

Then they started to go thru the drawers, all neatly assembled by underwear, socks, t-shirts, etc. Even his bills were arranged in order.

"Philadelphia", Longo said, "We've got to comb thru this stuff and camp out here."

"Uh-huh.". Tony said, amazed at what he saw.

"Ivan" Tony motioned to the super, "What does something like this go for?"

"Are you kidding me? A triplex in SOHO? "Ivan said. "When the market was at its top a few years ago, it was around 7 million, but now between 3.5 to 5 million."

"WHAT!!" Tony exclaimed. "Where did he get the money for this. After all he's a cop!"

"I believe that he had a co-signer or somebody was sub-letting it to him. I don't know. You'll have to ask the rental agent." Ivan stated.

"Okay, we'll do that." Tony said. "Who's the rental agent?"

"Cushman and Gold" Ivan said. "There's also some interesting people who live here in the building."

"Like who?" Longo asked.

"Like the singer Nora, the actor who played the Vulcan in the Star Trek movies, and even Justin, the actor."

Longo made a face like he was impressed.

"Ivan, one more thing." Tony turned to the super, "Did Griffin get many guests here?"

"I don't know. What do you mean by many guests? More than one?"

Tony looked at Longo and then asked Ivan," I'm guessing that you mean that there were many guests?"

"Well, he was quite the ladies man. I mean that there was a different girl here every day." Ivan mentioned. "Since he worked the night shift. I never saw many guys come here, but there was a lot of girls, a lot."

Again, Tony looked at Longo.

"What do you mean by a lot? More than one or two?" Tony asked.

"Oh yeah." Ivan said." I've seen him bring 2 and sometimes even 3 at a time here. I guess that he was into twosomes and threesomes . Must have been quite the stud."

"Apparently not on a cops salary." Longo mentioned. "Philadelphia," Longo motioned for him to come closer. "How come we live in such shit and he gets all of this nice stuff? Money, broads, all of this" He moved his arm all around to span the luxury apartment. "He must have been dirty."

"Yeah," Tony said. "Very dirty."

Everybody in the 9th precinct knew Griffin, whether those cops on patrol or those in the detective squads. He was big, burly with an attitude that said "Keep away or you'll be sorry." Most of them gave him a wide berth.

When Tony and Longo got back to the squad room, Tony walked into Loo's office.

"Loo, this guy is dirty." Tony said. "We just came back from his apartment in SoHo and it's like walking into a palace .You should see some of this stuff".

"Yeah," Longo said. "He's got 2 refrigerators. Who has 2 refrigerators?"

"Loo, we need to get a court order and camp out there." Tony stated. "And also do the same for the others involved in the accident."

Loo looked at them. "Okay, whatever you need. I talked to Cap and IAD and we're all on the same page." Loo said. "And Philadelphia, OT is authorized for this."

Tony smiled. He was going to go to the Detectives union if he had to work OT and not get paid for it.

"Also start looking at his arrest records." Loo stated to them. "We may just come up with something interesting."

Every time a police officer makes an arrest or does something like a stop and frisk, the officer is supposed to fill out a form to record the details and that is called a '61' or a complaint report ; if a Detective fills out a form, it's called a DD5 or "5, which is divided by color. The original '5' is blue, and when new information happens it is pink. Officers fill out the form by hand and the forms are entered manually into a database, called an Omni form. The precinct clerical staff, called a 124 room clerk, is responsible for taking the responding officers arrest report, or stop and frisk report, that's associated with it and signed off by a supervisor, and it is stored in a database of the criminal records section. After it is entered in the database, the original file is stored in the NYPD data warehouse.

Any police officer with access to a computer can access this database and find these arrest records.

Tony and Longo started to look thru Griffins arrest records.

"Wow." Tony said amazed that Angela was right. There were over 300 arrests credited to Griffin in less than 3 years. "Look at some of this stuff Longo."

"Reason for arrest –actions indicative of a drug transaction; reason for arrest – suspicious bulge; reason for arrest – inappropriate attire for the season; reason for arrest –carrying suspicious object; and get this one- reason for arrest- other!"

"The list goes on and on like this." Tony said not believing what he was reading.

Longo was looking at a separate database- resisting arrest charges. "How about this one, many cases of resisting arrest that he had, which states "Officer was justified in use of force. And the reason of why did he use force. Well the person was resisting arrest. That's a catch-all phrase Philadelphia."

There is a widespread pattern in the NYPD policies when resisting arrest charges are used to sort of cover up the officer's use of force. They say, why did the officer use force? Well, the person was resisting arrest.

"I think that we will also have to look at the other guys in his crew also. I'll bet we come up with the same stuff." Tony stated.

"You're right." Longo said. "We could be here forever on just this stuff.

"Uh-oh" Tony said looking at the arrest records again." This report also shows that Griffin has been accused of excessive force since he's been on the job. But Griffin added that resisting arrest charge in almost every single arrest case of his. That's not good. I bet if we went to Riker's and talked to the skels that he had arrested, we may find out some more stuff."

"Good idea." Longo said continuing to look at the database and writing down pertinent facts.

"Here's a good one Philadelphia." Longo continued to scan the arrest records."Jorge Rodriguez, was charged with unlawful possession of a weapon, possession of 404 decks of heroin, 17 additional grams of heroin, over 4 ounces of marijuana, 5 ounces of Ectasy and dozens of prescription pills and needles. He was also charged with possession with intent to distribute in a school zone and possession of drug paraphinelia. And added to this, resisting arrest. And get this. This was all due to a traffic stop."

"C'mon" Tony said. "They knew this guy was carrying. That's why they stopped him. Griffin must have had advance notice of this skel carrying all of this shit."

"Yeah, but who was the stoolie?" Longo stated.

"I don't know, but if we go to Riker's and talk to this skel, I'm sure that he'll fill us in." Tony stated. "Longo, this sounds too pat, too out of the everyday. Somebody higher up had this in for Rodriguez, and tipped off Griffin."

"You're right that's what it sounds like." Longo responded.

"And here's another thing." Tony added. "If this guy was carrying all of this shit, where's the money? To even sell all of this stuff, it had to be several thousand dollars worth. He must have sold a bunch of this stuff already. And I hate to say this, but I bet if we went to the property room here, that all of these drugs are gone."

Longo looked at Tony. "Do I hear you right , Philadelphia. That this will be going deeper than a few bad cops."

"I'm afraid so." Tony stared at Longo.

Tony and Longo went back into Loo's office and told him what they found.

"OK," Loo said to both of them," You two go to Riker's and see if this guy or any other who was arrested by Griffin will talk to you. This seems like a drug deal gone bad. Also check with the Detectives working narcotics if anything like this was known." And then in an afterthought," I can't believe something this big was not known to somebody."

Since the narcotics detectives were on the next floor up from them, that was the first place they went. The whip of the narcotics squad. Lt. William Barnett, was called" Billy Blue eyes," because his eyes were blue like a baby's eyes. And because of his baby blue eyes, he was able to attract many, many females, and to even get a different female in bed each night. He gave Tony a run for the money on being called a "horn dog'.

"Loo," Tony asked Lt. Barnett. "Did you hear of anything going on with a drug dealer named Rodriguez and a cop from this precinct, Charles Griffin?"

"Philadelphia," Billy Blue eyes said," I hear of stuff like this all of the time, but that's all b.s. from the drug dealers, trying to get a cop involved. Hold on, let me ask Sgt, Muldoon." He pressed the intercom." Muldoon, get in here."

Sgt. Muldoon entered the narcs office. "Do we have anything ongoing with a drug dealer named Rodriguez and a cop Charles Griffin?"

"No Loo." Sgt. Muldoon said." I would have brought something like that to you and IAD."

"Sorry guys." Billy Blue eyes said to Tony and Longo. "If we hear of anything we'll let you know."

"Thanks Loo." Tony said. He and Longo went out of his office back downstairs.

"They know something." Ed Longo said." They just want the collar for themselves."

"You think so?" Tony asked."

"I know so." Longo answered. "Muldoon and Baby Blue eyes go way back. I worked with both of them. They'll keep all or any information for themselves to make them look good."

"Ok, let's hope we get better luck with some of these drug dealers at Riker's." Tony said.

CHAPTER 5

Tony and Longo started to go to Riker's Island and was headed to Queens (Riker's is on an island between Queens and the Bronx) when they were stopped at a light and saw craziness happening again.

Two cops from the 17th Precinct were bashing in the head of a skel, one Robert McKinney.

Longo was driving, and motioned this to Tony, "What do you think? Should we stop?"

Tony looked at them and nodded. "Yeah, it's a full moon, and nuts and crazy's, even cops come out."

They pulled over and just as they got out of the car, one officer, Brian Adams, who was beating this skel incessantly, put his face inches away from the skel, and shouted,

"That's what you get for fucking with me, and remember, that I'm the one who did this to you."

"Hey, what's going on guys?" Tony said showing his gold shield.

The other officer, Anthony Cameron, who was also restraining the skel, told Tony. "This guy was resisting arrest, and tried to attack Adams with a cane."

"Where's the cane?" Longo said.

"Uh- it was here a minute ago". Cameron stated, looking around for the cane. Strangely, they would later write on their DD61, that it disappeared. Cameron who was also restraining the skel during the beating, then went along with a story in which the skel attacked Adams with a cane, justifying the use of force, according to the complaint.

"I think that you should just stop hitting him and take him in." Tony said.

"Yes, sir." Cameron said. Adams, picked up the skel and put the handcuffs on him.

As Tony and Longo went back to their car, Tony said, "I wonder what that was about. I've seen too much of this shit today."

"It's just our boys having fun." Longo shrugged. "What do you think that the skels are going to stop unless they're beaten senseless?"

"Yeah, but there's ways and then there's ways to handle this." Tony mentioned.

"Philadelphia," Longo said, getting back behind the wheel, "I never thought that you were a skel lover."

"I'm not" Tony stated. "But there's too many cops being harassed by IAD and the press for excessive force."

"True," Longo stated, "but I've never seen a skel that didn't deserve a beating for doing what they do and that is break the law."

"Longo, you're right." Tony said not wanting to get into fight that he can't win.

To get into Riker's Island most Contractor's and visitors have to get passes at 2 trailers before the bridge to Riker's, but police officers just have to show their badge, and say something to the guard, like "How's it going?" nod, and then continue across the bridge. Once across the bridge there is another checkpoint. After that the cops go to the specific building, but inmates go thru intake at the Western facility, a series of tennis bubble-like-buildings that handle inmate processing and admissions. Each bubble building is designated to serve a specific function: holding, processing, medical processing and staging for assignment to jail housing. A fifth building serves as a warehouse for supplies and equipment.

Everyone who comes into the intake unit is beat up. The idea is they let you know that when you come in they're not going to take any nonsense. Usually 4 corrections officers put the inmate in a cell, surrounded by them, and they punch and stomp on him until he is bloodied.

Now, until a prisoner is tried, he stays there at one of many buildings on the Island. Some stay there for years before their trial. Also, if a person is convicted of a crime that has a punishment of a year in jail or less, they stay at Riker's. Prisoners who get bigger sentences are transferred to other New York State facilities , like Dannemora or Sing Sing, in upstate New York.

Rodriguez was kept at AKMC, an old building that was maybe a 100 years old. A cop goes in to one of these buildings and immediately hands his gun to the guard who gives you a pass. They call up and bring the skel down to the attorney's room to be interrogated. Now you have to understand, that a prisoner gets a shower every couple of days, but they stay in their own clothes not prison uniforms, until his trial. He never gets to wash it, so he stinks real bad.

Rodriguez was brought into the attorney's room by a female correction officer. Most correction officers at Riker's are now female. They find that the males don't act up as much. Of course there are many cases of sex between inmates and correction officers because of that. One inmate, impregnated 4 female correction officers within one week, and he wasn't even charged with a crime; he said that it was consensual, and he must have been real good, because the female officers didn't object or press charges.

Rodriguez was brought in. He was small and wiry. Not Mexican, but maybe Columbian.

"Holy shit!" Longo said. "don't you bathe here?" he told Rodriguez.

"Fuck you!" Rodriguez said. "They don't let us wash our clothes here, so do you think that I'm going to smell like roses?"

"You smell like horse shit." Tony added.

"What do you want?" Rodriguez asked

"Officer Griffin." Tony said.

"Who?" Rodriguez asked.

"The cop who arrested you." Longo stated.

"Yeah, I know who you mean. The cop who pulled me over for no reason." Rodriguez answered.

"Well," Longo said. "There were a whole lot of reasons in your car, wasn't there?"

"Maybe." Rodriguez said. "But he had no business to pull me over. I wasn't doing anything. I wasn't even going the speed limit"

"Yeah," Longo said," trolling for kids to give them drugs."

"Bullshit. I'm a businessman" he stated.

"Look. We think that Griffin was banging away at your business and that's why he stopped you, in fact, he was working on you almost exclusively. Isn't that right?" Longo stated.

"I don't know what you're talking about" Rodriguez stated.

"The cops in this precinct, like Griffin, are giving you a business problem. All these arrests, all of the hassles." Longo continued.

"I got no problem," Rodriguez answered," except for you cops.""You people" Rodriguez said again, shaking his head, "Go back and tell your cop friends that I'm not paying anymore."

"Who's asking you to pay." Tony asked.

"You cops, the eyetalians, everybody." the skel answered.

"So was Griffin shaking you down?" Tony asked.

"Him and his crew and the others." Rodriguez said.

"By the others, you mean, the mob?" Tony asked.

"Oh yeah. We had to pay them, and all of your cop friends."

"Do you mean Griffin specifically?" Longo asked.

"No, not just him. All of the cops in Manhattan." Rodriguez said.

"C'mon, Rodriguez, ALL of the cops in Manhattan?" Longo said derisively.

"Yeah, almost every fuckin' precinct." Rodriguez answered.

"I can't believe that." Tony answered." Tell me more."

Rodriguez looked at Tony and then at Longo. "I ain't saying anything more unless I get off."

"C'mon guy, "Longo said. "With all of the shit in your car, you'll be lucky if you see the next century."

"Hey, you want info, then I want the witness protection program." Rodriguez told them.

"Hey, from what I can see that all you've got is a maybe, some cop tried to rip you off." Longo answered.

"I got more, much more." Rodriguez stated." The cop who pulled me over is working for them."

"You mean the mob? Griffin is working for them?" Tony asked.

"Yeah. He's on their payroll and he's also an enforcer for them." Rodriguez said. "When they want someone whacked, he does it."

"Bullshit!!" Longo said.

"No, it's true." Rodriguez stated.

Tony whispered in Longo's ear. "That's what Angela told me also."

"I'll talk to the DA and the feds and see what they can do." Tony said.

Longo got up. "We'll be back."

"Well you know where to find me." Rodriguez said.

On the ride back from Riker's Island, Tony said, "We've got to make a list."

"And check it twice- going to find out who's naughty or nice." Longo added laughing about the Christmas list.

"Exactly." Tony stated. "We need to see where this shit that Rodriguez said leads."

"And who's involved." Longo added.

"I mean he's talking about a lot of cops, a lot of precincts." Tony said. New York City police are divided into 74 precincts, 22 of them are in Manhattan.

"Do you believe him?" Longo asked.

"I don't know- but he's got my attention." Tony added. "Even if what this skel is saying is only half true, then this is bad."

"You know Philadelphia" Longo stated," if what he's saying is even half true, then these guys are scum, they're skels too, not cops, and they deserve anything they get."

"I agree." Tony said.

"I can use a drink after this," Longo added." Let's stop at Easy's for one, and after this, maybe even a couple."

"Good idea." Tony added.

When they got to Easy's, it was late in the day, and 2 other barmaids were on duty- Teresa and Kathy. Teresa had big boobs. She used to work at Hooter's across from Penn Station, but she got tired of guys always trying to feel those nipples. They were nice. They would stand straight up, pert, and peek thru her blouse and Tony could see why other guys wanted to touch them. Kathy was no slouch either, her ass was very inviting to Tony, and him and every other guy in the place would strain their necks to see it every time she bent over. Tony called her Kathy with a K instead of a C, and they both laughed at that. Most Kathy's are Irish and most Cathy's are Italian.

Once Longo had a few drinks in him (free of course!) his tongue would loosen up and the real Ed Longo came out from that big frame.

"Shit, piss, fuck—mother fucker!" he yelled.

Tony turned to Longo, "And this is directed to who?"

"Those scumbag cops!" Longo answered, his anger rising up.

"Lower your voice." Tony said," You don't know who's listening."

"I don't give a shit!" Longo said. "These fucks are all no good. I've been a cop for almost 20 years (he looks at his watch) okay 18 years plus. And I never took anything."(except for free drinks and food)

"Okay, calm down." Tony said to him. "They'll get these guys, it's just a matter of time."

"Time is what I don't have Philadelphia. I got a year plus until I retire." Longo answered." Do you remember the Knapp Commission? It took years to weed all the scum out."

"The scum rises to the top." Tony answered. "It'll be okay." Trying to calm him down.

"No. That's the cream rises to the top, not the scum." Longo said.

"Whatever." Tony answered. "Not to change subjects, so what major family do you think that they're into here - Gambino, Luccese, or Columbo?"

"My money is on Columbo." Longo stated.

"Why?" Tony answered." They're in Brooklyn."

"Yeah, but they control all of the drugs in the city." Longo answered.

There used to be an ambulance company in Brooklyn called Mayflower Ambulance and Tony knew the daughter of the owner, Marietta was her name. She was hot to trot and Tony would have loved to get into her pants but she was only going with guys who could afford the lifestyle that her father got her accustomed to. She even went with a Detective 1st grade who was like 20 years older than her.(Rod from the 6-9 in Brooklyn) When Joe Columbo was shot, Mayflower responded. They had always serviced the hits that the Mafia did and when they were looking to go legit, they forced the owner of Mayflower to make them "partners". But they ran the company into the ground because they're not businessmen, they're scum. And then they blamed the owner that it was his fault that it failed. So they killed him. And his daughter had to learn to live without a lot of the niceties that she had become accustomed to. Life changes. But she still liked to go out with the Dick 1, even though he was married and with a couple of kids.

Tony still lived in Brooklyn, in his old neighborhood, Bay Ridge. That part of Brooklyn was still safe, somewhat free from the crazies and the crime sprees that happen in other parts of Brooklyn, like Bed-Sty or Brownsville. It was still a place that you felt safe walking down the block, stopping at the fruit stand to pick out your fruit, or the butcher or the tailor. It was like if time stood still from 30 or 40 years ago, and you knew your neighbor, the people on the block that you said good morning to, and that they knew that you were a cop and it didn't matter to them. It was a profession that the people in the neighborhood looked up to and not derided it.

It was still primarily Italian, but a lot of Asians were starting to move in. He had had several broken romances from the old neighborhood, but none were marriage material. All of them were Italian girls from Brooklyn and Staten Island and they all had all this long, big black hair, and the heavy make-up and they all looked the same, like they were from a scene out of the movie "Working Girl" or "Saturday Night Fever." They just did not interest Tony for a long term romance. But Claire from Scores however did. He didn't care that she was a barmaid. For some reason there was chemistry between them, not only sex, but something more. He kept picturing her each night before he fell asleep.

The next day at roll call, Tony put in for 4-1/2 hours OT (overtime). You have to explain why you worked OT and get your supervisor to approve it. All supervisors have to explain why their people are working OT, because bottom line, it's all about the money; not solving crime, but the money. The Loo has to go to the Cap and explain it, the Cap has to go to the DI (deputy inspector) who has to go to the Inspector, to the Borough Commander, to the Chief of Patrol or Chief of Detectives, and eventually to the Police Commissioner.

"So Tony," Loo asked," Why are you putting in for so much OT?"

Tony answered," Loo, you said yesterday that it was authorized. Longo and I are busting our tails off trying to find out all about Griffin and his crew. And Loo, it looks pretty bad and pretty far reaching. It may not be just about them but involve a lot of precincts."

Tony went on to explain what he and Longo found out from talking to Rodriguez at Riker's Island. "Frankly Loo" Tony went on to say," I'm going to need more OT, not less to find out all about this, or we're going to need a lot more help."

"Okay, Tony," Loo answered, "I'll talk to Cap and IAD and see if we can get you more help. In the meantime, limit your OT."

Tony shook his head. "But Loo, I still have all of my other cases to do.

Loo looked at him." Well, you still have to get those done too."

Tony left Loo's office to tell Ed Longo. He would need the OT for his retirement, Tony thought. Most cops work 4-1/2 hours OT per shift. That's 22-1/2 hours OT pay per week. The NYPD takes the last 3 years pay including OT for his pension. So let's say if he was making $80K and $20K was in OT, the pension would be based on $100K instead of $80K. At ½ pay, that's a significant amount. But then a lot of cops fake a disability and then can collect ¾ pay for their pension.

"That bullshit!" Longo said to him after Tony told him what Loo said. "I need that OT; that money is going for my pension."

Tony agreed with him. "I agree. Maybe we should go to the union and see what they say."

"I know what they're going to say," Longo answered. "Slow down until they're forced to go to OT."

"That could be." Tony said. "On the way out, let's stop and talk to the union rep. I don't want to discuss this over the phone."

Longo nodded. "OK."

Tony still had 4 homicide cases to solve, but 3 were grounders. In one case, an off-duty cop, a sergeant from the 2-1 precinct (up to the 20th precinct they use the numbers, but after, they break it down in two numbers, like 2-1, 3-4, etc.) rams his car into his ex-wife's car, on 1st Avenue and 6th Street.(9th precinct jurisdiction) He gets out and fires 10 shots into the windshield killing his ex. However, his 7 year old daughter was in the car at the time. He had 9 kids with her, ages 7 thru 24, and he was upset that he wasn't getting custody.

It was a simple "grounder" and this was typical of these cases. Open and shut- 2 to 3 days and done; case closed. But you still have to prepare a whole folder on each case for the DA to prosecute, and you still have to appear before the Grand Jury, even though it is an open and shut case. That's why Tony was bitching about not being able to work OT.

Cops always have to testify to the Grand Jury and in most cases the ADA (assistant district attorney) who presents the case to the Grand Jury, relies heavily on the testimony of officers. Most cops in the past have lied to the Grand Jury and in the trials that occurred afterwards, defense attorney's question the reliability of such testimony.

In this particular case the defense attorney at the trial, asked Tony, "Did you actually see the defendant kill the victim?" No was the answer. Well how can you be sure that the defendant is the shooter. Because he still had the gun right after he shot 10 times into the windshield and killed his wife. Well, since you didn't actually see the crime, how can you testify to it. Because other cops did. Where are these other cops. They're not here. Well since the "other cops" are not in the courtroom, and since you didn't actually see the murder, then Judge, I ask for a dismissal of the charges. The Judge didn't agree to this, but it happens sometime like this. Especially in high profile murders, like actors or billionaires.

Jimmy "The Gent" Lonnigan, was the union rep for the Detectives Endowment Association.

"You have no choice. Slow it down!" He told Tony and Longo." If the brass wants you to do 30 jobs at once, then slow it down until no cases get done, even the grounders."

"He's absolutely right." Longo said looking at Tony.

"Absolutely!" Tony agreed.

Longo tells Tony as they're walking to their car," Some guys just don't have patience. Now me, there will always be another case, another tomorrow in this business. You just have to pace yourself; you respond to emergencies, but don't kill yourself. Get there safely, maintain a level of composure and control."

"So you're saying fuck the brass, and do what you can. Especially if they cut your OT." Tony responds to him.

"Absolutely!" Ed Longo answers.

CHAPTER 6

The IAD had gotten a court order to survey all of the apartments and houses that the cops involved in the car accident were in. Tony and Longo went to the Realtor, Cushman and Gold, of the apartment that Griffin lived in and showed him the court order.

"The owner of the place is Paul DeMarco. I don't know if he's sub-letting it." Josh Cushman said.

"How long has it owned it?" Tony asked.

"About 3 years." He said.

"That would seem to click with all of the arrests that Griffin had." Tony said to Longo. And then in an afterthought," Paul "Big Paulie" DeMarco is the acting head of the Columbo family."

"I would like to know if the other crew members also were sub-letting apartments." Longo said to Tony.

Tony asked the Realtor, "Can you tell me if Peter Ryan, who lives at 109 Green Street apartment 1N,is one of your firms listings?"

The realtor looked it up." Yes", he said. "And the owner is also Paul DeMarco, the same as Mercer Street."

"And what does that go for? Market price." Tony asked.

"Around 3 million." was the answer.

Tony looked at Longo," We're in the wrong business." he said.

"That's for sure." Longo answered.

"We'll check on where these other cops live also." Tony mentioned.

"Good idea." Longo said.

Pete Ryan's condo at 109 Green Street was similar to Griffin's condo but at a much less magnitude. 109 Green Street is in the shadow of the Williamsburg Bridge and it wasn't the best as streets go, but still worth 3 million plus dollars. Since he was still alive, but in critical condition, the Tony and Ed Longo had to tell the super that they are getting a court order to search the apartment but they needed to at least get in to look around. The super, a Russian by the name of Mersak, looked at their gold shields and let them to Ryan's condo.

They followed the super and it was on the first floor all the way in the back, apartment 1N. He had a similar apartment as Griffins, but much less expensive furniture. This was still too expensive for a cops salary, but for some reason he had 2 refrigerators also. It was decorated more like a college fraternity place with basketball courts inside, hockey goals nets, etc. It seemed that Ryan was a sports geek. They told Mersak, that they'll be back with the court order and more cops.

The two other cops in the accident was Shaun O'Donnell, who was killed, and Brian McDonald, who was on a ventilator and not expected to survive. O'Donnell lived in Tottenville, Staten Island was married ,as well as McDonald, who lived in Oyster Bay, Long Island. Both places were nice, too nice to be on a cop's salary, but they weren't up to the same caliber as was Griffin's or Ryan's condo's.

"So how do we handle these 2 cops, Longo?" Tony asked him.

"Well,let's do O'Donnell's place first, he lives in Staten Island, and then we'll do McDonald." Ed Longo told him.

"Okay." Tony said." We'll have to be careful when we talk to his widow, since I am sure that she's upset enough as it is."

"Right." Longo told him. "But we'll treat it like any homicide in talking to the relatives."

"Gotcha." Tony said.

Tony called both wives.

When they got to O'Donnell's house, it still was pretty nice for the area. Well manicured lawns and shrubs (by an expensive lawn service who was there every day to pick out every single weed and insect), nice new siding and a black wrought iron fence, that had an electronic gate to be able to get in.

Tony rang the buzzer, and looked directly at the video security camera," Mrs. O'Donnell, Detectives Philadelphia and Longo, we called earlier and would like to talk to you for a few minutes."

The gate clicked open and swung wide to let them in. They walked up the Belgian stone driveway up to the door and rang the bell. Robin O'Donnell opened the door. She was without make-up and you could tell that she had been crying.

"Yes, what is this about?" she asked.

"Can we come in?" Tony asked.

She opened the door and motioned for them to come into the house. It was nicely furnished, not to Tony's taste, but looked like money and looked like it had been recently decorated.

"Mrs. O'Donnell, we would like first to offer our condolences about Shaun." Tony said.

"Thank you." She said.

"We're investigating some claim by drug dealers, that Shaun was involved in some robberies of drugs and money." Tony told her.

"Detectives, Shaun would never do that." She said. "He was always working overtime and loved being a cop."

"I'm sure he did, ma'am." Ed Longo said," But we have to ask you some questions that might be embarrassing."

"Okay." She answered.

"I see that you have a nice house, with a nice lawn, you live in a nice neighborhood, how were you guys able to afford this?" Longo asked her."

"We..uh..manage." she answered, and didn't elaborate further.

"I hate to ask this, but do you have money problems?" Tony asked her. "I mean this house must be a fortune to just maintain."

"No." she said. "We don't have money problems and I do not like that line of questioning either Detective. Shaun took care of all the bills and I just stayed home. But he was a worker, and he provided for me, so I didn't have to worry about money."

"I'm sure he did Mrs. O'Donnell. "Tony said." But Shaun was only making $50,000 a year and some overtime, that doesn't add up to how you can afford this house."

"Well, we have a mortgage and we took out a home equity loan, that much I do know." She told him.

"Mrs. O'Donnell," Ed Longo said." I'm sure that Internal Affairs is going to ask you to produce monthly bills and savings accounts to see where he got the money to pay for this."

"Detective, I object to your inferring that my Shaun was a dirty cop." She told him.

"Ma'am, I'm sure that he wasn't." Tony said." But we're just trying to find out where he got his money to pay to live here."

"Detective," she told him." We're not living in an extravagant home- we're ordinary people and I object to you inferring that Shaun got the money from robberies."

"Ma'am," Tony said." We're not trying to insult you or your dead husband. But we're the nice guys. Internal affairs is not going to be so nice, and if they find out that he was dirty, it will jeapordize his pension".

"You can't do that!" She screamed at him. "Shaun worked hard for the money, always putting in extra overtime when he didn't have to keep me safe."

"Ma,am," Longo told her." We've got a job to do, and meaning no disrespect, but he was involved with a bunch of other dirty cops, who were robbing drug dealers for the money."

"Detectives," she told him," I'm going to ask you to leave. Shaun would never be involved with dirty cops."

"Okay, Mrs. O'Donnell." Tony mentioned to her," But Internal Affairs will be contacting you."

When Tony and Longo went back to their car, Tony said,

"She knows something- I mean I know that she's trying to protect his name…"

"and his pension." Longo added.

"You're right." Tony said." And his pension, but somehow this Staten Island housewife reminds me of that TV reality show," The Real Housewives of Staten Island."

"You're right, Philadelphia." Longo said. " Again, big coffured hair, nice, really nice business clothes, nails done and she just had an air about her."

"A Staten Island attitude." Tony added." That's why I never date girls from Staten Island. Besides the accent, usually very heavy make-up, like they're whores, and other things."

"But I wouldn't throw her out of bed." Ed Longo said.

"Now who's the horn dog." Tony said.

"I'm just saying." Longo told him.

"Right, Longo." Tony added. "You accuse me of trying to fuck every woman, but you're just as bad."

"What can I tell you, I'm horny and every woman's pussy looks good to me now." Longo said.

"Longo you're a pig." Tony laughingly said.

"Oink, oink." Longo laughed also.

The next day they went to Lisa McDonald's house in Oyster Bay, Long Island, only about an hour from the city, but it could have been on a different planet. McDonald was still alive, barely, but on a ventilator, but by now he was brain dead, and it was just a matter of time until Lisa McDonald had to pull the plug on him.

The McDonald's house was right near the water, in a spacious house that again no cop, except for maybe the Police Commissioner could afford. When they pulled up, they saw a 25 ft. boat that was on a boat trailer, ready to be launched.

"Nice!" Longo said." How come we don't have yachts, Philadelphia?"

"Boats, Longo, boats- that's not a yacht." Tony said.

"Whatever." Ed Longo commented.

They pulled up to the house that was 2 stories, plus it backed up to Oyster Bay. They rang the doorbell and Lisa McDonald answered. She was platinum blonde, with long hair draped down past her shoulders. Stuningly beautiful, she wore Capri pants and escorted them to the living room showing a fantastic view of the ocean.

"Mrs. McDonald," Tony said," like I explained to you on the phone, we're investigating a complaint against your husband Brian, brought by several drug dealers."

"I understand Detective," she said," but why would you believe a drug dealer?"

"Mrs. McDonald," Tony began," we don't, but by law, we have to follow up on every complaint, whether it's true or not."

"Well I can tell you that Brian did nothing wrong." She told him.

"I don't mean to say that he did, but can I ask you a personal question. How can you afford this place on a cop's salary?" Tony asked her.

"Brian worked a lot of overtime, and he got some money from an inheritance." She said.

"Mrs. McDonald," Tony told her," Internal Affairs is also investigating this and they will be more suspicious than we are. By the way, how much does this go for on the market?"

"Probably 5 million," she said matter of factly.

"And Brian's inheritance was that much?" Tony asked her.

"No, but we took out a big mortgage and we figured that with all of his overtime, that we could afford it." She said.

"Yeah," Longo said," but you can't count on overtime, especially a lot of overtime to pay for this."

"Well Detectives," she mentioned," I have a small business on the side that keeps us solvent."

"Can I ask what kind of business?" Tony asked her.

"Personal success. We cater to many rich people." She told them.

"Oh." Tony said." Can I ask like who?"

"Oh people high on the social scale. I can't divulge their names, Detective, that would be unethical."she said.

"Ok." Tony answered.

(IAD would find out that Lisa McDonald is running an escort service and she was supplying the women that Griffin saw.)

"Well, I understand that Brian is still on a ventilator, any word on his condition?" Tony asked.

"Not good, I'm afraid." She said, showing no emotion.

"Ok, Thank you for your time, Mrs. McDonald." Tony said.

"Yes, thank you." Longo said.

After they got back to their car, Longo said," She's dirty too."

"I agree Longo." Tony said "Personal Success business. I bet that's a secret word for an escort service."

"Yeah." Longo said." I bet she's supplying hookers to Griffin and the mob, right out of this house."

"Yeah," Tony said. "Did you see she was cold as ice- she was no emotion about Brian- no boo hoo, nothing at all."

"I'll tell you Philadelphia," Longo said,"this gets deeper in shit all of the time."

"You're right Longo." Tony said,"But what do you think of her, she's beautiful."

"And you'd love to fuck her also." Longo mentioned.

"Of course." Tony mentioned. "Wouldn't you?"

"In a hearbeat." Longo added.

On a 12midnight to 8AM shift, cops get mixed up with prostitutes and also junkies. They can offer a cop the only human contact that they would have, so why wouldn't they all know each other. Tony and Ed Longo was going to find out who were Griffin's hookers, who hired them and did he tell them anything that they could use. The problem was that Griffin was dead and even though they suspected that Lisa McDonald was running an escort service, they couldn't right come out with that and ask her, just in case she knew something also.

They went back to Griffin's Soho apartment and had to ask Ivan if any of them had signed in. In a building like this, every visitor had to sign in, said the management.

"Sure everybody signs in unless they are accompanied by the tenant into the building." Ivan stated.

"Can we see the sign-in sheet for the past month, let's say." Tony asked.

Ivan went behind his desk and brought out a large folder. "Here." He said." Knock yourself out but you can't take it from the premises."

"OK, Ivan."Tony said.

Tony and Ed Longo went through about two months and came up with about two dozen names. But the names appeared to be phony. Names such as Tiffany Diamonds and Georgia Peaches and Too Loose What the Heck.

Tony and Longo dutifully copied down the names and what times they signed in and out.

"We'll be back Ivan." Tony said.

They went back to the squad room and looked at the little book that Griffin kept. It had these hookers names and phone numbers and a little asterick next to each name to signify what she was good at.

"I bet each star means something." Ed Longo said.

"Yeah, how good they were, if they were good at blow jobs, and if they took it in the ass."Tony said.

"Hey Philadelphia, look at this one- 3 stars next to it."Longo said."She must do it all."

"OH why can't we find something like this." Tony said.

"I know." Longo said.

Tony and Ed Longo got the list of hookers from Ivan and point blank called Lisa McDonald if she knew them.

"Yes," she told them." They work for me on a contract basis."

"You're right." Ed Longo said." They're hookers and you're running an escort service."

"No." She said." I just cater to successful men who need coaches to inspire their youth and vigor."

"Yeah, I'll bet." Tony said." Okay, here's the thing, Mrs. McDonald. If you do not cooperate with us,, we'll arrest you for running an illegal prostitution business."

"Success business." Lisa McDonald told him.

"Ok, whatever you want to call it."Longo said.

"Okay, what do you want." Lisa said.

"We got the names of the hookers that Griffin saw each night, and we just want their phone numbers to talk to them, and ask them a few questions about him." Tony said.

"Ok." She said." Who are the names that you need phone numbers on?"

They gave her the names and she supplied the phone numbers. He called and asked to speak to each one of them in person.

One was a striking blonde with a smile that said," Fuck me now!" She had skin tight pants on and a pleated blouse. She could roll her shoulders so that her breasts moved in unison. Her breasts were large and you could see that her nipples were a pale pink that deserved a male's mouth on to suck.

Another wore a black wrap around dress, taller than most, with an ass that begged to be gotten into. Her muscles rippled as he moved. She had black hair and shapely legs.

The third piece of ass was a Russian who strutted as she walked and licked her tongue around her like to say that she wanted your cock in her mouth. She held her bouncing breasts, one in each hand and wouldn't let go of your stare. She purposely stared at you until you dropped your stare and not the other way around.

The last one that Tony and Longo saw was a light skinned black, skinny and in her mid-30's. She wore little make-up. She didn't need to since she was drop dead gorgeous. Both Tony and Longo started to get erections and she strutted past them, grabbing each one's cock.

"Want some?" she asked each one and Longo ran his hand through his hair and whispered to Tony." I want to fuck that one." He said.

"Me too." Tony added. "Let's get out of here before we get into trouble."

"I'm willing to get into trouble with this one." Longo said drooling at her.

"Come on Longo. Keep it in your pants and let's go."

A lot of people want to put a label on today's cops as more violent, or aggressive in making arrests than cops of years ago. Maybe they are, and some say that the "quality" cop has all but disappeared, but cops like Tony and Ed Longo are still what cops should be.

Most active duty cops get a lot of complaints against them, and the first thing that skels do when they get arrested is to make a complaint of brutality or corruption, hoping that they can use it as a bargaining chip. The CCRB(Civilian Complaint Review Board) looks at complaints about bad cops. The thing about the "coffin cops" is that all of them had cases against them, and not even one time, but multiple times. IAD gets these cases after the CCRB, but in most cases, does nothing. Again, the 'blue laws'. Don't do anything to a cop, even if he seriously injures a civilian(not a skel) in the process of arresting them.

The usual procedure is for cops to put handcuffs in the back so that skels can't move. But there are some who are low threat or who have some physical hardship that the NYPD recommended front-cuffing suspects even as it stressed its danger. Street savy suspects prefer front cuffing and often contort themselves in extraordinary ways to maneuver their arms from rear to front. They do this to try to escape or to put up resistance. It seems to play to their desires. A front –cuffing suspect can be as much of a threat as if the suspect was not cuffed. Most times, front cuffing is used in jails, with prisoners legs shackled as they are taken to court appearances.

One of the big drug dealers Edwin Ramiriz, was being transferred from Riker's to the Courthouse on Park Row, but was brought in by the narcotics squad to the 9ᵗʰ precinct to try and get some information from him. However, the standard for big drug dealers getting arrested is to say nothing even if confronted.

Ramiriz was in a room and Ed Longo got permission from the Narcotics cops to interview him.

He looked blankly at Longo.

"The cops in this precinct are causing you problems" Longo said." All of the arrests, the hassles, lost product, lost man-hours, legal expenses."

"What?" Ramiriz said." I know nothing- nothing."

"I'm here to tell you that your problems are going to get worse." Longo told him." We're going to be all over you, like flies on shit."

"I know nothing, nothing" Ramiriz said again.

"You know nothing? Right" Ed Longo said sarcastically." Who's asking you to pay, Rossi? Is he shaking you down?"

"You people." Ramiriz said.

"What? You mean us cops?" Longo said." What's your reason - your right to sell drugs to kids?"

Ramiriz looked up at him, grinned, and then said," I now nothing, nothing."

CHAPTER 7

Back at the squad room, Tony tried to find out where the" coffin cops" meet to plan their robberies; the old coffin company. He looked up defunct coffin companies in New York City –there were 3.

He discounted the two in the Bronx and Queens, focusing on the one near the shadow of Police Headquarters.

"Hey Longo, this is something." Tony said," this place that they look like they're meeting at is close to 1 Police Plaza. They're thumbing their noses right at the top brass."

The defunct coffin company was right near the East River, just north of the South Street Seaport, on Cherry Street. He went on Google Earth and you could even see the DEP waste treatment plant on Ward's Island from there. It was an 1800's era building that had a huge "For Rent or Lease" sign on it.

Longo came over to Tony's computer and looked at the site. "This must be the place." he stated. "We'll have to do a stake-out."

Tony nodded in agreement. "Can we stop at Easy's for a couple of minutes?" He asked Longo.

"Sure." Longo said then looked at this watch. It was almost noon." I could use a brew."

But Tony wasn't interested in booze; he was interested in sex and especially in Claire. He was getting erections constantly thinking about her and her nice rounded ass. He figured that any pretense to see her is good. He was going to ask her out on a date. A real date with dinner and wine and then maybe a nice long roll in the hay.

He called Easy's and asked to speak to Claire. I was almost 12 noon and he knew that Claire only worked until 12PM.

"Claire –hi!" he said to her when she answered the phone, "The Easy Score!"

"It's Tony Philadelphia, hi again. Listen, I'm coming up there in a few minutes. Can you just hang out for a few. I need to ask you something."

"Sure Tony." Claire said. "I'll be here." When she hung up Claire wondered what he wanted to ask her. For a date- for something else like sex. She wanted to see him also. She was going to say to Angela that Tony was coming up there, but decided against that. She wanted him all to herself.

The Easy Score had a bunch of cops from different precincts. The word gets out quickly from all of the precincts in the city, Easy's is the place to go after your shift ends (or even before) to get free drinks and maybe a feel of some of the dancers. The bar at Easy's (in addition to the tables) was in a horseshoe shape and the dancers could also extend their runway strut there to give a cop a quick moment's look to put a dollar up their tights. Sometimes they just bent over with their ass's in the cops face. This way a cop was pleased and the dancers made the most money from doing this. The cops had to wind down from their tours and relive the nights highlights and you talk with another cop who is reliving a fight with a skel and soon it's past midnight or even past noon and they're drunk.

When Tony and Longo got to Easy's, Angela wasn't there by then. Thank God, Tony thought to himself. He wanted to see Claire alone. Kathy and Teresa were already serving the lunch crowd.

"Hi guys." Kathy with a K said to Tony and Longo, putting down place napkins on the bar. "What will it be today?"

"I'll have a beer on tap." Longo said.

"Me too." added Tony, and then said," Where's Claire?"

"She's in the back, where the dancers are." Kathy said.

"Okay, thanks, Kathy." Tony said and started to walk around the back of the bar. The music was always playing loud, so loud that you couldn't hear yourself think. But the dancers liked it and so did the clientele, who was much too interested in the dancers and not the music.

Tony found Claire near the dancer's dressing room.

"Hi Claire." Tony said, eyeing Claire in her street clothes and not the skin-tight barmaid uniform she usually wore.

"Oh hi Tony." Claire said. "What did you want to ask me?" She had already guessed.

"I was wondering if you wanted to go ou   nner with me tonight or maybe tomorrow."

"Sure, I'd love it. But I go to bed at 5PM   I have to start work at 12AM." She answered.

"Oh, I don't get off work until 6PM   wered." So maybe we can get together then on Saturday   ound 6PM."

"That sounds great, Tony. Where do you want to meet?" Claire said smiling at him.

"There's a nice Italian place on West 63rd Street and Broadway, called Il Italiano, right near Lincoln Center. It's a nice place." he said.

"Great!" Claire said,"I love Italian food. Okay, I'll see you then."

"OK. It's a date." Tony said smiling back at her.

Tony was getting an erection just talking to her. He turned quickly so that she wouldn't see it and went back to the bar. He smiled at the dancers as he went thru their dressing area. Some of them winked at him. Angela had also spread the word to them about Tony.

Longo was already on his 2nd beer. "I needed this." Longo mentioned to Tony as he settled onto his bar stool. Tony and Longo surveyed the cops at the bar, but none of them looked familiar except for Bobby O'Mara, the goofy looking one.

Tony whispered to Longo,"Let's follow this one when he leaves and see where it leads."

Longo looked at this guy and asked Tony," How come?"

"He was a little too inquisitive in what Angela was saying to me about Griffin." Tony answered.

"Gotcha." Longo said.

Bobby O'Mara was already sloshed, after downing a number of Scotches. Nothing but the best- 12 year old scotch. He tried to get up, but dropped back in his bar stool. Finally, he got up and weaved over to the exit door.

Tony and Longo followed him. Again, he sauntered down the street to his car. Fumbling for his keys, he missed the lock, but on the third try was able to open his car. He got in, turned the ignition on and pulled out into traffic.

Tony and Longo got into their car and followed him.

He started downtown once he got on the West Side Highway.

"Probably headed to that old coffin place." Tony stated to Longo.

"Sounds it." Longo said.

O'Mara was headed to the old coffin place, Tony was sure after he got on the FDR drive and headed uptown toward the South Street Seaport. He got off near the Seaport exit and drove to Cherry Street. Then he got out of the car and went inside.

Tony and Longo parked a few car lengths from the place. The old coffin factory at 45 Cherry Street, was in a completely isolated spot in the center of abandoned buildings. A dumpster in the corner overflowed with pizza boxes and beer cans, the tale that this operation had been going on for quite some time. But before they had a chance to settle in, three cars pulled in, two marked and one unmarked. To Tony it looked like Midtown South and Midtown North precinct cars.

Some cop cars have initials which help identify them, such as MSN for Midtown South and MTN for Midtown North.

Tony was amazed at what he saw next. It was John Rossi, the detective from Midtown North who came out of the unmarked car and looked around right at them.

"Look who's fucking here." Longo said. He had worked with Rossi also at the 3-4 some years back.

"Yeah, Rossi. That asshole." Tony mentioned.

"Uh-oh." Longo said. "I think that he spotted us."

"Yeah." Tony said. "But he's not making a move to check us out." Rossi then went into the building along with the other cops, from Midtown South and Midtown North. The one from Midtown South, Tony recognized as Sgt. Roy O'Fallon. He had made Sgt. when Tony made detective.

"I guess that Sgt's pay isn't that good anymore." Tony said, pointing out O'Fallon to Longo.

Most cops on stake-out are paranoid about being tagged as watching them. Cops sense that they're being watched. It comes from years of being in uniform, feeling eyes on you. The coffin cops started to get aware of people watching then. Rossi told them at the meeting.

"We may be getting watched." He said

"You know this for a fact." Sgt. Fallon asked him.

"No. "Rossi said." It's just a feeling. Maybe we should lay low for awhile."

"Nah." Sgt. Fallon said." We got a good thing going here, and besides no other cop is going to rat us out."

"Maybe." Rossi said. "But stay sharp guys."

"Ok, OK." Fallon said. "You worry too much Rossi."

"That's why I'm in charge, Sgt., because I do worry." Rossi responded.

"I'd love to be a fly on the wall inside that building to hear what the fuck that they're talking about." Tony said. "I bet that they're talking about the others getting into that accident, and what to do next."

"We're going to have to get that place bugged so that we can find out what's going on." Longo said.

"But, the only problem is that they're cops and they may look for bugs and sweep the place." Tony mentioned.

"I know a guy in CSU who can plant a bug that will resist sweeps." Longo mentioned."

"We'll have to get him involved in this caper."

"Sounds good to me." Tony said.

"You know, I'm wondering how all of these cops from who knows how many different precincts were able to get together on this." Longo mentioned.

"There has to be a common thread." Tony said. "Most of these cops, maybe except for Rossi, are Irish. Could it be the Emerald Society thing?"

"I don't think so." Longo mentioned. "I'm half-Irish on my mother's side and I belong to the Emerald Society and I ain't seen any money from this stuff."

Almost all of the Irish cops belong to the Emerald society, the black cops belong to the Guardian society, the Jewish cops to the Sharim Society and the Italian cops to the Columbia Society. But Tony did not belong to the Columbia society, he felt it was too much like the Mafia.

"You know," Tony mentioned." It could be from when other cops got transferred to other precincts for OT. For the 'Safe Streets" thing a couple of years ago."

"Yeah, I remember it now." Longo remembered. "The Mayor wouldn't hire enough cops, so they thought that they would double up on OT and that would save his administration. He just should have hired more cops."

"So how can we get more OT?" Longo added.

"I guess that you've got to be a crook, like these skels." Tony mentioned.

When cops talk to one another, or their partner, either in a cruiser or on patrol- it's mostly something b.s., anything except what is going on.

"So did you hear about Ryan?" Tony asked. (Ryan was Detective 2nd grade Rod Ryan, 49, married with 2 kids carrying on an affair with a 25 year old from Brooklyn)

"Yeah," Longo said. "He's got some sweet deal. She loves to fuck, and she takes it in the ass, and sucks like a water pump. He's lucky. I wish that I had some piece of ass like that."

"How did he find her?" Tony asked.

"I heard it from the grapevine that he was cruising off duty in Brooklyn and she was stopped for a light." Longo stated. "She winked at him. He gets out of his car, shows his badge, drags her out of the car, and just left the car there running. Then he takes her to a secluded spot near Dyker Beach Park and fucks her. "

"Wow." Tony said. "Did she report him?"

"No." Longo said." Obviously she loved it, because she kept coming back for his monster cock." Then he added," Why can't I get someone like that? "

Tony agreed. "You know I heard of 3 cops from the 2-7 who did the same thing. A twenty something girl smiled at them on their shift and they gang raped her. And she didn't even report it either."

"I guess that it has something to do with the uniform or the badge." Longo added. "And some women are a suckers for that. I keep telling these females that get raped, don't smile at anyone, because it's going to get you into trouble."

"Do you think that it's going to help?" Tony said.

"Nah." Longo said. "Like I said, they're a sucker for uniform or the badge."

"No," Tony added." I meant for any woman?"

"Hey pal, that's what makes the world go 'round. Women want a guy's cock but he's got to be a knight in shining armor for them to give their pussy to him, and guys just want pussy." Longo added.

"I wish that I was a knight in shining armor." Tony said. "then I'd go for any pussy that's available."

"Me too," Longo added. "Then I could get pussy everywhere. Hey, listen to this, there was the time when I was working at Brooklyn Downtown, there were these two black cops on duty then, and I think that you know the secretary there, Nicole. Well she did both of them in the stair well, front and back at the same time. She didn't get fired, but the two black dudes did. But these black cops were stupid and so was Nicole. Didn't they realize that the stairwells are monitored with video cameras. They had all of them on camera, so they couldn't dispute it. I guess that their little heads down there, made them do it."

"Remember that movie where the guy played by that famous actor, he kept saying stupid is as stupid does. Well they were all stupid. She must like black cock." Tony said. "Yeah, I remember her from the old neighborhood. She's a whore, but I guess that I would still fuck her in a second." Tony thought about Nicole's nice rounded ass and putting it in there.

"So would I." Longo agreed, thinking about Nicole's ass too, and wondered how he could get some pussy.

All cops are cocks men, because they get the opportunity to get laid a lot. Just as they get free coffee and free meals, they get a lot of free sex offered to them. And of course they take up on it.

A lot of people look at what's going on in the NYPD today and wonder why; why would they do this or that since they know it's illegal or against the law. People do what they do for different reasons. It's just people being human, letting that thing that's most weak in them get the better of them. Sometimes an officer or a woman has poor self-esteem and taking a risk makes them feel powerful, or an officer gives a woman adoration that they crave. Sometimes they get off on the thrill of taking a risk. Corruption happens or is borne out of a desire for money or sex or both. Either way, as long as there are cops, there are crooked cops.

Just then 2 cops in a cruiser pulled into one of the other dilapidated buildings on Cherry Street. They got out and pulled what looked like a fat Italian slob out of the back seat and escorted him into the building, at 39 Cherry Street. Tony couldn't see what precinct they were from. All of a sudden a gun shot rang out. And then 2 minutes later, both cops got back into their cruiser and went into the old coffin company building.

Tony looked at Longo. "We have to find out what happened."

Longo said, "If we go out now, our cover will be blown. We have to wait."

"You're right." Tony said.

Surprisingly, none of the Coffin Cops came running out to investigate.

After more than 2 hours, the coffin cops came out, and went into their cars and went in separate directions.

Tony and Longo got out of their cars and went into the building.

'Holy shit!!!" Tony says coming up to the fat Italian; he was dead. "What's this, they shot him in the chest and walked off. Shot him like he was a dog, like he wasn't even human."

All police have this same idea to, "Shoot him! Do not take him alive." Even if it was a hit that was ordered by the brass or even the Mafia. The Columbo family had gotten so many cops on the payroll, that it was easier for them to get a cop to whack somebody that they didn't like or who had crossed them, rather than do it themselves. Who was going to blab? Certainly not the cops. So it was a good investment, for them and the cops .But there were times that the Mafia got too big and also tried to get the cops to kill a prosecutor who was going after 5 family members, but they were told no, too risky. So they settled for some "greasers" from the other side (Sicily) and did in the prosecutor while he was in a John in the Federal Building; shot him 22 times as he was taking a crap. But they got nabbed by the feds as they were trying to leave. What idiot greaser shoots someone 22 times, especially in a Federal Building. Two shots to the head and walk away is normal. But not them, they wanted to make a statement; so they got stopped and were caught. Who says crooks are smart.

Longo bent down, and felt for a pulse. There wasn't any. They went thru the building checking for anyone else left there. They couldn't say that they were on a stake-out, so they waited until they could speak to Loo, back at the squad room. Meanwhile, they made an anonymous call to 911 to say that there was shots fired in 39 Cherry Street and there was a dead body in the building.

Back in their car, they discussed what was next.

"We've got to talk to the Major Case Squad and maybe even the FBI to see what they got on this Columbo thing." Tony said.

"Yeah." Longo agreed. "They must know something and are keeping it to themselves."

"You know, "Tony said," We all work to get the skels and every different squad or agency wants to do their own thing."

"I hear ya." Longo agreed." They want the collar themselves. They're afraid that if they share it with you, then you'll get the collar. How about splitting the collar. That makes sense."

"No, they'll never go for that unless some brass makes them do it." Tony answered.

"You're right, wishful thinking." Longo said.

They called Loo and told them what had happened, and he told them to go to Major Case Squad to see what they could find out.

Major Case Squad of the NYPD is located at One Police Plaza on the 10th Floor. The parking lot for the entire building holds 700 cars, it goes on for 10 stories below ground, and is in a very dilapidated condition because the city didn't have money to fix it. It would leak like a sieve when a heavy rain hit. So when the big Hurricane hit, 700 cop cars were flooded in there and destroyed including the Chief's car. Who said the city doesn't believe in penny wise and pound foolish.

CHAPTER 8

Tony and Longo parked in the temporary parking lot below One Police Plaza and had to walk up the 100 steps to get to the main floor lobby. They reported to Lt. Rory Calhoun, of Major Case Squad, and explained to him what was going on and could he tell them what info he had on the Columbo family ties to hired killings by cops.

"Do you mean the 'coffin cops'? " Lt. Calhoun said.

Tony and Long looked at each other, and it was if they both knew what they had talked about was true. Major Case was keeping this for themselves.

"Yes, exactly Loo." Tony said.

"I'm going to have to talk to the DI to see if we can share it with you." Lt. Calhoun stated. The Task Force had a DI (deputy inspector) assigned from the NYPD to head the city's part in it.

NYPD Major Case squad works together with FBI, ATF and DEA in a special task force to wipe out the 5 Mafia families in New York; the Columbo family being only one of them. As Lt. Calhoun called DI James Sweeney, Tony and Longo looked at the pictures on the Loo's wall of the Mafioso they were following. Longo elbowed Tony to look at one of the pictures at the bottom tier of Columbo soldiers, Vinny"Fat Vinny" Carouso. It was the dead guy at 39 Cherry Street.

Tony looked at Longo. "Should we tell him?" he asked.

"No." Longo said. "Let them find out for themselves. Obviously, they're not going to share anything with us."

"The DI said that we'll get back to your Loo, after we talk with the FBI." He said.

"Ok thanks Loo." Tony answered. "But can you tell me at least is Charley Griffin involved."

"I can only say that a bunch of those guys are involved." LT. Calhoun said, and then in an afterthought, "Very heavily."

Longo and Tony turned and left his office. "I knew that this was a waste of time." Longo mentioned. "They want the collar."

"That's what it sounds like." Tony said.

Tony and Ed Longo were going back to the squad room but they stopped when they saw 3 NBA players coming out of a trendy Manhattan night club and being accosted by cops from Manhattan North. One cop took his baton and broke the leg of Atlanta Hawks player, Christian Both. They pulled their car over and flashed their gold shields.

"Guys, what's going on? Don't you know that these are NBA players." Tony said.

Officer Dalton told them," They were disobeying a lawful order to leave the area."

"I moved out of the area," Chris Both said," and then I was grabbed by these officers and taken to the ground. Then this one officer broke my leg with his baton."

"He wouldn't move fast enough." Office Dalton said.

"Then you should have called for back-up and arrested him." Tony said.

"Do you want the collar?" Dalton asked."

"No." Tony said." Get him to a hospital- fast."

The three NBA players were arrested for obstructing government administration, disorderly conduct and resisting arrest.

Detectives do not work weekends unless they are getting OT. There are 2 shifts for detectives who want to work OT, on Saturday and Sunday. Even if a case is hot" Sorry – that will have to wait until Monday" they will tell whoever, unless it's from the Chief of Police or if it's a high profile case.

Tony still had to work on his other cases. And he had to round up people for the lineups in each of his homicide cases.   Each borough command receives a monthly allotment to pay for "fillers". "Fillers" are the people who detectives pay to stand next to real suspects in police lineups. The cash is usually distributed to the robbery and homicide squads. The pay is usually $10. There are 5 fillers, or $50 worth in a lineup. The problem is that if he can't get enough "fillers", the suspect goes free. This is called the "343" rule, which states that when a prima facie case cannot be established without a lineup, the suspect has to be released – on the spot.

So the arrest is still on the books and the detective and the squad and the borough command are happy because their arrest records are sky high, but so are '343' cases. And to make matters worse, the city cut down on the amount of money that they paid for "fillers". Catch 22.

One of Tony's cases was almost like this. A skel plunged a knife into a couple just walking down the street. He killed the husband and severely injured the wife, who survived. Tony had to take the money out of his own pocket to pay for the fillers, and luckily he did. When the wife recovered enough to see the line-up to id the skel, she yelled,

"That's him!" pointing to No. 3 in the lineup.

And he couldn't put in to get reimbursed for it, that's how crazy the 343 rule is.

When the present police chief came in, he put in a lot of different reforms. What used to be safe and loft (robbery cases) became different types of robbery dependent on the amount of money involved. So if it was like $10,000 or less, one detective squad worked on it out of the robbery division, usually a bunch of 3rd grade detectives, since they got training out of it. If it was over $10,000 another detective squad worked on it, and maybe some 2nd grade detectives worked on it, and if it was like hundreds of thousands of dollars, then major case squad worked on it, which was like 1st grade detectives or above.

Then also, murder investigations changed. What used to be robbery/homicide became different types of homicide cases .Cold case had a squad devoted entirely to it, as well as crime scene unit, and then there was ordinary homicide cases that Tony handled. Even grounders cases took a lot of work, and the homicide detectives were all backed up with many cases each. When there was a rash of murders in the city, the Police commissioner had like 15 detectives to each murder on it. But that was unusual; usually, there are only two detectives assigned per case, unless it is a high profile case.

A lot of times, a detective will make a decision to go out and do observations on his own, without any back-up, or anyone with him, or nearby, or even knew where he was. Tony usually followed the rules, but a lot of times he would go out on his own to look for activity in the case while his partner, Ed Longo was eating pizza around the corner. So you could suggest that he behaved in a reckless manner, but to him, it was all about trying to solve the case, not trying to break the rules. That's what happened when Tony and Longo were at a pizza place near where Griffin lived on Mercer Street.

He left Longo and went door to door asking Griffin's neighbors what they knew about him, besides him being a cop.

"I heard that he was a pro wrestler before he became a cop." Justin told him (yes that Justin, the actor). "I saw him put this guy in a chokehold once, lifting him off the ground. I gave him a lot of leeway after that whenever I saw him."

Another neighbor, who played the Vulcan on Star Trek told him, "I saw him once bite somebody in the neck, trying to rip their carotid artery out. It bled all over the sidewalk. I was scared to death every time that I saw him."

The singer Nora, who lived in the floor above Griffin, said," I saw him shove his thumb into this guy's eye socket to gouge his eye out. Nobody wanted him living here, but what could you do. You just avoided him, like you would any bully."

Tony was amazed at what each of them said, and could only say. "You don't have to worry about him any more –he's dead. Killed in a car accident. Most cops are not like that." They all commented with a "Thank God."

Tony went back to the pizza place where Ed Longo was on his fifth slice of pizza (all free of course), and filled him in on what Griffin's neighbors said. Longo looked up and wiped his mouth from the tomato sauce, and said," I wondered where you went."

"This guy Griffin was some bad ass, Longo. I wouldn't want to meet him in a dark alley."

"Why, are you afraid of some shit head cop, who should never had been made a cop?" Longo said and took another bite of pizza.

"No" Tony answered. "This guy was some sort of psycho. You couldn't figure what he was going to do."

"I could tell you what this guy was going to do. He was going to swallow his gun when IAD found out about all of this shit that he did." Longo said.

"I don't know." Tony replied. "He had some powerful friends in the mob. They would have protected him. What do you think?"

"I have no clue." Longo said to Tony as they got back in their car. "If the city would hire more cops, the right type of cop, they wouldn't have this type of case going on."

"I wish." Tony said." But we couldn't get OT with more cops on this case."

"Very simple." Longo continued." We fuck it up so bad, they'll either order us off of the case, or put someone else to take it over."

"Well," Tony uttered," If we fuck it up, then it will go on our records."

"So what." Longo said. "You want to make Dick 1 or Sgt? You don't have any family rabbi to help you, so you're not going to get it."

"I know." Tony responded." But what else can we do with the case that we got."

"Like I said," Longo repeated," We'll fuck it up."

"And how do we do that?" Tony inquired.

"Again simple." Longo added." We just do our regular cases, put in our report, and give it to the next guy."

"Yeah right, for now." Tony added.

"You paying lip service to me Philadelphia?" Longo's voice raised.

"No. I hear you. You have the right idea." Tony said.

"Yeah, right." Longo again derided Tony. "If I'm right then why aren't you saying something. I know you Philadelphia, you're a goodie two shoes."

"No, I'm not" Tony responded." But I can see what you're saying, but I always want to get the case solved and we won't get this case solved."

"So IAD or Major Case will solve it. So what? You've got how many commendations already. You don't need several more." Longo added.

"It's not that Longo." Tony commented," You have a little less than two years..."

Longo interrupted him," No that's not right, 1 year, 7 months, 1 week, 1 day, 16 minutes and 12 seconds."

"Ok, whatever." Tony responded. "You don't give a shit if a case comes out good or bad because you are leaving shortly. I do because I still have a number of years left until I leave the job."

"So what? You're worried more about your fucking bosses than doing the job?" Longo added. "Fuck them and fuck you too."

"I have two words for you Longo, and they're not good morning or happy birthday." Tony laughed.

"So what? You're afraid to say fuck me? I'm a big boy. I can handle it." Longo stated.

"Ok. Fuck you Longo. "Tony said.

"Ok, for that, you've got to buy me a drink then Philadelphia." Longo laughed.

"OK Longo, Easy's it is. Drinks on me" Tony added knowing that they were going to be free for them.

Detectives don't solve cases like they used to and it's not like on TV; it takes weeks. There is always pressure from the brass to get cases solved and go onto the next case, because there is ALWAYS a next case. Detectives work on dozens of cases at a time. Although this particular case is not about a murder, homicide is still most often about love, hate and greed. Narcotics also have long played a role in murder and killing over drug turf and is common.

The basic work that detectives do after a killing, like cordoning off the crime scene and photographing it, collecting evidence and canvassing for witnesses, have changed little over the years. Also, investigators can lift fingerprints and find ballistic evidence, like bullets and shell casings. Also they can trace property taken from homicide victims, use phone records, and DNA can link killers to victims. But real detective work is talking to people and putting the pieces of the puzzle together.

In this case of cop corruption however, unless you have a witness or one of the cops who are involved to spill the beans or wear a wire, you're not going to get anywhere. Tony and Longo can watch and photograph corrupt cops, tail them to their meeting places, get rental records and phone records, and see whom the meet. They can also interview neighbors for unusual stuff, like in Griffins case, and see which drug dealers will tell them what happened. But unless they have an inside man, they will get nowhere, because of the 'blue laws'. The code of conduct amongst cops not to rat out a fellow cop. The problem is that the atmosphere does not yet exist in which honest cops can act without fear of ridicule or reprisal from fellow officers. Cops are in danger from other cops. That was true when Serpico and the Knapp Commission was there, it was true when the Mollen

Commision was there and even today. The reality is that cops almost never testify against a brother officer. And for good reason. You call for back-up and there isn't any, you wear a bullet-proof vest, even at home, and you check your locker every hour for bombs. You get paid back for being a rat. One NYPD sergeant, who worked at One Police Plaza in the Organized Crime Control Bureau, jacked off in the stairwell, and then threw his semen onto a female cop who had testified against another cop, who was not only stealing drugs, but dealing and using drugs. "Here's some cheese to go, rat." He yelled at her. Nothing was done to him, even though he threw it at her in the main lobby of One Police Plaza.

It is pervasive in the NYPD, everything from cops committing armed robberies on duty, to even kidnapping people on duty, to killing people, to stealing drugs, selling drugs, and of course, brutalizing civilians without provocation. Cops will routinely turn a blind eye to what they see other cops do.

Ed Longo was right. Your career gets advanced by making arrests, not by uncovering a scandal at the police department.

CHAPTER 9

After imbibing of several beers at Easy's, Tony and Longo went back to the squad room. As they approached the 9th precinct, a cop on patrol was in the process of arresting a middle age woman, Peggy Goldman. She was arrested for answering back to a cop, especially this newbie cop, maybe 21 years old. She had been running for a train, and simply asked the officer, if there was a tunnel to the downtown side. Obviously, these are fighting words to a cop trying to get some zzz's leaning against a pole. When he said, "Most people know the downtown from the uptown side." The problem is she responded, "Oh don't be an asshole." Which you don't tell a cop, even a newbie. He grabbed her arm and said," You're under arrest for disorderly conduct." and put the handcuffs on her, very tight. As she was brought into the precinct, she was thoroughly searched- pockets pulled inside out, entire body groped, crotch sort of goosed in a couple of swift upward strokes, and very humiliated. She started to cry.

Tony heard this exchange and told the cop who he didn't know," Words aren't criminal officer."

The officer responded bluntly, "Yes they are - She called me an asshole. She didn't have any respect for being my high status of a police officer."

Ed Longo started to laugh." Hey, asshole! High status! Yeah." Pumped his fist in the air and shook his head as he kept laughing and walked up the steps to the 2nd floor squad room.

Tony followed him up the steps. When they got into their area, IAD was waiting for them in Loo's office. Lt. Ian McGregor, also a big man, well over 6 feet four inches, was sipping on a soda supplied by Loo. He was waiting for some juicy information that Loo had told him about.

"So Philadelphia," he said, "What have you got here?"

Tony looked at his Loo and then to the IAD Loo. "I don't know Loo, but it seems that Griffin was into a lot of shit."

Lt. McGregor stared at him. "Well Philadelphia, Loo here says that more cops than just Griffin are involved. Do I got that right."

"Probably true, Loo. But I don't have that information yet to say that others are involved, but it doesn't look good. Loo, it looks like the Knapp Commission all over again."

"Philadelphia," Tony's Loo said, "Tell him what you heard from that barmaid at The Easy Score."

"That a lot of cops were involved in a bunch of shit, like stealing from drug dealers, even killing for hire and also informing the mob of stuff coming down the pike." Tony mentioned.

"And do you have any solid facts, not from that barmaid, that we can build a case on?" IAD asked.

"No, Loo" Tony responded. "Only that Griffin and his partner lived in some very fancy dwellings that they couldn't ever afford on a cops salary."

"Yeah." Longo added." This guy had two refrigerators in his place."

"Longo," IAD Lt. said, "that means shit. I have two refrigerators- one for cold beer and one for food."

"Never thought of it that way." Longo added. "that's not a bad idea."

"Loo," Tony said to IAD." Forgetting the two refrigerators, Griffin and his partner were living in multi-million dollar SOHO condo's that they could never afford. It was being paid for by someone in the Columbo family mob. Obviously for services rendered."

"And also," Longo added, "talking about services rendered, they were being serviced daily by a bunch of hookers, again supplied I think by the mob."

"How do you know it was the mob?" IAD asked.

"Because we went to the rental agent, and the owner is Paul DeMarco, who as everyone knows is acting head of the Columbo family." Tony responded.

"Did you talk to Major Case or Organized Crime Unit about this?" IAD asked.

"Yes, we talked to Major Case, but they wouldn't give us any information. Next we'll talk to the Organized Crime Unit." Tony added.

"I see that you're signing out personnel folders." IAD said to Tony.

"Loo gave us permission to look into their personal lives but more of going thru their collars." Tony responded.

Tony would photocopy the personnel folders and then head to the break room.

"Longo," IAD Loo asked. "Did you also look at their personal folders?"

"Yeah," Longo responded." It doesn't hurt to check it twice. There were a lot of collars; a ton of collars- over 300. We needed to do a survey of the type of collars."

"Were they 'good' collars?" IAD asked. (a 'good' collar is one that won't come back and bite you in the ass by the judge or district attorney who would throw the case out)

"They were all dealers" Tony said." And the skels deserved being arrested. But the thing is that these dealers were being robbed of drugs and money by this crew. They call themselves the 'coffin cops'."

"Where did they get that name?" IAD asked.

"Loo, they work out of an old coffin factory down on Cherry Street." Tony responded. "We don't have a bug in there yet, but we think that they decide which dealers to hit there and when."

"OK." IAD responded. "My people will put a bug in there and I'll contact Major Case and Organized Crime to find out what they have on this."

Longo whispered to Tony." Of course, they want the collar."

IAD told them." OK, we'll let you know what happens. Meanwhile, keep us informed of whatever you find out."

"Sure thing Loo." Tony said. As Tony's Loo walked IAD out of his office, Longo added,

"That's the problem Philadelphia. IAD now knows, Major Case knows, and Organized Crime Unit knows. Soon every cop on the force will know about this. And when that happens word of mouth follows and these guys will find out about it."

"Longo, there's nothing we can do about it. It's probably out of our hands." Tony said.

"Nah," Longo said," Nothing ever gets out of our hands. They'll want us to do the dirty work and then they'll take the collar."

"Probably." Tony mentioned then looked at his watch. "It's almost quitting time. Going back to Easy's for a few?" he asked.

"Absolutely!" Longo mentioned. Most cops once they hear of a place that will cater to them, will keep going back there for the free booze. But then they become closet alcoholics from all of the booze on the house, not counting the tits and ass that they see.

Tony thought of Claire and decided to call her and leave her a message to confirm Saturday's date; even though he knew that at 6PM when detectives get off of duty, she was probably asleep by now. He wished that he could be sleeping next to her. And also fucking her.

On Saturday, after Tony and Claire had dinner, they went back to Claire's place in Chelsea on West 24th Street. There was definitely chemistry between them, because as soon as she opened the door, they were on each other, kissing and feeling each other up, pulling clothes off and moving towards the bedroom.

Tony pulled her panties off and started to go down on her, pursing his tongue into her outer lips, then putting one finger, followed by two fingers inside there and moving it around and around. She was groaning already, with one hand he was grabbing her breasts and touching her nipples. She grabbed his cock and started stroking it, hard. Finally, she couldn't stand it any more, and moved him off of her and started to go down on him.

Tony liked the way that Claire had long dark hair that draped over his groin as she was sucking his cock, and she was good at it! She did not bite him or have her teeth rub against the head, but sucked it like a water pump. She really went down on him all of the way, her head bobbing up and down. He only had to guide her head down on it, not push her head down on it, like with other women.

"Do you like that babe?" she said long enough to come up for air.

"I love it. You're good!" Tony said.

She kissed him and went back to giving him a blow job. She wanted to please him because she knew that he was going to please her with that big cock of his inside her.

He laid her back on the bed and entered her, in a slow deliberate motion, that drove her crazy. Screaming in pleasure she said,

"Oh fuck me babe!"

"That what 'm going to do to you." He said pounding it into her.

She didn't care that he didn't have a condom on him, she wanted to feel him inside of her.

He took her 4 or 5 times, big and hard, and thick, in different positions, one after another.

Afterwards, just laying on the bed breathing heavy, she said, "My God that was good! Where did you learn to fuck like that?"

He laughed. "I don't know. I read a lot of books."

"Yeah, right." She answered." Books my ass; you didn't learn those moves from books." She told him." So, what do you want for breakfast?" she asked turning to him and smiling, hinting that she wanted him to spend the night with her.

"You." He answered, kissed her, and went down on her again.

The next time that she saw Angela, she told her that she had gone out with Tony.

"You're right." she said. "He is DEFINITELY a stud."

"I told you so." Angela said. They both giggled.

After Tony left Claire's place on Sunday, (again, Detectives do not work on weekends) he was walking to the subway near 14th Street and 7th Avenue, when he spotted 22 year old Tyrone James surrounded and being beaten, by a swarm of police officers from the 10th precinct. Tony hears James screaming "Grandma!" as he lay on the ground. A second later, another police squad car arrived with more cops and an officer yelled out," You're getting the fucking taser." And another officer shouted," Tase that motherfucker!"

Stupidly, Tony goes over to the scene and flashes his gold shield to them.

"What the fuck do you want?" one of the cops said angrily looking at Tony.

"I want you to stop beating him and arrest him." Tony responded.

"Fuck off detective." One of the other cops from the 10th precinct said. "Why do you want... do you want this collar? This is ours."

"What the hell did he do that you're beating him senseless?" Tony asked.

"Jaywalking." One of the other cops answered.

"C'mon." Tony laughed." You're beating him for jaywalking? That's the dumbest thing I've ever heard." Tony added.

"If you must know detective, I was giving him a summons for jaywalking, and he tried to walk away." Officer Johnson stated." I told him that he was under arrest for interfering with a police officer's duties, and then I told him that he was resisting arrest by walking away. My partner caught him and tried to put the cuffs on him, but he cursed at us."

"So then you punched him?" Tony asked the now 6 or 7 police officers.

"Well, he wouldn't let me put the cuffs on him, so we had to make him, by any means possible."

"And that's the truth, detective." Patrolman O'Leary stated.

Tony nodded and started to walk away. He thought, 'why should I get involved in this, let it be referred to Internal Affairs'.

Later at the 10th precinct station on West 20th street, all of these cops would swear that James fought with the arresting officers and tried to bite one of them on the forearm. However, there were no" bleeding wounds" on the officer's arm so IAD was not able to pursue it and dropped any investigation. And all of the 7 police officer's would get an 'assist' for helping with the originating officer's arrest. That's why you see so many cops pile on to one cops arrest. They also get points on their career record for assisting another police officer.

Tony got off of the subway and started to walk along 5th Avenue in Bay Ridge to pick up some food for dinner. He stopped at the fruit store and was choosey of what fruit he took. His mother had taught him how to pick out the 'best' fruit in the bunch. Press the fruit in to see if it was ripe and not hard. He still liked to shop at the neighborhood stores and not go to the large chain supermarkets unless he had to. The store keepers knew him and even told him which was the freshest to take. Like in the fish store, he selected those fish that had clear eyes and not cloudy, because that's how you knew they were fresh, the shop keeper told him. The baker would even hold some rolls for him, because he knew that Tony loved bread. And Brooklyn bread had substance, because of the water; it wasn't fluff, but the real hard rolls, that you could dip into coffee or put a sandwich in it. Tony wondered how long this neighborhood would stay the same, because the chain stores had forced out a lot of local shops. But as long as he could stay here, he would, and not live in the 'real city, Manhattan, or move to Queens or Staten Island. He really didn't like Queens, except for maybe Howard Beach, which was a lot like

Bay Ridge; primarily white and Italian. Staten Island was still okay, was the same ethnic male-up as Bay Ridge, but it was hard to get around there. And Staten Island girls all looked the same with the big hair and the heavy make-up. Bay Ridge was similar, but it was still home. You could take the person out of Bay Ridge, but you couldn't take Bay Ridge out of the person.

New York City cops have to live in either the 5 boroughs of the city, Nassau or Suffolk County in Long Island or the upstate county's of Westchester, Orange or Rockland.

The next day, Tony and Ed Longo went to the Organized Crime Unit which is in a separate building near 1 Police Plaza. Members of the FBI, NYPD, DEA,ATF and Customs are put in there to monitor not only the 5 major crime families of the Mafia, but also the Bloods and Crips gangs, the Highbridge boys, the Jamaican rodeo gangs and others.

Captain Terry McGuire runs the NYPD contingent.

Tony asked for him was escorted to a separate office outside of a bullpen "squad" desks of the other agencies manned by members of the FBI, NYPD, DEA, ATF, and Customs.

"Cap", Tony said," Detectives Tony Philadelphia and Ed Longo of the 9th Precinct homicide squad."

"Hi detectives", Cap said, "What can I do for you?"

"Cap," Tony said," we are investigating a really bad auto accident on the West Side Highway, including cops from the 9th precinct."

"I heard about that", Cap said, "Really tragic."

"Thanks Cap." Tony answered. "But," Tony continued," when we were investigating it because they were from our precinct, we came across possibly some cops being paid from the Columbo family. DeMarco, in particular paid for some SOHO apartments that Griffin and Ryan were living in and sub-let it to them."

"For nothing, I guess." Cap said.

"Exactly." Tony answered.

"Yeah, Cap," Ed Longo added," These were real fancy SOHO condos, that in no way that they could afford."

"What else were they getting?" Cap asked.

"Well," Longo answered," they were getting hookers every night supplied to them."

"At no cost to them?" Cap inquired.

"Exactly- sometimes 2's and 3's" Longo added.

"They must have been doing some serious stuff for them to rate 2 and 3 pros a night." Cap said.

"Yes sir,"Tony said," We think that they were whacking guys and also tipping the mob off to drug raids."

"Well we know DeMarco well, but this is the first time I've heard of cops being on their payroll." Cap said. "Let me get Agent O'Conner of the FBI to come in here and see what he knows."

He picked up the phone and said," Agent O'Connor, can you step in my office a minute?

Sean O'Connor came in with the standard FBI uniform, blue suit and tie, thirty-ish, sandy brown hair, and also around six four.

"This is Detectives Philadelphia and Longo of the 9th Precinct." Cap introduced them.

"Do you have any information on the Columbo family, especially DeMarco, having cops on the payroll?" Tony asked.

"Cap," Agent O'Connor said," We have lots of information on the mob paying cops. Since the original Godfather days."

"Agent" Tony asked. "How about officers Griffin and Ryan on their payroll?"

"Could be." Agent O'Connor said," but you know that their dons and capos don't talk over the phone. They have an intermediary physically go and send the messages back and forth."

"Much like old times." Longo said.

"Yeah, these old mustache Pete's don't trust phones." Agent O'Connor said.

"Agent," Tony said," We know for a fact that Griffin and Ryan are on their payroll."

"Detectives," he said," haven't heard anything, except for some chatter that the Columbo mob has some cops on their payroll to do stuff for them."

"How about whacking?" Longo asked.

"We know that 2 cops from the Gambino family did murder. You know the fat one who played in the film about the mob. He and his partner are in prison for life." O'Connor stated.

"Yes, I remember those guys." Longo said.

"So you're saying that we have similar case here?" Agent inferred.

"Yes Agent." Tony remarked. "We know that there are those who have been supplying information for the Columbo family and these two are part of the crew."

"Okay, why don't you pass what you have onto Cap here and we'll check it out."

"Thanks, Agent." Tony said. Looking at Longo. When the agent left the room, Longo whispered to Tony.

"He knows. He just wants the collar for himself."

"Yup." Tony mentioned.

"Cap" Tony turned to the NYPD Captain." Since this is now more of an IAD investigation, I'll have to get permission from them to turn over what we have to the FBI."

"Absolutely." Cap said. "If anything pops up, I'll let you know."

"Thanks, Cap." Tony said.

"Thanks, Cap" Longo said, and they both turned and left to go back to their car.

When they got back to their car Tony mentioned to his partner, "Longo, I know of some people from the old neighborhood that maybe can help us."

"Who?" Ed Longo asked.

" I know of a woman who is the daughter of one of the guys that the Columbo family killed. They also killed her husband too in a blood feud." Tony mentioned." She hates them, and maybe, she might be able to know something, even if it's in a backhanded way."

"Wow. That would be great. Do you think that she would rat on them, after all, you know the way that some of those Mafia family members are." Longo said." They clam up as well as their relatives do."

"Well this one was brought up believing in La Cosa Nostra law- never go against the family. And that code of honor, to her, runs thicker than blood." Tony mentioned. "This one believes in the old rules of payback and maybe will be willing to work with us." Tony said.

Tony and Longo drove into Brooklyn and Tony gave Longo a history of the blood feud between different members of the Columbo family. During the storied Columbo war- a power struggle between acting boss's left a dozen gangsters dead on the streets of Brooklyn in the late 1990's and early 2000's and when it all shook out, DeMarco was left as the head of the crime family. They stopped at a house on Ovington Street near 13th Avenue in Bay Ridge.

"She still lives here." Tony said as they got out of the car and walked up to Barbara Marino's house. Tony rang the bell, no one answered. A few minutes later he rang the bell again, and a woman opened the door a crack, and said curtly ,"What do you want?"

"Barbara, it's me… Tony Philadelphia, do you remember me?" he said.

The woman behind the small opening in the door looked at him closely and said, "Tony, of course." and opened the door wider. The years had been kind to her; she was still strikingly beautiful, mid-40's, with jet black hair that was probably dyed, and a figure that boasted of too many spaghetti dinners. Her ass still jiggled as she moved, deliberately or not. She looked out into the street and from side to side and also looked at Ed Longo who smiled at her. "Who's this?' she asked.

"This is my partner, Detective Ed Longo." Tony mentioned.

"What can I do for you Tony?" she said.

"Can we come in? I need to ask you some questions about DeMarco?" Tony said.

"That piece of shit- may he rot in hell." she told him." Of course, come in."

"You look good Barbara." Tony said to her.

"Always the flatterer, Tony, but thanks anyway." She said to him as she led them into the kitchen that was right off of the main entrance. "Sit down- can I get you anything?"

'No, thanks anyway Barbara. What can you tell me about DeMarco paying off cops?" Tony asked her.

"They all pay off cops." She said laughing." How else do you think that they're still in business."

"No Barbara, specifically, did you hear of the cops whacking people for the family."Tony mentioned.

"Of course they all do it." She said.

Tony and Longo looked at each other.

"Look, I'm Italian. I may be born here, but I'm still from Italy and I believe in the Italy rules." She said." But they're all dead to me after they killed my husband and my father. In fact I'd love to run into them now. I can't tell you what I would do, but you would have to arrest me."

"I know you Barbara, and I wouldn't put it past you." Tony said.

"But these fucks protect him", she continued." I will do whatever I can to hurt him."

"Barbara," Tony asked, "do you really want to get back at them? We know that you still go to their hangouts and bars."

"That's because my sister-in-laws go there. I talk to them every day." She mentioned. She has 4 sister-in-laws that are still married to made men in the family. A made man in the Mafia is one who has been inducted by killing someone. Barbara's murdered husband (also named Tony) had 4 brothers- Frankie(' the Barber'), Anaphrio('Patch)', Emelio ('Big E') and Augie ('little A') Marino. They were in on the hit on Barbara's husband and father. They all had crews of their own. Her sister-in-laws were Kitty, Rose, Diana, and Angie.

"Barbara," Tony said astonished," you mean to tell me that your brother-in-laws killed your husband and your father?"

"Yes." She said." So they could become higher up in the DeMarco gang."

"So that's why you're now willing to get back at them,"Tony said.

"Yes." She mentioned.

"Barbara, if you really want to get back at them, would you wear a wire?" Tony asked.

"I would hide it in my pussy and show it to them, just so they knew it was me to turn them in," Barbara said.

"Barbara, but how could someone kill their own brother." Tony asked astonished.

"In the Mafia, you do what you're told or else you get whacked, even if it's family." She said.

"So when is DeMarco going to get killed?" Tony asked her.

"As soon as someone has the coulionies(balls) to do it." She told him matter-of-factly.

"Do you think that some of your family is planning this now?" he asked.

"Come back and see me when you're off duty Tony and we'll talk more about it." She said smiling at him.

"Sure thing Barbara." Tony responded. "I'll stop by later, okay?"

"Great" she said. "come for dinner; I haven't made dinner for a man in a while. We can talk about old times." She winked at him.

As they left, Longo said to Tony." She is built like a brick shithouse."

"I know," Tony said," she always looked good." She was a good ten years older than Tony, but still liked him a lot; more than a lot if she wasn't married when they knew each other.

"And she has the hots for you Philadelphia, I can tell the by way that she kept looking at you, almost devouring you." Longo told him"

She's a widow who probably hasn't been fucked in a long while. You betta keep your cock in your pants, because she is determined to fuck you."

"I'll try," Tony answered." But she's got some nice body to fuck."

"That's true." Longo added.

Later that evening, Tony stopped by at Barbara's house and was ready to hand her a nice bottle of Chianti , but was quickly given a greeting more like former lovers and not just friends. She hugged him and kissed him fully on the mouth as he got in the door.

"It's really great to see you Tony." She said looking at him, but still holding onto him. "I wonder why you never came around after the funerals."

Tony had made the dutiful trips to the viewings and the funerals of her father and husband, but years tend to come right after one another, and he didn't want to disrupt her mourning period, which to an old fashioned Italian family, is for life. Most of the time she still wore black, but tonight was the exception. He knew that she wanted him to fuck her.

"I'm sorry, Barbara, but it was too soon, and I didn't want to interrupt your mourning period." Tony mentioned.

"Well, come in- let's open that wine." She said.

"Great." He said. As she went first into the kitchen to get the bottle opener, he couldn't help eyeing her ass jiggling in the pants outfit that she wore. She got two glasses and let him open the wine. They toasted each other' salud!'and he followed her into the living room where they sat side by side on the sofa. Before he could even settle in, she put her glass down and was all over him; on him, kissing him and licking him and unbuttoning his shirt.

"Barbara, wait." He said in between kisses.

"Why?' she mentioned." I always wanted you; and I can tell that you always wanted me."

He proceeded to caress her breasts, and kiss her neck and lips. She unzipped his fly and grabbed his cock and started to stroke it. As he fumbled with pulling down her pants, she went down on him and started to suck his cock. It was fully erect in a second. He layed her back on the sofa, and pulled off her pants. He then went down on her licking her pussy and fingering her ass. By the time she was moaning and screaming, she pulled off her blouse and bra. He stopped eating her long enough to suck on those beautiful nipples.

"Oh fuck me baby!" she yelled.

He mounted her and she let out a scream of passion that her husband could hear in his grave. Over and over again he pounded her, and kept it in her a long time. Then he made her get up and leaned her across the sofa, plunging his big cock into her pussy to the hilt. She screamed,

"Oh I like it like that!." And screamed even more. He kept fucking her for a good half-hour before he finally came in her. She loved it and wanted more.

"Give me a second, hon." He said as he laid next to her, momentarily out of breath.

"I always knew that you were a stud, Tony." She said.

She turned to him and gently touched his stomach and chest and then reached down and grabbed his cock again. She stroked it and put her mouth on it, sucking it deeply, over and over, until it was erect again. He started to go down on her again spreading her pussy with his tongue and grabbing her breasts and caressing it. She got up and sat down on his cock so that she rode it like a cowgirl. He raised her ass up and down to push his cock all the way in as she screamed words of encouragement again and again.

"Oh fuck me again baby." she screamed. "Oh wow, you are the best! Give it to me!"

Once again, he let her ride him for a good 20 minutes or more, she kept coming and he kept saying to her,

"Want more baby?"

"YES!" was the answer and he kept pounding it into her. He turned her back on the sofa again and spread her legs really wide and plunged it in again from the front. He knew it was all the way in by her expression and screaming. Finally, she couldn't take it any longer, and got up and took him by her hand into her bedroom. She just threw him on the bed and was sucking his cock again and stroking it. She couldn't get enough of him today or anyday. She had to make up for many years of not doing it. "Turn over honey." He said. She complied and again he started to lick her back and went down to suck her pussy this time from the back. He then mounted her from the back, and again plunging it into her. Moaning, she said to him.

"YOU ARE A SEX MANIAC!"

"You just keep turning me on Barbara." He said and came in her again. They both came at the same time.

"Okay, let's take a break for a few seconds." She said out of breath. "So what do you want me to do Tony?" she asked.

"Well for starters, I want to fuck you like this every day." He laughed.

"Any time!" she told him. "You know that I always wanted you even when I was married, I used to dream of you each night before I went to bed."

"That's great. It's a deal. But, to get back to what I'm doing at work, would you wear a wire and find out from the family what's going on." He told her. "You don't have to push it by forcing questions, just hear what is doing, okay?"

"Tony, most of my sister-in-laws just constantly talk about getting laid." She mentioned.

"That's good too, but don't tell them that we're doing it." He said to her.

"Okay honey." She said.

The next day back in the squad room, the first thing that Longo asked Tony was,

"So did you nail that piece of ass last night?

"Definitely" Tony answered. "And you were right, the widow lady wanted it a lot."

"I told you." Longo added. "I know when a woman wants it."

"Well, she certainly wanted me." Tony said. "I should have gone to see her years ago. She would have kept me satisfied for quite some time."

"Why do you have all the luck with the ladies Philadelphia? I'm lucky if I get laid once in a blue moon." Longo added.

"I don't know Longo. I just flatter them until their panties drop." Tony laughed.

"But every woman?" Longo asked.

"I wish." Tony responded. "Can you imagine that Longo, fucking every woman you see, like a male deer does?'

"That would be great!" Longo mentioned. "Too bad human females aren't like that, even though we are."

"I know."

Another thing that cops do all of the time is retaliate against witnesses who observe police officers doing either illegal acts or using excessive force. A woman recently videotaped a man who was choke hold and died. This video was played all over the news. But police remember such instances.

Tony and Ed Longo were driving from their 9th precinct down to SOHO and passed the 1st precinct near Ericson Place, when they observed this woman, Tamika Garner, being harassed by a police officer, Thomas O'Brien. She had been walking down the street near a store, when he said to her,

" Oh you're the bitch that filmed that video aren't you?"

Tamika ignored the comment, but wondered why was he singling her out. At that point, the officer falsely stated,

"Ok, now you have a warrant out for your arrest." Without checking her identification to run her name in the system. She tried to walk away, when several other officers nearby, grabbed her and threw half her body over a fence, twisting her arms as she 'screamed in agony'.

Tony and Longo pulled over and ran to the scene, as several officers started to beat her with a baton and dragged her to their police car.

"WHOA!!" Ed Longo said showing his gold shield. "What the fuck is going on here?"

"She's the bitch who filmed that video of the choke hold." Officer O'Brian said.

"Wait a minute." Tony added. "What did she do now?"

"We think that there is a warrant for her arrest." O'Brian stated.

"You think or you know? Did you run her name through?" Longo added.

"No, but we know she is wanted for something." Another officer said. "Any bitch who would film an arrest is probably wanted."

"Well then cuff her and book her- don't beat her." Tony said.

"Do you want this collar?" O'Brian added. Most detectives will take the collar of a patrol officer to get arrest points on their record and leave the hapless patrol cop waiting for his turn.

"NO!" Longo stated. "Guys, this is bad, cops don't beat up women."

At that point they stopped hitting her.

Tony and Ed Longo went back to their car, and Tony said,

"This is what gives all cops a bad name."

"You're right. Some of these cops do not belong on the force." Longo added.

Later at the 1st precinct, a Captain told another officer that they did not have the right person, but since all those officers who beat her swore that it was her, they made this woman plead guilty to disorderly conduct and obstruction charges.

CHAPTER 10

Tony and Longo went back to the SOHO apartment of Griffin armed with a court order to look for evidence. Once they initially got in they would call for a crime scene unit to search everything, including garbage, toilet paper, etc. everything.

"Ivan" Tony said to the superintendent. "Here is the court order allowing us to search Mr. Giffin's apartment."He showed Ivan the court order "Let us into his apartment."

"Ok', Ivan said looking at the official looking document.

He brought them up to Griffin's apartment. Once he got to the elevator landing and the door opened Tony said,

"Ivan, you can go. We have a lot to do here and we'll be getting some back-up here in a few minutes. Please let them in here also."

"Ok". Ivan said and went down, back to the 1st floor.

"What do you make of this guy?" Longo asked.

"He's okay I guess, typical gate keeper; keeps the skels out in this high end condo." Tony answered. "OK let's start going thru drawers and stuff and see what we can find before the CSU guys get here."

"Sounds good to me." Longo added. "I'll start in the bathroom. You never believe how much shit, pardon the meaning, that you can find in a bathroom. People will hide things in air conditioning ducts, behind radiators, in medicine chests, even in the toilet bowl."

"I didn't know about toilet bowls." Tony said.

"Yeah," Longo mentioned." One time I found out that you can hide something under the toilet bowl, where it meets the floor. You have to pull off the bowl part where the gaskets are. This drug guy had hid some keys of heroin in there. I'm going to start there. I wonder if Griffin was as smart as he thought."

"OK. I'll start going thru his drawers." Tony answered.

Longo was a big man and he had no difficulty in pulling off the bottom of the toilet bowl after he shut off the water. A vitreous china toilet bowl can weigh more than a hundred pounds without water in it.

"Bingo!!" Longo shouted after he pulled off the toilet bowl. In it was a gun, stashed between the flexible gaskets that seal the toilet bowl. He took some toilet paper and lifted the gun gently. Then he took his pen and put it thru the trigger and carried it out of the bathroom.

"Look what I found!" Longo exclaimed. Tony looked up to see a Glock 9MM semi-automatic gun.

"I wonder why he hid it there; it's not his service revolver." Longo mentioned.

"I wonder if it was involved with any of these mob rub-outs." Tony said. "We'll give it to the CSU guys to check it for fingerprints and see if they also match any ballistic imprints from those mob murders."

Longo went to the kitchen to find a large plastic bag and put the gun in there.

Tony, meanwhile was going thru Griffin's drawers, and was looking for anything unusual, like receipts for stuff that you wouldn't ordinarily keep from other receipts. Griffin was a neat freak and he should have kept all of his receipts in one place, and not spread in different areas. He removed each drawer and dumped the contents onto the floor, flipping the drawer over to see if anything was attached to it. Then he looked into the empty drawer cavity, again looking to see if Griffin pushed something to the back of the drawer. One by one he took each drawer out and painstakingly did the same method of detective work.

And then something caught his eye. It was a full length mirror behind him, that was slightly off center. Griffin being a neat freak would never have allowed that. Tony put down the drawer and went over to the mirror. He took it off of its wire hinges and spun it around to reveal the back of it. Two things glared at him. There was a vault behind the mirror and an envelope taped to the mirror. He opened the envelope and he found what looked like a safe deposit key; to what bank he thought.

He called to Longo," Guess what I found." Longo came in from the kitchen and saw what Tony had found- the key and the vault."

There is no name on this key, I guess that we'll have to first see where Griffin banked and try there. Otherwise, we'll have to start calling banks to see if he had a safe deposit box there."

"I wonder what's in the vault?" Longo said. Just then the CSU (crime scene unit) guys arrived. (actually it was two guys and a female)

All CSU people are detectives, just like Tony and Longo. It was the 3-Rs that came this time. Reagan, Ryan and Roseanne. Roseanne was a petite blond that Tony wanted to fuck her body, but so did every other dick.

"Hello people," Tony said to the CSU as they came in.

"What are we looking for?" Timothy Reagan asked.

"Everything" Tony answered. "This guy is a dead cop and possibly a dirty cop."

"Uh-oh. That's not good." John (Jack) Ryan mentioned.

"Well, if it isn't the Tony awards." Roseanne DeMucci said.

"Hi Roseanne." Tony said." How's it going?"

"Good." She said.

"I need something blown." He added.

"I hope it's not your cock." She laughed.

Everybody laughed at that remark.

"I wish." Tony said. "But no. There's a vault behind the mirror that needs to be opened and the contents emptied out. And I also need this" he showed them the safe deposit key." We need to find out which bank this is from."

"That looks interesting" Jack Ryan said. "A vault AND a safe deposit key. Wonder what is in the safe deposit box. He was really trying to protect something. What's he hiding?"

"That's what we're thinking too." Longo added.

"Not a problem." Reagan answered. "Let's crack the vault first and see what's inside."

Roseanne grabbed a crow bar and a stethoscope from her CSU bag of tricks. She put the stethoscope on the tumbler and tried to listen for the combination. After several tries, she folded up the stethoscope and said to her teammates" NG. This is a really good lock. You're turn guys."

Jack Ryan also grabbed a sledge hammer out of his bag of tricks and a chisel. He first tried using the crowbar several times. "Damn, this is a really good safe." He looked at the manufacturer." Moser. They make good safes. Okay Reagan, it's yours."

Reagan selected a chisel from the bag and placed it on the vault hinges. One hefty blow and the safe door opened and fell to the side, hanging on by one hinge. "I guess that it's not that safe." He smiled that he cracked it open.

Roseanne started to empty out the contents of the vault to catalog it, much like an autopsy is done by a pathologist.

"Okay, I see a lot of cash here. Ryan, why don't you count it. I next see a passport." She opened it. "He recently made a trip to Italy." She handed it to Reagan, who cataloged it and put it in a glass-line envelope. "I next see a gold bar." She tried to pick it up "Damn, it's very heavy. Must be at least 10 pounds." She handed it to Reagan. "I next see a gun. Snub nose revolver." She handed it to Reagan."

"I count $50,000 in 100's here." Ryan said.

Roseanne continued emptying out the vault. "I see a lot of small envelopes with white power in it." She opened one envelope and tasted it with her finger. "Cocaine." she said. "Must be about 50 envelopes in here." she again handed it to Reagan who started to count the envelopes. "There is a list here of telephone numbers. Must be several pages long. "Again she handed it to Ryan. "There is also some DVD's in here, maybe 5." She turned and put it on the night table. "And he has a bunch of gold coins here." She handed the stacks to Reagan. "And there is some miscellaneous papers here too, actually, they are US Treasury Bonds, and stock certificates."

"Nice haul." She mentioned. "That's about it on the contents of the vault." She said.

Reagan turned to Tony and Longo. "Ok guys, we'll start going thru all of the apartment, catalog it and give you a report."

"Thanks, guys." Tony said

"Thanks" Longo added. They called for the elevator and went down to the first floor. They saw Ivan and told him, "The CSU people will probably be there all day. They'll let you know when they're finished."

"OK" Ivan said.

Tony and Longo went back to their car.

"Easy's?" Longo asked.

"Absolutely." Tony responded

Most tits and ass bars are open 24/7 to make as much money on drinks. Also, there is food, and the kitchen is open for at least several hours during the early morning hours, but you have to buy a drink to look at the dancers.

Tony waved to Angela, but wanted to talk to Claire. He motioned to her to go to the end of the bar. He kissed her and said.

"How about lunch tomorrow after you get off at 12PM?"

"Actually that's dinner for me, but sounds great." She answered.

"Ok, I'll pick you up here and we can go someplace."

"Good." She answered "What can I get you now to drink, hon?"

He motioned to Longo to come sit where he was. Longo already was nursing a beer that Angela gave him.

"Just a beer on tap, honey." Claire went to get a glass and fill it from the myriad of beers on tap.

There were cops already at the bar and at tables eying the dancers perform their struts and picking up dollar bills being shoved in their tights.

"What do you think Philadelphia? With what CSU found?" Longo asked.

"Not here. Too many ears. Let's talk when we leave."

"Yeah, you're right." Longo said turning around and looking at the cops who were trying to listen in on their conversation.

Bobby O'Mara was there as well as SGT. Fallon. You have to watch everything that you say in a bar, especially, if cops are listening in.

Later in the day, Tony went with Longo and stopped off at Barbara's house again to give her the wire and show her how to do it. Tony researched how Barbara's father and husband were killed. The mob had only intended to hit Barbara's father, but they hit Barbara's husband too because he was with him, and they take every opportunity to do it. But it had to be a set -up, because Barbara's father also had some "zips" (Sicilian hit-men) as protection, and they mysteriously went to the bathroom while it happened.

"I know how to do it." She said." Do you know how many family members have flipped?" (turned to be a government witness)

"Okay, honey, but you don't need to put it in your pussy like you said, it's small and you can wear it hidden in your bra." Tony added.

"Do you want me to fashion it for you?" she asked knowing that he wanted to fuck her again.

"That would be nice? Tony said.

Barbara removed her blouse and her bra. They were still erect even though she was in her '40's. Tony said amazingly, "I can't believe that you're breasts are still so perfect." He said admiringly.

"genes" Barbara said, putting the small wire into the cup of the bra.

"It has a range of 10 miles so you don't have to worry that it won't pick up even the slightest voices." Tony added. He also gave her a tiny tape recorder and enough tapes for like six months. "I'll see you at least once a week, and I'll collect the tapes, okay honey?"

"You can come every day babe." She looked at him with desire in her eyes and grabbed his cock from outside his pants. It was erect already. "Hmmm. It's big already. It'll be a shame to waste such a nice big cock." She kissed him passionately on the mouth. She opened his zipper and pulled his cock out, got on her knees and started sucking it. She was good too, Tony thought, and she knew that he wanted it.

He lifted her up from her kneeling position, pulled off her pants and panties, turned her around and quickly plunged it into her from the rear.

She started screaming the moment he entered her, "Oh that feels so good."

"You like that honey?" he asked her as he kept plunging it into her to the hilt.

"It feels wonderful. Oh my God that's good." She screamed.

After a long while he came in her and waited until she came. "Not yet babe. Keep it in there honey." She demanded. Finally, she was satisfied and let out a big sigh. "Wow, you can keep coming back for this every day, my love."

"I'm going to." Tony mentioned zipping up his pants. He kissed her and said,

"I wish that I could stay longer, honey, but I have to get back to work. My partner is waiting for me outside in the car."

"Okay, my love, come back whenever you can. I'm here for you." She said, and then added, "Always."

Tony smiled and blew her a kiss as he shut the door behind hm.

As he got back in the car Longo said,

"You knocked off that piece of ass again, didn't you?" he laughed.

"What can I tell you, she wants it." Tony answered. "And I love giving it to her."

"Fuck you Philadelphia, you get all of these women to fuck. I want some too!" Longo stated.

"They are out there, you just have to find them and cultivate them." Tony laughed as Longo pulled away from the curb. "You just have to listen to them until her panties fall off."

"Damn you !" Longo added, and shook his head at Tony's luck with women.

Barbara was true to her word; she wanted to get back at the family for what they did to her husband and father. She started to go their hangouts with her sister-in-laws.

Before she left to go to these joints, each day she would say into the tape,

"This is Barbara Marino, the date is Friday July 17th. Tony and Dad, this is for you."

The family still accepted her even though her husband was dead, especially since all her brother-in-laws were still connected. The 'boys' would play gin-rummy and talk about what scores they were going to make, or what scores they had just pulled off. Or even what their future plans were for the family. Because the 'wire' was so sensitive, Barbara could pick up each conversation.

"So what are we going to call this caper." Emilio (Big E) asked.

"Well since Griffin is dead and we know that Ryan will soon be dead, let's call it the Rossi." Frankie (the barber), who was the eldest of the brothers, told him. "He should take over as head of his crew of cops."

"But he didn't get all of the bene's that Griffin did; with the condo and the broads." Augie (little A) stated.

"So give it to him." Anaphrio (Patch) said. "He deserves it- for one, he's Italian and not like all of those other Mick cops. And he's also a Detective, so he'll hear more of what's going on than the other cops who are just on the street."

"Agreed."Emillio stated. "And this is gin." Putting down the 10 cards of 4, 3 and 3 of each suite on the table.

"Aw, fongu." Frankie mentioned.

" Emillio." Patch said, "where did you get those cards from- up your sleeve."

They played for a $1 a point.

"Just lucky I guess." Emillio answered, as he marked down on a sheet of paper what he had and how much each card was worth in points.

All of the made guys had mistresses, and their wives knew it. It was just accepted. They didn't like it, but they accepted it. So all of the time, when the sister-in-laws got together, all they talked about was sex, and their lack of getting laid.

Bay Ridge in Brooklyn was still a tight knit community. Even though there was a large influx of Asians lately, everybody knew what was going on. Especially, since all of the Marino family lived within blocks of Barbara, so they knew, like detectives, that Tony was continuing to visit Barbara, especially the sister-in-laws.

"Barbara," Kitty Marino said," who's that guy that I see coming over to your place- new beau?"

"Oh no,"Barbara said," that's Tony Philadelphia. You remember him, he's an old friend. Just catching up on old times."

"He's a cop." Kitty added.

"So what? Do you know how many cops that the family has on its payroll?" Barbara stated.

"A lot." Rose answered. "But what is he coming around now."

"He just wanted to re-new an old friendship. We knew each other from the old neighborhood." Barbara answered.

"He's still good looking." Angie said. "So is he sticking it into you?"

Barbara blushed." No. It's not like that. He's just a friend."

"But he comes over a lot." Diana said.

"Not a lot." Barbara answered. "Maybe once a week, and what is it your business. I don't have a husband- you all do. So let me ask you; are any of you getting laid? I bet not, because your husbands all have mistresses."

"No that's not true." Rose answered.

"Yeah, right." Barbara answered curtly. "You all must be delusional, but your husbands all have a piece of ass on the side."

All Mafioso do have a mistress. And Barbara, since she was Sicilian, knew all too well that they did. But the sister-in-laws did not want to admit it. But they knew.

Tony liked fucking Barbara because she was a nice piece of ass, and he knew that she really enjoyed being fucked by him. But he really fell for Claire in a big way. Not only did she let him fuck her every way, but there was something else that he could relate to. She was closer in age to him than Barbara or Angela, and he couldn't put his finger on it, but wanted to continue seeing her. But he still wanted to have a piece of Barbara and Angela on the side. Most men are horn dogs, ready for sex at the drop of a bra.

When Tony went to Easy's to pick up Claire, Angela waved him over.

"Tony, I need to speak to you." She motioned for him to go with her to where the dancer's dressing room was. He followed her, but it was hard for Tony to concentrate with all of the naked women. And they were all smiling at him.

"I heard something." Angela said." That the mob knows that you're seeing one of the Columbo family widows."

"Who said this?" Tony asked.

"The goofy looking cop, Bobby O'Mara." Angela answered. "He mentioned this to other cops at the bar."

""I went to see her because I know her from the old neighborhood. She's an old friend- nothing more." He lied. "I didn't ask her to do anything for me."

"Okay Tony, I'm just trying to tell you what I heard." Angela said.

"Rumors find a way of getting turned around." Tony said.

"That's for sure." Angela added.

"Thanks, honey. Keep telling me what you find out. I appreciate it." Tony said. "And Angela, if you find out some more info, I'll have the Dane come over and pay you a call." He winked at her.

"I'll make sure to get that stuff for you then." Angela said to him, blushed and giggled.

Tony came over to Claire. "Ready?" he asked.

"Am I ever." She answered. "Where are we going?"

"There's a Cuban place on West 46th Street that's not bad."

"Sounds good." She said." I like Cuban food."

"So do I." Tony answered and led her out to his car.

"What was Angela trying to tell you?" she asked.

"Cop business on a case that I'm working on." He answered." But you probably know these guys- Griffin, Ryan and that goofy looking cop."

"Oh yes. Bad people. Really bad people." She said.

"So I'm finding out." Tony stated slamming her side car door after she got in.

As he started to pull out a cop car with 5 cops in an SUV passed thru a stop sign and T-boned (broadsided) a vehicle. The NYPD car occupants had just left The Easy Score and was without flashing lights or a siren. All 5 cops got out of the SUV and proceeded to ask the driver if he had been drinking. They were smelling of alcohol and they asked him if HE was drunk.

Tony looked at what was happening and told Claire." Wait a second honey. I need to see what's going on here."

Tony got out of his car and flashed his gold shield to the 5 cops who recognized him as being from the 9th precinct.

"Hi Detective. We observed signs that indicate that this driver may be intoxicated." Officer Wiggins said.

An arrest for driving under the influence usually has a driver who smells, not of alcohol, but of an "alcoholic beverage." More often than not the driver is described as having "watery, bloodshot and or glassy eyes along with slurred speech". A quick check of the booking photograph will show the way a person's eyes looked the time of the arrest and they don't always appear in the way they are described.

"He has red watery eyes, slurred speech and the odor of an alcoholic beverage." Officer Wiggins said.

"I didn't drink anything." The driver, one Bill Raymond stated.

"And he's swaying." Another cop stated.

Tony approached him and said to the other cops." I don't smell anything on him, but all you guys reek of booze." He looked at the skel." He doesn't have bloodshot, watery eyes either, but give him the standard DUI test."

"Do you want the collar detective?" another cop asked in order to save their badges.

"No. Just put in an accident report." Tony shook his head in disgust and went back to his car.

"What was that all about babe?" Claire said when he got back in the car.

"I think that those cops were trying to make an improper arrest in order to cover up the accident that they just caused." Tony added.

"And what did they ask you?" she asked.

"If I wanted the collar." Tony said.

"You know that they are lying pieces of shit. They have been getting away with so much for so many years." Claire added.

"I know." Tony said. "What can you do, it's that way with a lot of cops."

"But not you." Claire said.

"No." Tony said. "I'm one of the good guys."

"I know." Claire mentioned, smiling at him. "That's why I'm going out with you."

When he heard her say that, he smiled at her knowing that he was going to get laid again later.

He didn't get too far when he noticed another disturbance a few blocks away that he decided not to get involved in.

"Don't look honey. It's another disgrace to the uniform that I wear." Tony said.

"Why do they let these bully's join the police force?" Claire said as she couldn't help but look.

"That's because bully's as kids grow up to be cops." Tony answered. "They should be vetted and thrown out."

A plainclothes narcotics cop by the name of Fred Dale, had pulled over a car driven by John Charles, for no apparent reason except he needed to show something that he did for the day on his report. He called for back-up and they found prescription medication for anxiety and pain.

"I have a prescription for the meds." Charles said.

"Fuck you, shut up. We've had enough of you!" Dale shouted at him.

The cops threw him in the back of the van and took him for a "rough ride'. That's a police term for deliberately driving erratically and recklessly by repeatedly accelerating and decelerating abruptly, slamming on the brakes, making sharp turns and speeding around corners. What happens is the skel was sent rolling around the interior like a rag doll, slamming into the back doors of the van, the front metal separating the rear compartment, and two benches that faced each other. At the end of that ride, the skel was unresponsive. The cops thought that he was faking it, but in reality, he had suffered a fatal injury to his spinal cord. The cops tried to think of ways to cover this up and came up with the brilliant idea of that he deliberately injured himself while in police custody to be able to sue the city.

Meanwhile the Organized Crime Task Force Unit was starting to get pictures taken of Tony and Longo going into Barbara Marino's house. And when he went back there alone for dinner and to rig her with the wire, they also noticed. It's hard not to notice when you're the daughter of a former crime family head.

The NYPD Organized Crime Task force Captain, showed Tony's Loo the pictures. "What do you make of this." He said.

"He's just trying to get information from her." Loo stated looking at the photos of Tony and Longo with Barbara Marino.

"Well," Cap said, "He should give any information that he gets from her to us. This is our collar."

"I'll tell him that Cap."Loo responded.

"Just between you and me Loo, the extracurricular activities of these cops that are linked to the Columbo crime family, range from tipping off these gangsters about a murder probe to helping cover up a mob or cop hit, or even running license plates for loansharks." Cap stated.

"I know; it sounds pretty bad. IAD is also involved in this Cap." Loo answered.

"And also that Griffin regularly provided information and services to DeMarco and the other members of his crew, like the Marino brothers." Cap said. "Philadelphia and Longo should also know that one of these cops, I believe O'Donnell, lied to the FBI about DeMarco's cover-up, a second cop ran plates on loan-shark victims and a third hired one of these gangsters in an arson plot. This allowed DeMarco to find debtors and collect money, sometimes by burning their cars or beating them senseless." Cap stated again.

"Cap" Loo said. "I'll make sure that Philadelphia and Longo report anything they find to you personally.

"Very good Loo. Carry on." Cap stated.

Loo got to the dispatcher as soon as Cap left and told her to have Philadelphia and Longo report back to the squad room as soon as possible.

Longo was still where Tony had left him, at Easy's , imbibing on his sixth beer and free lunch and ogling the dancers, or should I say trying to feel them up with dollar bills.

Tony and Claire had finished lunch and they were starting to eat one another's genitals when Tony got the call.

"Don't answer it." Claire said, taking enough of a breath to suck his cock again in the 69 position.

"I've got to hon." Tony said rolling her back over onto her bed.

"Philadelphia!" Tony answered curtly and out of breath.

"Tony" Dispatcher Cheryl Nielson said over the phone. "Loo wants you and Longo back to the squad room immediately."

"I'm in the middle of lunch break." Tony stated. "I'll be there as soon as I can."

"Roger that." She said.

"I can't believe this." Tony complained to Claire, shutting off his phone. "I can't even catch a break here."

"We'll make it a quickie and then I'll let you go." She said still stroking his erect cock.

He mounted her and although he wanted to stay longer inside her to make her enjoy it more, he came almost immediately and got off of her.

Tony picked up Longo at Easy's (he was already sloshed); they stopped at a coffee shop to get black coffee for Longo (free of course) and it took him like 3 large black coffee's to even get half-awake. Tony gave him a roll of mints that he carried in his pocket, to stop the smell of beer. Over the years and many women later, this roll of mints would instantly stop the "pussy eating breath". This to him was a proven method to get rid of the genitalia smell that was a giveaway that he just had sex. But as usual, whenever you are in a rush to get somewhere, fate always throws something in your path to delay you.

Passing thru Midtown North, an officer pulled over a woman for failure to signal a lane change. He was short on his daily ticket quota and he thought that this would be an easy one. The woman, Jenny Goode, started to question him for pulling her over. The officer Brian Leary, argued with her over her smoking a cigarette in the car.

"Don't you know that's illegal." He told her.

"In what state?" she said. "This is my car and I'll do whatever I damn please in it as long as it's not against the law."

"Well you're puffing smoke in my face and to me that's illegal, so stop it now." He added.

"Like hell I will!" She angrily responded puffing more smoke into his face.

"Get out of the car now!" he screamed at her.

"I will not!" she stated.

"I'm going to yank you out of there." Leary shouted.

"Ok, you going to yank me out of my car" Goode replied. "Ok. All right. Let's do this."

The officer pulls out his gun. "I will light you up!" he shouted before she finally steps into the street. The officer did not know that Jenny Goode was the head of "Black Lives Matter" and was going to resist this cop by any means possible.

Tony and Ed Longo saw this develop and immediately stopped and get out of their car.

"What's going on?" Tony said flashing his shield.

"This bitch is refusing arrest!" he said.

"Take it easy-"Longo said." Cuff her and put her into your car. Don't make it develop into an IAD case."

The two still shouted at each other as the officer puts the cuffs on her.

"You about to break my fucking wrist!" she shouted. "STOP!!"

This is another example of "resisting arrest without violence", which is that a person charged with this crime can face a year in jail because they "refused to stand up" or they "tensed their arms" while being handcuffed.

Just then back-up arrives and Leary puts her in the car.

"You want this collar." He said to Tony.

"No- just process her." Tony said to him.

As Tony and Longo went back to their car, Tony says to Longo, "You know we all know that some cops are foolish men, but to argue with them is more foolish."

Tony finds out several days later, that she" hung" herself in her jail cell because of the humiliation. It appeared that they made it look like a suicide and the cover-up within the department to lynch her dead body up. Death should not be the penalty for non-compliance in America.

There are 2 kinds of truth, the truth and a police version of it.

CHAPTER 11

When Tony and Ed Longo got back to the squad room, Loo was already on a roll about them not coming back even though it was on their lunch break.

"Guys." Loo said," You're not just cops, you're Detectives, which means you are like management."

"Geez, Loo." Longo said. "When did we get a promotion to brass?"

"You know very well, what I mean- Longo." Loo retorted. "It means wherever you are, even if you're in the can or on lunch break, you come back to the squad room."

"We got here as soon as we could Loo." Tony said. "I was in the middle of a delicious sandwich and I couldn't get it to go." He lied, he just couldn't tell Loo that he was in the middle of fucking Claire.

"Yeah, I'll bet Philadelphia." Loo knew that Tony was a horn dog and that he was probably fucking somebody.

Tony grinned. "So what was it that I had to leave my sandwich there?"

"Cap from Organized Crime Scene Unit was here and he showed me pictures of you and Longo at Barbara Marino's house." Loo stated.

Tony and Longo looked at each other, surprised that they were being watched. "We were there to find out anything from her, since she hates DeMarco for killing her husband and father. I know her from the old neighborhood." Tony said.

"Well did you find out anything from her? Loo asked.

"She agreed to wear a wire when she goes to the joints that the Columbo family owns and find out anything that she can." Tony responded.

"Well did you inform IAD about the wire?" Loo asked.

"No Loo." Longo answered. "We didn't have a chance since it happened so fast."

"Where did you get the wire then? Loo asked.

"I know somebody in CSU who gave me a very sensitive wire." Long answered.

"And we're also going to plant a wire at the warehouse where the coffin cops plan all their capers." Tony added.

"Just inform IAD guys. I don't want them coming back to say that this was their collar." Loo stated.

"Sure thing Loo." Longo answered.

"Yup." Tony added.

"Okay, you can go. But remember when I call you, forget those free beers and forget fucking some whore and come back here." Loo added.

"Sure thing Loo." Tony answered, and looked at Ed Longo who was trying to hold back a laugh, since Loo knew what his guys were up to.

Tony and Longo then went to drive back to the coffin cops hideout on Cherry Street. Again, as they were riding there, two cops pulled over a car for a traffic infraction, and the officer smells the "odor of marijuana" coming from the car. Smelling marijuana is grounds for a police officer to search a car during a routine traffic stop. These two officers claimed that they smelled marijuana through their air conditioning vent that was coming from the car that they just pulled over. The" I smell pot" ploy is nothing more than a way to get around looting that vehicle. This is especially true if the officer asks to look through the car and you say no. Then they'll pull out the smell nonsense and it usually holds up in court if it's challenged.

"I'm not getting involved in this." Ed Longo says to Tony.

"You're right. Keep going." He said.

But as they past some street near the South Street Seaport, they witnessed something that they had to stop and get out of their car. Four cops on patrol from the 1st Precinct, had surrounded a man in a wheelchair, and were using bean-bag rounds and a Taser on him.

As they approached the scene, they could hear shouts coming from the cops,

"Take that you fucking son-of-a bitch!'

The wheelchair bound man was kicking his legs and screaming at the cops.

"Hold it!" Longo said showing his gold shield. "What the fuck are you doing?"

"This asshole spit at us." The officer replied.

"And you're using a Taser on him for that?"

"He wouldn't submit to being arrested." Officer John Edwards said.

"What did you think that he was going to leap out of that wheelchair and attack you?" Tony said.

"Well you never know with these skels." Officer Brian Sullivan stated.

"Was he going to run over you with his wheelchair or do you consider yourself incapable of capturing him or too slow to avoid getting run over by a wheelchair. C'mon guys!!" Ed Longo said.

"Do you want the collar for this?" Officer Edwards said.

"No! Just process him for spitting on the sidewalk." Tony said, turned and walked back to the car.

Once in the car. Longo said to Tony. "What the hell is going on with these young cops?"

"I guess they're taught at the Academy that they can do anything they want." Tony answered.

Since the coffin cops hide-out was on Cherry Street, there's a lot of abandoned buildings there. And there's always abandoned cars just parked there too. Tony and Ed Longo were going to plant a bug inside the old coffin warehouse when a patrol car from Midtown North with

2 of the coffin cops pulled behind one of these abandoned cars. But it wasn't abandoned. There was a skel sleeping in there. Officer Kevin Darcy walked behind the car and then banged on the windshield with his gun, which broke it to awake the sleeping skel inside. He opened the door and then said,

"Get up you mother-fucker. You're under arrest for driving with a broken windshield."(which he just broke)

The skel, Vincent James, wakes up and says, "I wasn't driving."

"Bullshit!" Officer Darcy says, and reaches in and starts to punch and kick James.

The officers arrested James at the scene on assault, resisting arrest and drug charges. They couldn't find any drugs, but who else would park a car near an abandoned building and not be doing drugs. Also, he was adjacent to their "place of business" and they didn't want anybody there.

Tony and Longo look at each other in amazement.

"Did you just see what I saw?" he said.

"Don't blow our cover." Longo said. "Let's wait until they leave and then we'll try to go into the building."

Tony nodded agreement.

A few minutes later, after they left, Tony and Longo approached the building by foot. Longo says to Tony,

"I'll stand watch outside. You go in and case the building."

"Got it." Tony says and nods. He pulls out his gun and goes in the building's door that's cracked open. There's an office just inside, and then the warehouse where they stored the coffins. It's a large warehouse with spaces for stacking hundreds of coffins up to the rafters. The place still smells of the wood coffins, even after a number of years. A quick look around and Tony sees that there is no one in the building. He gets on his radio,

"Longo, there's no one here."

"I'm coming in." Longo says, taking another quick look in all directions.

"Do you have the wire?" Tony asks him.

"Yeah, right here." Longo answers and pulls out a thin wire from his jacket pocket.

"Where should we put it?" Tony asks.

"I would love to put it in the office, but they'll probably find it." Longo says. He looks up in the warehouse and starts to climb up a few of the racks. For a big man, Ed Longo was very agile, much to the chagrin of many skels who thought they could outrun him by climbing over a fence. Like a monkey he climbed on the edge of the steel structure, and sticks it behind one of the rack's steel columns about 12 feet off of the ground. He pulls out a roll of grey duct tape from his pocket, and tapes it so that blends in with the steel.

He climbs down and is proud of himself. "I dare them to find that." He dusts himself off.

"Great." Tony says. "Let's get out of here."

They get back in their car just in time, as some of the coffin cops arrive to plan their next heist.

On tape the coffin cops are discussing a new heist.

An unnamed cop is saying," I got these 2 guys, you know? They're out of the 2-6; they run plates, they do a lot for us."

Another unnamed cop asks," Is he stand-up?"

And the other cop say," I think he is. I mean, you know he's a cop too. He does favors for people. You know what I mean?"

Still another cop is asking him," To see if he could help burn a house."

"How much is it worth?" the head cop asks.

"I think that he could easily get $5,000 for burning down a house."

"Okay. I'll let the family to give us the money."

"Sounds good. I'll let him know."

"So how are you doing with the other jobs?" the chief cop asks.

"Good." The cop answers. "Sometimes we got in by verbally threatening these people. Other times, we would break in using any tools we have in the patrol car- battering rams, crowbars. There would be nights when you could do two or three raids a night."

"Great!" the chief cop responded. "Keep up the good work."

Tony says to Longo," Do you hear this? They're spilling their guts. This is better than that undercover FBI agent who taped the mob families."

"That's for sure." Longo said. "But let's ask Loo and IAD how long that we have to do this for."

"Sounds good." Tony responded.

Back at the squad room, Tony and Ed Longo tell Loo what they heard.

"The problem is." Loo said. "You must be able to identify who the cops are, either with photographing the cops going into the building or having a cop inside who will flip."

"Loo," Longo stated. "I'm sure that IAD was photographing this already."

"Did you talk to IAD?" Loo asked.

"No, but we'll do that right now." Tony added. "But we'll also take pictures of who is going in and out of that building."

"And what if we can pinpoint voice recognition?" Longo said." I know that CSU can usually help with voice ID."

"Then that will work." Loo said.

"Did you fill in Cap of what's going on here?" Tony asked.

"Yes he knows all about it and he's not happy." Loo stated.

"Is he going to tell the brass about these cops?" Longo asked.

"He already has; all the way up to the borough commander, and the Chiefs of Patrol and Detectives." Loo answered.

"That's great." Tony said. "We'll get these dirty cops off of the street."

"It'll be soon." Loo said." That's what Cap and the brass are telling me."

"Sounds good." Longo mentioned also.

This will probably not happen for years to come, because there are pockets of police corruption everywhere in the NYPD, and because of willfully blind supervisors who fear the consequences of a corruption scandal more than the corruption itself. The "blue laws" of not ratting out a fellow cop still persists and will always persist since the mentality of a cop is them against us.

To get into a Mafia family or even be close to a Mafia family is very hard, because you have to know somebody who knows you. Just because Barbara Marino is seeing Tony that doesn't qualify, especially because he's a cop, and because she's a woman. So, for instance if somebody who's "connected" says that he's a stand -up guy, or that he won't rat out anybody

is a plus. Most of the coffin cops who knew Tony, knows that he won't rat out a fellow cop and that he means what he says, even if they think that he's a goody two-shoes.

Tony knew a bunch of wise-guys growing up in the old neighborhood; Tony as an Italian knew what the Mafia was. Every Italian in Bay Ridge, Bensonhurst or Park Slope knows somebody in the mob. Mafia in Italian means, "My daughter." This goes back several hundred years when they protected their daughter's honor from being raped. They would kill anybody who tarnished their daughters honor. Hence, "Ma Fia" or "Mafia." As a teenager he played cards, played pool and knew guys who were mob guys. He knew how Mafia guys acted, how they, walked, how they talked; much like cops do. Like they're the big man who nobody messes with.

Frankie "the barber" Marino, the eldest, was the underboss of the Columbo family under Paul DeMarco. "Patch" Marino was the consiglieri or advisor. Most wise guys walk down the street with a chip on their shoulder daring anybody within sight to knock it off.

Much like cops do. That's why the Mafia and cops are much like the other; they are thieves and liars in their heart.

Barbara Marino was going out every morning and every night to different places that the wise guys hung out. Their social clubs, their owned nightclubs, even their restaurants. So after a few days, she had gotten a lot of information for Tony and she looked forward to seeing Tony again. She knew that he not only was coming to get the tapes, he was coming also to fuck her again. And she loved the way that he treated her, like a desirable woman, and not like the "bull" type of wise guys, but with respect, the way a woman wanted to be treated. And his big cock was a plus to her. Also, the way that he went down on her (she told him that he loved to eat pussy- he laughed), and that he took her many times in many different positions- even her dead husband Tony never did that- just straight fucking. She found out after he died that he also had a mistress on the side whom he did everything to.

Barbara knew his knock on the door and her pulse sped up because she knew that he had come to fuck her.

"Hi babe." she said as she opened the door for him. He grabbed her and kissed her in the doorway. Bad idea because everybody was watching, especially her sister-in-laws of the Columbo family, as was the FBI, and IAD.

He pushed her inside and kicked the front door shut.

"I missed you." He said to her. "Want some?"

"You bet I do- I missed you too." She answered.

He kept kissing her as he led her to the bedroom, and then picked up her housedress, and pulled off her panties.

"I've been waiting for this." He said as he pushed her down on the bed and started to go down on her.

"Oh babe, so do I." she said and put his big cock in her mouth, her head bobbing up and down. Moaning, she continued to suck it and then looked up at him.

"Put it in honey. I need you."

He mounted her and shoved his cock full in to the hilt of her pussy.

"Oh that feels nice." She screamed out.

"I need this." He blurted out pumping her in and out with his big, erect cock.

"So do I!" she screamed.

Back and forth, in and out he rammed his cock in her.

"Oh sweetie- that's good." She screamed aloud again.

Not waiting until she came in that position, he flipped her over so that he was under her and she was straddling him, riding him up and down on his erect cock.

"Like that honey?" he asked pushing it into her and moving her ass up and down to get it in further.

"I love it!!" she yelled. "I'm fucking you now!"

After a while she came a few times, exhausted, and looked at him. "Where did you come from? You're a sex maniac!" she blurted out.

But he wasn't finished with her yet. He leaned her against the bed and plunged it into her from the rear.

"Oh my god! Oh my god!" she screamed again. "Oh fuck!"

"Feel good hon?" he said plunging it into her again and again. All you could see if this was a porno flick was his two balls erect and his cock shoving it into her.

"Oh it's delicious!" she cried out.

Finally he came in her and they both lay back on the bed exhausted.

"Where do you get the energy to do that?" she asked exhausted.

"I go to the gym." He said. "That's why I have a lot of stamina."

"Well keep going!!" she gasped." I want you to do this every day!"

"That's a deal." He laughed.

"Listen," she told him, "The family knows that you're seeing me. I told them that you're just a friend, but they're not stupid, they know by now that you're fucking me."

"So what." Tony responded.

"Well, they're protective of me." she mentioned. "They may want to know what your intentions are."

He nuzzled up close to her. "My intensions are to fuck you every day."

"I thought so." She laughed. "No, they may invite you to a family dinner. Again, to ask you what you're intentions are with me, sweetie."

"Look Barbara." He said," I enjoy seeing you, and coming here, but we're just friends for now."

"That's what I told them." she said.

"Friends with benefits." he added.

"Exactly." She said. "Speaking of benefits, how about another round?" she asked, grabbing his cock and starting to suck it again.

He started to get erect almost immediately.

"I want that cute little ass of yours." He told her and then turned her over and took her in the ass.

"My God! My God! Keep it in, keep it in!! she screamed.

He felt his cock slip into her anus and then go down the ribbed opening of her ass. At first it hurt her, but then she loved it.

"Keep it in! Keep it in!!" she hollered again.

He shoved it in to the hilt.

"Don't come in my ass babe. Come in me." She ordered.

"Okay." He pulled it out and came on the back edge of her pussy

He got up to see his semen dribbling out of her pussy.

"Wow!" she said, "That was intense!"

He looked at her." How come you didn't want me to come in your ass" he asked.

"I didn't want to waste all of that beautiful semen in my ass." She told him.

"You never took it in the ass before Barbara?" he asked her.

"Not since before my dead Tony." She mentioned. "It was nice for a change."

He got up and went to the bathroom to wash off his cock, and handed her a wet towel to wipe herself off.

"I can't wait for the next time." She told him with a wink." What are you doing to me sweetie? I let you shove it up my ass and I'm enjoying it."

"I think that you like it." He said.

"Maybe I do." She told him. "I'm going to suck your cock again, babe." And she grabbed his cock.

This time he wanted to come in her mouth but she pushed his cock into her pussy again. " I don't want to waste it, honey." Tony started to wonder what was going on, but decided to leave it alone.

After a while, he took a quick shower, took the tapes and then went to relax a bit before he would see her again. All of the tapes that Barbara did and also what Longo and Tony did had to be dated and recorded as an official document, because if the case goes to trial, it has to be made available to the defense attorney's.

Angela was good in the sack and so was Barbara. But he really enjoyed fucking Claire. There was definitely a lot of chemistry there and he wanted to keep seeing her and fucking her.

"You got the tapes Philadelphia?" Ed Longo asked.

"Yes, a lot of information there." Tony answered.

"And you fucked her again, didn't you?" Longo said.

Tony nodded.

"Fuck you Philadelphia! How do you get these women to let you fuck them again and again. You're not a ladies man." Longo complained.

"No, I'm a good guy who treats them nice, and that's hard to find according to them." Tony answered. "But you know Longo, something strange, she wouldn't let me come in her mouth or her ass. "Tony wondered. "She said that she didn't want me to waste it."

"Uh-oh, that means trouble. Did you wear a rubber?" Longo asked.

"No. She said that she wanted to feel me inside." Tony responded.

"She must be in heat, and wants something more." Longo said. "If I were you, Philadelphia, I'd wear protection, just in case. You don't want to knock her up."

"That's true. Good idea." Tony responded.

Rookie cops are given a 2 year probation period. That is, any infraction in 2 years and they are off the police force. It's like a teacher who gets tenure after like 3 years. They can be let go, but after that they are untouchable. And cops who do pass their probation period, will start to slack off, knowing that they can't be let go for no reason. And they know that no other cop will rat on them, so it's a free ride until they put in their 20 years and retire on ½ pay. More, if they can prove that they have an on-the-job disability, which most cops will try to do. And they do succeed in it. That's why cop pensions are so over-bloated.

Tony and Ed Longo are on their way back to the coffin cops hideout to take some pictures when another disaster unfolds before them. Officers Thomas Flannigan and Keith Bratton are beating a skel who had just been stopped for not having an up to date inspection sticker on his car. The skel had his hands up to surrender and the officer doesn't care. Flannigan is bashing the head of the skel on the car hood and also punching his eye socket, so hard that it eventually broke it.

"Take that you mother-fucker! You want to resist arrest, I'll show you what you get!" Flannigan screamed at the skel, one Percy Johns, an aspiring hip-hop artist.

Tony has Longo stop the car and gets out showing his shield." What the fuck are you doing Officer? Are you trying to kill him?"

Officer Keith Bratton acknowledges Tony. " Detective, this skel tried to resist arrest. He didn't have the proper inspection on this car, and he cursed at me."

Longo joined in." So you're beating him senseless because he cursed at you?"

"Yeah. He's disrespecting the uniform." He said.

Tony asked them. "How long have you guys been on the police force?" figuring that they're rookies.

"Almost 2 years. We have 2 days left on our probation." Flannigan stated.

"And for this, you're probably gonna lose your job." Tony said.

"Listen Detectives, take the collar. We need this job." Bratton asked.

"I don't want the collar! " Tony screamed. "Book the guy now, and we'll let this pass. But take him to the hospital- he's bleeding from his face."

"Yes sir.' Flannigan said.

"Thank you." Bratton said.

"Fucking rookies!" Tony said to Longo as they walked back to their car.

"This is what's joining the police force?" Longo said to Tony in disgust. "Thank God I'm retiring in less than 2 years."

"Longo. You amaze me. "Tony told him. "You forgot to be exact. What happened to the 1 year, 7 months,0 days, 10 minutes…"

"and 27 seconds. Fuck you Philadelphia." Longo answered him back." I KNOW exactly how much time I have left in this job. Just wait until you're in my position."

"8 years left." Tony stated to him."

On one of the tapes that Barbara gave to Tony, Augie Marino is telling Frankie Marino, the underboss of the Columbo family,

"You know, we may have a possible problem here; all of our wives are saying that Barbara is seeing a cop. You may remember him, Frankie , that kid Tony Philadelphia from 77th Street."

"You mean the little skinny kid? The cop who shot those 5 bank robbers?" Frankie asked. "Yeah, I remember him from the funerals for Tony and Barbara's dad. He seemed like a stand-up type of guy."

"Yeah, that's him." Augie answered. "He's a Detective now in the same precinct as Griffin and the others."

"Yeah, the 9th precinct. We got a lot of cops on the payroll there. Do you think that she would flip if he asked her?" Frankie asks.

"Never." Augie says. "She's still family and still believes in the old ways. And this cop Philadelphia has had many chances to rat out a fellow cop and he hasn't."

Frankie thought on that a moment, and says, "Well, being a woman, she needs someone, and it's good that he's Italian at least and not a Mick cop."

"So what should we do about it then?" Augie asks.

"Tell Barbara to invite him to dinner. We'll see if he's just looking to be a friend or if there's more to it than that." Frankie orders. "I can spot a good cop from a bad cop. Let's hope that he has larceny in his heart."

"Sure thing Frankie. I'll go and tell our wives to tell Barbara to invite him for dinner."

Tony was going to Barbara's every day at her insistence. Later, after they had sex, and they were lying on the bed, he asked her how come she didn't have any children. She started to cry.

"Tony. We did, but the baby was stillborn. It broke my heart; I didn't want to live anymore. We tried again and again, and all I kept having was miscarriages. Seven times a miss. Do you know what that does to a woman who wants a baby? It was horrendous and then my Tony was killed."

"Barbara, I'm so sorry." He told her and held her in his arms very tightly.

"I miss my husband." Barbara said crying. "It's been hell since he died, I didn't want to live anymore."

"I feel for you Barbara." Tony added. Barbara turned to him.

"Tony I want you to give me a baby." She told him.

"What!" he said.

"Babe you are young and your sperm is potent, I can tell. You come so easily. I don't want you to waste that sperm. I'm still young enough to get pregnant." She said.

"Honey, I don't know if I can get you pregnant." He said to her.

"Well, we'll try every day to get the deed done." she said.

"But why me?" Tony asked.

"It will be like part of it is from my Tony. You're a Tony and you're Italian, and you look a little like him, so it will be like it was from my Tony." She told him.

"You mean that you want me to be a surrogate for your dead husband? He asked.

"Yes."

"Barbara, you don't understand. Even if I did get you pregnant, once these tapes are made public, the Feds will put you in a witness protection program. I will never see you again, or the baby, and you'll be alone with the baby, by yourself, with no family." he told her.

"I know that, and I'm willing to make that sacrifice to have a baby." She said.

"You know that I have a life too, maybe it's not that great, but I have a life." He mentioned.

"Tony, if you don't do it, then I won't give you the tapes." She told him.

"So you're blackmailing me." He said.

"You can call it that, I'm calling it that this may be the last opportunity I have to be a mother. Tony I need you to do this for me." She told him.

"Let me think about this Barbara." He said.

"Tony there's no thinking about this. I want you to come over two times a day, in the morning, I'll make you breakfast after we do it, and then after work, I'll make you dinner after we do it." She told him." You can even sleep here if you want. And on the weekends, we can do it several times a day."

What she proposed was like a couple who were trying to get the woman pregnant and the husband had to perform sex every few hours. It was rough work, getting it up on call. The female of any species wants to be a mother and will do anything to become one.

Tony started to get up and get dressed. He looked at her naked on the bed. She still had a body that begged to be fucked. Longo was right, she was built like a brick shithouse. "I'll let you know later." He said.

"I'll make you dinner honey." She said. "Don't let me wait too long. I need you."

He nodded and went back to talk to Ed Longo.

"Philadelphia, I thought that was what she wanted." Ed Longo told him. "Hey, sex two times a day with her, every day, what are you complaining about?"

"But she's using me." Tony answered.

"So?" Longo asked.

"These fucking guineas are all alike, even their women. They want to steal your everything, even your manhood." Tony sighed.

"Oh stop it!" Longo told him." Just make her pregnant and let's get the tapes."

"I wish that it were that simple." Tony said.

"Don't tell me that you're falling for her?" Longo asked.

"No, I want Claire." Tony said.

"So tell the wop bitch." Longo added.

"I will, right after I fuck her in the ass." he said. "And I'll do it without any lubricant."

"Oh you're a bastard." Longo laughed." I love the way that you do things Philadelphia."

"Longo, you don't have the problem." Tony said.

"You're right, but I wish that I did. Fucking a sexy woman two times a day minimum- stop complaining!" Longo told him.

Like the dutiful good guy that he was, Tony started to go to Barbara's two times a day as she requested and fucked her several times. He had the ability to come so easily that she even loved sucking his cock to get him erect again and again. A female in heat and determined will do anything to get laid.

"Barbara, I like you a lot, you turn me on, and you're always ready for me, but I'm not ready for marriage yet." Tony told her.

"Babe, we'll just pretend to be married." She answered him.

"And what about your family?" he said.

"I'll take care of my family. You just provide the baby." She told him.

Tony's sperm was potent, and after a few days, Barbara was anxious to take the pregnancy test. It showed positive, that she was pregnant.

"Look at this sweetie." She told him showing him the telltale blue on the pregnancy test. "I'm pregnant! You're going to be a papa!"

"That's great," he answered. "Now can I have my life back?" he asked curtly.

"No." she said. "I'm going to make an appointment with the doctor to take a blood test. I want to be sure. Let's continue this until I know." She told him.

Tony obliged again and fucked her. Both of them didn't know but that she was going to have twins, fraternal twins, which means the pregnancy happened on two different occasions.

After the sex, she told him about the family wanting to meet him. And the invitation for dinner on Sunday.

"So if I go do I meet DeMarco?" Tony asked her.

"No, you don't." Barbara responded.

"How come?" Tony asked again.

"He's the boss and nobody talks to the boss except for Frankie Marino who's the underboss and Patch Marino, who's the Consiglierie." Barbara replied.

"So how are we going to get him on tape?" tony asked

"Don't worry sweetie, I will." She told him.

"I'll have to let you know Barbara." He told her.

"Okay sweetie; tell me later." She told him.

Disgusted, Tony went driving with Ed Longo along 1st Avenue, going back to the squad room, when he saw another distraction that he just wasn't in the mood for. Officer James Finnigan stopped a skel for no apparent reason just to check his license and registration. Any cop can do that without justification. This particular skel was unarmed and going home to his 12 children, all of which were by different mothers.

His partner Officer Thomas Reed overheard Officer Finnigan say,

"I'll put a hole in your head you mother fucker!"

Then for no apparent reason, Finnigan shot him in the head. His partner said,

"What the fuck did you do that? Are you crazy?"

"He made a move to open the glove compartment and I thought that he was reaching in for a gun." Finnigan said.

"He was reaching for his registration idiot!" Reed stated.

"Well what are you going to do?" Officer Finnegan stated." One less skel to cause trouble."

Tony and Longo pulled over to the street, and went rushing over with their gold shields displayed.

"What the fuck did you do to warrant this officer?" Longo said.

"I thought that he was reaching for a gun." Finnigan told him.

Tony went around to the other side of the car and looked into the glove compartment.

"There's no gun in here, schmuck. Only his registration and insurance card." Tony said.

Officer Reed stated." Do you want the collar?"

"No idiot; I don't want the collar! "Tony screamed at him." How are you going to explain this, tell me. "Tony mentioned. "Now this is going to have to go to the Review Board"

Longo went to call for back-up and ask for a supervisor to come immediately. The Review Board will want to know all of the details of this "homicide."

Officer Finnigan was described as being "extremely proactive" with traffic enforcement. This is cop lingo for saying that he would give out tickets, anytime, anywhere, way more than his monthly quota. Some also described him as being a "money maker" for the city. And yes there is a monthly quota for cops to give tickets. The city needs the money. So the cops get an unwritten code to give out as many traffic violations as they can in order to bring in money.

Only 10% of cops fire their guns and kill somebody in the line of duty. 90% of cops do not even fire their weapon outside of the firing range. But cops still draw their guns even though they don't have to, so they can show that "they" are in charge.

They only drove maybe two blocks and another cop has pulled over a black female for failing to stop at a stop sign. Actually she did make a full stop, but it was 1'-0" past the stop sign. To this cop, Officer Drew Pettigrew, that was a chance for a ticket.

As he got to the car, he told her," I smell marijuana here."

"I don't have any pot." She stated.

"Get out of the car now. I have to search your car." Officer Pettigrew told her. He couldn't find anything in the car, but called to his partner, a female, Officer Lisa Martin, who was pulling up her trousers from just being laid by Officer Pettigrew.

As the driver got out of the car, he told his female partner to strip search her. "I smell pot on her. It's probably inside her." He said.

"Get on the ground." Officer Lisa Martin ordered the driver. The female cop then handcuffed her and forced her to the ground, where she pulled off her skirt and pulled down her panties. Then she put gloves on and felt inside her vagina and her anus. "It's clean inside and I don't smell anything, but let's book her for making us strip search her. That's resisting arrest." She said triumphantly.

"I agree." Officer Pettigrew told his partner, with whom he had just had sex in their patrol car minutes earlier.

Even now more disgusted Tony said to Longo." I need a drink after this shit."

"I'm with you partner. What an idiot that these cops are." Longo told him.

Tony added," I also need to see Claire."

"You didn't get enough pussy, Philadelphia?" Longo laughed.

"No it's not like that. I haven't seen her in a few days, and I want to tell her what's going on." Tony told him.

"You're going to tell her that you're fucking Barbara Marino a minimum of two times a day?" Longo again sarcastically said.

"Of course not! I'm just going to tell her that I had to go undercover for an assignment and that's why I didn't get a chance to see her." Tony declared.

"And you were so deep undercover that you couldn't call her right?" Longo added.

"No. I'll tell her some of the truth, that it was a high profile case, and we couldn't jeopardize the case." Tony said.

"I'll tell you Philadelphia, you have some line of shit that you tell these women. But I got to hand it to you. They come begging for your cock. So you must be doing something right." Longo mentioned.

"Oh fuck you Longo." Tony added.

When they got to Easy's, Tony waved over Claire to meet him by the dancer's entrance to the stage.

"Hi, I didn't mean to ignore you honey, but I've been on this undercover assignment and didn't get a chance to tell you."

"That's okay Tony. I know that we're an item and you would call me when you had a chance to" Claire told him. "Angela had said that it's the problem with dating a cop. You never know."

"We are an item? Glad to hear that Claire." Tony told her. "So how about Saturday night we go out?"

"Great! She said.

Tony picked up Barbara for the short ride to Frankie's house and was making small talk.

"So why do you want to get back at DeMarco and your brother-in-laws?" he asked.

"Because they killed them both." She said matter of factly. Barbara Marino's father, Joseph (Joey Pitts) Marino was killed by DeMarco and his crew, who were sick of working for him.(Frankie said," he would always nickel and dime you. He would never give you a chance to earn more money)

"You mean to tell me that your brother-in-laws killed your father and your husband?" he asked dumbfounded.

"Yes, so they could become the boss and underboss of the family." She said.

"So that's why you're trying to get back at them." Tony answered.

"Yes, to get back at them. I talk to my sister-in-laws every day and when I see my brother-in-laws, I want to spit in their face, and cut their heart out." She told him.

"But how could somebody kill his own brother?" Tony asked utterly amazed.

"In the Mafia, you do what you're told or else you get whacked." She told him.

"So when is DeMarco going to be killed?" Tony asked.

"As soon as somebody has the colonies(balls) to do it." She answered him.

Frankie "the barber" Marino's place had a nice big yard for Bay Ridge, and it could hold the entire family's brood for a dinner. Tony didn't have to drive far from Barbara's house to get there since it was only a few blocks away. But Tony could tell this was a boss or an underboss's house because of all the 'gumba' security outside of there. However, since the gumba's knew Barbara, Tony was waved in.

"Hi Barbara." Angelo "Jello" Vitale, a soldier in Frankie's crew, greeted her.

"Hi Angelo." Barbara said. "This is Tony, a friend of mine." She pointed to Tony.

Angelo nodded that it was okay. And some of the other soldier's on duty also nodded. When a mob family person says that they're 'a friend of mine' means that they are vouching for them, even if they are being accompanied by a woman; which is unusual in the Mafia. But because of Barbara's dead husband, and because the family protected her, this was allowed.

Barbara escorted him into the yard, which was all set up with tables ready for food to be brought in by the wives of the family. She brought him over to the four brothers, and introduced him to them.

"Tony," Barbara said," this is Frankie, Anaphrio, Emilio and Augie, my brother-in-laws. Guys, this is Tony Philadelphia."

They all nodded, and Tony nodded also.

"Let me go introduce you to my sister-in-laws. They're in the kitchen cooking." She added.

"Barbara." Frankie told her. "You don't have to do that, they'll be out here in a few minutes with the food. You can introduce them then. Why don't you go into the kitchen and see how is it coming. This way we can get to know Tony here."

"Okay Frankie." Barbara said meekly, not really wanting to leave Tony alone, but figuring that the family wanted to see what this guy she was seeing was made of. Tony shot her a look, of don't leave me here with them, but she let go of his hand and went inside the house.

Numbers defeat numbers, four against one.

"You're a cop." Frankie said.

"Yeah, so what." Tony replied.

"Nothing, just mentioning it to you; I'm a barber." Frankie added. "And I hear from others that you're a good cop."

"Well, I'm a Detective." Tony mentioned." So that should stand for something."

"Too bad about Griffin getting killed." Frankie told him trying to make small talk.

"Not to say something bad about the dead, but he was a drunk." Tony added." A lousy drunk at that."

"I know." Frankie said. "He liked his booze and the broads."

"That's what I hear." Tony mentioned. The other brother-in-laws were letting Frankie set the stage.

"Detective," Frankie started, "Can I call you Tony?"

"Of course, I've known Barbara for many years, even before her husband died." Tony mentioned.

"Yes, we remember you were at the funerals for Tony and her Dad. It shows that you have respect. You used to live on 77th Street, wasn't it?" Frankie asked him.

"Yeah that's right." Tony answered.

"Well respect is important to us." Frankie added.

"Frankie, I've known about your family for many years." Tony mentioned. "I see that you're trying to be pleasant, and so am I."

"Tony, we take care of our own, and that includes watching over our dead brother's wife." Frankie told him.

"Again, Frankie, Barbara and I are just friends from the old neighborhood."

"Tony let's get down to the basics. You're not wearing a wire are you?' Frankie asked.

"No, I'm off duty and I wouldn't disrespect Barbara's family." Tony added.

"Thank you Tony. I believe you, but just to be sure Augie is going to pat you down." Frankie told him.

"No problem Frankie." Tony said extending his arms out wide for Augie to pat him down.

"He's got a gun!" Augie told them, feeling Tony's leg.

"I have to carry a gun even off-duty. "Tony answered putting his arms down.

"Ok, other than that he's clean." Augie told them.

Most mafia bosses do not carry guns because that's an automatic prison term if they get caught. But they do carry knives, large knives to cut your heart out.

"Tony, we don't allow guns here." Frankie said.

"Well because you guys know that's an automatic prison term. But you do carry knives." Tony answered.

"Well, I'm a barber." Frankie replied.

"Anything over 4 inches is a weapon, and I guess that you have one that's at least 6 inches long, right?" Tony answered.

Frankie pulls out his knife which is like one of those extra large Jim Bowie hunting knives. He smiles at Tony. "Okay. You got me."

Just then the women start to bring the food in to the table.

"Later, we'll talk, okay Tony?" he said.

"Sure thing Frankie." Tony replied curtly.

'Patch' Marino whispered to Frankie, '"He's got some balls; he doesn't back down, this Tony of Barbara's.

"I agree. We'll talk about him later." Frankie told him.

When the women all came in, Barbara introduced her sister-in-laws to him.

"Tony, this is Kitty, Rose, Diana and Angie. Girls this is Tony Philadelphia." They all nodded and took their seats next to their husbands. The women poured wine into their husband's glasses and they all lifted them up in the air and made a toast 'salud' (good health). Tony said,

"Hey, this wine is good, smooth and no bite at all."

"That's because it's home made in Italy. There's nothing like stuff made in the old country." Emilio stated.

"Do they sell this stuff in the stores?" Tony asked naively.

"No. This is a special wine, made exclusively for us." Patch told him.

This was a typical Italian 7 course meal. The women brought in each course and served it to them. the appetizer, the salad, the pasta, the brigiole, the veal and the meatballs, the lasagna, the pastries, the fruit, cheese and nuts. And the espresso, spiked with some grappa.

"Wow," Tony exclaimed." I haven't eaten like this in years. It was very good, thank you all for inviting me."

Barbara told him," I'm glad that you liked it; get used to it."

Frankie and the brothers looked at her and figured that Tony was here to stay. They didn't know yet that she was pregnant with Tony's twin boys.

Barbara strolled by Tony, smiled and made sure that he got enough to eat.

"Mangia(eat) Tony." Angie told him.

"I'm stuffed." He said.

"You don't like the food?" Rose asked.

"No it's great. I just don't eat this much anymore."Tony mentioned.

After the meal as the women were cleaning up, Frankie asks Tony, "Do you play cards- like gin rummy?'

"Of course, but I haven't played in years. I always used to play when I was a teenager." Tony mentioned.

"Ah, you never forget. It's $1 a point, is that okay? Frankie told him.

"Sure, no problem." He replied.

When Barbara came nearby, he whispered to her,

"I just got suckered into a game of gin rummy."

"So what." Barbara told him." That means that they're warming up to you. They just don't invite anyone into their game. This means that their accepting you as my beau."

"Barbara, I'm a cop and I know who they are." He told her.

"Tony, everybody here knows that you are a cop, but they are giving you a pass because you are here with me." She told him. "Otherwise they would have killed you already"

"Gee thanks" Tony mentioned.

"Don't be surprised if they offer you some sort of deal, that only family members get." She mentioned also.

"What to become made?"

"No. Tony they have half of the NYPD on their payroll." She told him.

"What?" he said in surprise.

"Well, maybe not half, but a lot." She told him.

Frankie was talking about one of the Columbo soldiers," He's a good operator. He knows what he's doing and he's also a good earner."

"Yeah, he definitely knows what he's doing." Augie said.

The family started to make small talk with Tony.

"So Tony how long have you been a cop?" Emilio asked.

"Twelve years." Tony said.

"That's good. And you're a homicide detective right?" Patch asked him.

"Yes." Tony replied. As they started to shuffle the deck of cards.

"I bet that you've worked on some interesting cases then." Frankie asked him.

"No. Not really, most of them are open and shut." Tony replied. "But each case takes time. You have to check every detail, no matter how minor or else it comes back to haunt you."

"I can relate to that Tony" Frankie told him. "A lot of things done wrong, comes back to haunt you."

"So Frankie, let me ask you since we're getting all friendly here. Since you know that I'm a cop and I know that all of you are in "the family" let's say (he emphacized the family) what are the pros and cons of living the "family" life." Tony said looking down at his cards and putting one card down and picking another up from the deck of cards.

"There's a lot of good, Tony and there's a lot of bad," Frankie tells him. "One bad thing Tony, the one bad thing is , every day you wake up and you don't know if they're gonna knock on your door and take you away for 50 years." Frankie takes a card from the deck of cards and puts down one card on the pile. "Goes with the territory." He looked straight at Tony, who didn't move his gaze away from him.

"Another thing Tony, you have to be cautious about taking advantage of your position as a "family" guy." Frankie told him.

"Frankie, you mean "a made" guy right?" Tony asked. Picking up another card and dropping one more on the pile.

"That's right Tony." Frankie mentioned. "Once you get that thing (become a made man) you can't abuse that privilege and go around sticking your chest out like some guys do."

"So you're saying that caution is the ticket." Tony added.

"Right." Frankie answered holding onto the word. "Make a wrong move as a "made" guy and you'll get your legs chopped off."

"Then Frankie, "Tony asked," what are the rules to live by if you're a made guy?"

"Well Tony," Frankie tells him, "There are several basic rules to live by, and since I know that you're not recording this, I'll tell you. Don't become an informer, don't fool around with another made guy's wife and don't strike a made guy. Although the last prohibition can be resolved with an apology. The first two" Frankie said, "are the things that get you killed. Everything else can be worked out."

"Well that's not a lot," Tony told him "I guess that it's not like the 10 commandments to live by."

"No." Frankie said. "You do your thing and stay out of trouble, you can get some good rewards."

"That sounds good." Tony replied.

"So let me ask you Tony, I've been on the level with you, can I ask you to do the same with me?" Frankie said.

"Sure, I'm on the level with you here." Tony replied.

"No I meant what's the deal with you and Barbara? Are you going to stick around with her?" Frankie asked.

"Well, I'll be blunt Frankie, I like Barbara a lot and it may grow into something more, but for now it's still just friendship." Tony replied looking down at his cards which were close to a gin rummy hand.

"If we sweetened the deal with you, would you stick around a lot more?" Frankie mentioned.

"What's the deal Frankie." Tony asked.

Frankie layed out what he was going to offer Tony. "I guess you know that Griffin had some nice benefits, money, broads, a nice place. I hear that you like broads a lot too Tony, and that's why I'm asking."

"But I'm seeing Barbara."He said.

"Tony, Tony. Let's be real. I know that you're seeing those two barmaids at The Easy Score. We can offer you a lot more on the side" Frankie told him.

"Can I ask how you know that Frankie?" Tony asked.

"Tony, we own Easy's. Nothing passes by us without we knowing. In a way, we're like the FBI, seeing all, hearing all."

Tony, not wanting to give away his hand, looked at Frankie and said. " Frankie, you're not the FBI, not even close."

Frankie undeterred said to him.

"Tony, if you stay with Barbara and marry her, we'll have you supplied with a place to go fuck them and have any woman of your choosing each night, just like Griffin did."

"Not a bad deal. Is that what you guys have?" Tony asked.

"More if you know what I mean." Frankie stated.

"And besides Barbara, what else do I have to do in order to give you a reward for these benefits?" Tony said sardonically. He was now one card away from gin rummy.

"Well if you're going to be in the family Tony, we may ask you from time to time to help us out." Frankie mentioned.

"Like what, whacking somebody Frankie?" Tony asked, and put down the last card that he had. He was holding a gin rummy hand, but did not want to piss them off by saying aloud 'gin'.

"Nothing of the sort Tony, we would just want some information that you are privy to" Frankie said.

"Frankie, I'm a homicide detective, I just do murders; I don't do narcotics or robbery, so I don't know what information I could be of service to you." Tony told him.

"Tony, a lot of times cops hear things like who is going on trial, who put what into the property room. All we want is the information, we'll take care of everything else. That's why we have a bunch of cops to do that stuff for us. You won't be involved because you'll be part of the family." Frankie told him.

'Patch' broke in."Take the deal Tony; it's a good deal, and it will cement your relationship with the family and with Barbara, who really needs a husband."

"And we're all in fucking trouble right now." Emillio added. "We're all in the same fucking boat. The only thing that we got is our honor."

Augie also had his say about dealing with law enforcement. Like the time that authorities raided his house. "They come with a no-knock warrant, 5:30 in the morning, break my front door down..It was 16 of them with guns, fucking guns 5:30 in the morning, broke the whole front door down. My mother was there. My kids were there. It put everybody in shock, including me. I thought that I was getting whacked; they wrecked my whole fucking house. They ransacked and they were there for five and a half fucking hours. They had me handcuffed to the bannister in my underwear. They strip searched everybody. I blew my top over this. I ripped the whole bannister down because I said, listen , you fucks, if you're gonna lock me up do it fucking now.My poor mother almost had a heart attack. They hadda call a paramedic. They destroyed my house. They did about $15,000 worth of damage In the house.. punched holes in the fucking walls, looking for silencers,looking for bullets, looking for machine guns. Who do you think lives here, John fucking Dillinger?" Augie told him.

"And when it was over, the house was in a shambles,"'Patch' added." And it was all for naught. They dropped the case. It never went to fucking trial Nothin' they couldn't find nothing."

"So Tony," Frankie told him. "That's why we need somebody from the family to warn us of this type of shit."

"I can see that you guys were upset. That shouldn't happen to anybody's house."Tony said. " I'll have to let you know." He started to get up. "Oh by the way, and that's gin." He put down the 4 and 3 and 3 of each suite of cards.

"Fongu." Augie said throwing down his hand of cards. "I needed that" motioning to the king of Clubs that was in Tony's hand.

"And Tony" Patch again added," You see that Frankie, he only wants to take care of his family, you know what I mean? And he ain't bothering nobody. They should just leave him the fuck alone. Frankie's just concerned about people eating and making a living for their family."

"I can see that." Tony added."I want to thank you Frankie and all of you for inviting me .It was great. I enjoyed it. Let me go pay respect to your wives, who prepared a delicious meal."

"Thank you Tony." Frankie said extending his hand to shake. Tony reciprocated and shook hands with all of them.

As Tony went to find Barbara, Frankie said to the brothers," I can't read him too well. He says all of the right things, but in his heart I still see an honest cop."

"I agree Frankie, but I think that he cares for Barbara and will do whatever she wants to make her happy." Patch said.

"Same here" Emillio stated. " I believe that he's fucking Barbara now and he wants to keep doing it. But if push comes to shove, he still believes in the old ways ,as does Barbara, and will come across to us."

"Could be."Augie added. I'll ask Rossi to find out what he thinks is going on with Tony."

"Good idea Augie. For now let's give Rossi Griffin's condo and the broads." Frankie told him. He looked at Tony kissing their wives and telling them what a delicious meal that had prepared. "Tony is a horn dog and he wants pussy all of the time. Tell Angela and Claire to be good to him. Maybe fucking 3 women at once will change his heart, and come around to our way of thinking."

As Tony escorted Barbara back to his car, he mentioned to her," You know Barbara, the others talk like Frankie is going to be the next DeMarco."

"They all want that." She told him as he held the car door open for her on the passenger side to get into.

When Tony got in the car, he told her," Frankie asked me to marry you."

"Well I like that very much." She said smiling at him.

"Barbara, I like you very much, I really do, but I can't marry you, even if you have my baby. You would have to go into the witness protection program and I'll never see you or the baby again." He told her.

"So why don't you come with me. I'll make you happy, I know that I will." She said to him, grabbing his cock and smiling.

He pushed her hand away from his erect cock. "Barbara, you know what you do to me. You know that you turn me on constantly." She grabbed his cock again. He pushed it away again.

"Barbara. I can't; I'm a cop and I like my job." He told her.

"But wherever we went you could become a cop there also couldn't you? She asked him.

"Of course I could. Everyplace in the USA needs seasoned cops. But it would endanger you and the baby. Also I'm starting to see somebody. It's not there yet, but it could be"Tony said.

"And you're fucking me at the same time?" she intonated.

"Barbara, I love your body, I always have; you turn me on like no other woman. I really mean that. "Tony told her. She smiled at him and grabbed his cock again. He pushed it away.

"Barbara- NO!" he told her. "After you have the blood test, let's see what develops. In the meantime I'm going to tell Frankie that I'm going to marry you and move in with you."

"Babe, I like that very much, but what about your new crush? Won't she be angry?" she asked.

"I told her that I'm going undercover. She bought that." He said to her.

"Tony I really care for you. I want you to be my husband and for us to have this baby." She looked at him.

"So do I Barbara, but it can't be. For your sake and the baby's. I told you that." he said to her.

"I know but I want a family." She said.

"You want Tony's family." He said.

"I know." She said and started to cry. "I miss my husband."

"I know that you do honey." He said holding her. "But I'm not him. I'll go back to your place and I'll stay the night"

"Thank you sweetie." She kissed him and held onto him very tightly. Again from holding her close, he felt her warm breasts and her body that was filled with desire. He immediately got another erection which she felt. She again grabbed his cock and this time he didn't push her away. She kissed him and then unzipped his pants and started to give him a blow job.

"Oh shit. You know what you do to me." He said feeling his big cock get bigger and swollen with passion.

"This is mine." she said holding his cock. "I'm laying claim to it."

"Ok, I give in." he said pulling up her dress and pulling down her panties.

"You know sweetie that I'll be good for you," she said lifting her body up for him to pull off her panties.

He went down on her as he had many times before."Better get us home quick babe. I need that big cock of yours in me NOW!!" she screamed.

"Okay," he smiled and put the car into gear. She grabbed his cock again and started to take it into her mouth, her head bobbing up and down, immune to the traffic. As soon as they got to her house, holding hands going up the few stairs to her house, he put her on the floor and entered her.

"Oh my God that is so good!" she screamed, feeling his big cock pump her in and out deeper and deeper. When he came in her, she cried out.

"I can't let you go Tony, you're the love of my life." She told him.

He nodded, but wondered how was he going to do this. He picked her up and brought her to her bed and lay down next to her for the night.

But during the night he got that feeling again, that he wanted her body for his cock. He touched her and she was up ready to go again.

"Want some more?" she asked.

He nodded and they stated all over again, sucking and fucking. "I could do this every night with you babe. You're going to have to marry me." She told him cradled in his embrace.

"I know." He murmured, but wondering what was he going to do about Claire. He really needed his cock in her too. "Barbara, I want to meet DeMarco before I agree to anything." He told her.

"I'll tell Frankie in the morning."she said ,starting to fall asleep in his arms.

CHAPTER 12

Tony asked Loo what should he do. " Should I go thru go this "fake" wedding and keep finding out about the mob and the crooked cops or don't."

Loo looked at Tony," For that I have to go talk to the FBI. You know having a 'made' man working for the mob and actually being an NYPD undercover is intriguing." He said."But it's really up to you Philadelphia."

"Loo that's not me." Tony answered him. "That's not me; not who I am. I'm not used to undercover work. I know that Barbara Marino has a vendetta against Paul DeMarco and his crew including her brother-in-laws, for killing her husband and father; but she wants me to marry her, have a baby and have a new life somewhere else. I'm not geared for that – I have a life." Tony said to Loo.

"Yeah, but sometimes you have to sacrifice for the greater good." Loo told him. "To have a NYPD cop become a 'made' man in the Mafia, is like Christmas coming in July and every month. Do you know what you could learn from that operation? Everything about the Mafia that's been hidden for generations."

"Yeah, but Loo, to become a 'made' man in the Mafia, you have to kill someone and that's not me; I'm a lover and not a killer."

"We know that all too well Philadelphia." Loo mentioned about his horn dog status that's known all thru the NYPD.

"Okay, Loo." Tony replied." But I'm going to have to think about this real hard."

"Take your time Philadelphia." Loo told him. "But just remember, stuff like this kind of gift to us happens once in a lifetime, so don't take too long. I'll confer with the FBI and get back to you."

Tony nodded and went to find Longo.

"I was just in with Loo, and of course the brass wants me to go ahead with this thing about going undercover and marrying Barbara Marino." Tony told him. "What do you think that I should do?"

Ed Longo thought about that for a minute." Philadelphia, you've got to do what you've got to do. "he said. "Only do what feels right to you. I know that fucking that Mafia broad has got a lot of benefits, namely to me, she sucks like a water pump, she takes in it the ass, and she's a nymph about your cock. So for those reasons alone, I'd say go thru with it. But, why give the brass a gift that will haunt you the rest of your life."

"How so?" Tony asked him.

"Well, you may get all of the dirty cops and all of the mob guys too" Longo told him." But your name will be shit on the force for ratting out a bunch of cops, even if they were dirty."

"So I'm getting from what you're saying that even though it sounds good, don't do it?" Tony asked.

"I can't tell you what to do, Philadelphia." Longo told him. "I'm just saying this for your own protection. You know all too well what happens to a cop rat. You have to watch your back at all times."

"Yeah. I know." Tony said. "When Serpico called for back-up, no one came, and he almost got killed. He had to leave the force and go into the witness protection program."

"Well the only good thing that would happen if you go thru with this is that you'll make Dick 1".Longo told him. "That is, if you can get a cushy job at Headquarters and not be in the line of fire."

"Well, I'm going to have to think long and hard about this." Tony said and walked back to his desk.

He started to go thru the pile of other cases that were on his desk. Maybe, forget about this for now and just concentrate on this other work, he thought.

One case that he caught was about a gang member who shot another dead, took a knife and sliced off the ear of another, and also sliced open his throat, and then stuck a screwdriver in the eye of a third all because they were stealing drugs and money from him, when it was really the coffin cops who did it. But this guy didn't want to listen to that. No excuses, he said. But he was still on the run, and made it to the FBI's most wanted list. Tony thought that this guy was way out of town by now. So let it become the FBI's problem.

Tony decided to go to Easy's alone and to see Claire. He missed seeing her and he wondered if he should tell her the truth about what was going on. But what if she didn't want to hear the truth, Tony thought.

He had just turned up West 35th Street near Midtown South's other precinct when he saw another disturbing event. Midtown South precinct has two buildings with about 150 officers in each. One is on West 35th Street between 8th and 9th Avenue and the main one is on West 30th Street between 6th and 7th Avenue. Two cops from Midtown South were hogtieing a white man inside an ambulance so that he couldn't breathe. His face was buried in the mattress of the stretcher. There was a strap over the back of his head. His hands and feet were hogtied so that he couldn't move those either.

Tony pulled his car over and got out showing his gold shield. "Guys, this guy can't breathe, why did you tie him up like that?"

"He was acting up Detective. We had to restrain him." Officer Peter Edwards told him .

"And what are you bringing him in for?" Tony asked.

"Disturbing the peace. He was yelling like crazy and we had to restrain him."

"But he isn't yelling now- release him." Tony told them.

Unknown to anyone the guy was an asthmatic and couldn't breathe face down on the mattress. He was already dead when Tony felt for a pulse. "This guy is dead!"

"Detective, do you want the collar?"

"No I don't want the collar. Better bring him into the holding cell and book him even though he's dead." Tony shook his head in disgust and got back into his car.

When he got to Easy's, all of the bar stools were filled up, but he elbowed his way to the bar, waved at Angela, and motioned for her to call Claire to come over.

"Hi sweetie." Claire said and planted a big kiss on Tony." The other cops all looked at this and wondered how come this guy gets all of the pussy.

"Hi honey." Tony said. "Get me a beer on tap, and come over to the end of the bar."

"Sure thing." Claire went and got him the beer, and then met him at the service area of the bar.

"What's up?" she asked.

He took a big gulp of the beer, wiped his mouth, and said." I need to see you when you get off."

"Of course." She told him. "What's going on?"

"I can't tell you here, but I need to ask your opinion on something." he said, holding her hand.

"OK," she told him." I can get off for a few minutes now. I'll have Angela cover for me."

"Great." Tony said.

Claire went to talk to Angela "Can you cover for me while I go talk to Tony for a couple of minutes." Angela nodded. Claire put her apron down under the counter. They both walked out to the kitchen and back out onto an alley that faced West 52nd Street.

"So what's going on baby?" Claire said.

"I'm in a kind of bind and I don't know what to do." Tony told her. "Like I mentioned to you, I've been undercover trying to weed out a lot of dirty cops and also get the low-down on some mob guys."

"Ok' she said.

"Well, here's the thing. I collected a bunch of evidence and the brass want me to stay undercover and help them get all of them." Tony told her." But if I do, then I'm shit out of luck staying on the force."

"How come?" she asked.

"Well the brass would like it, but the regular cops would think that I'm a rat, and that would put me in danger." Tony told her.

"Tony," she looked at him," I don't want you to do anything that will put you in danger. Just try to get out of it if you can."

"But I'm in very deep already. I don't know if I can get out." he said.

"Look, you can always get another job, or get transferred to another precinct." She told him.

"That's true, but I really like what I do. It's just that I don't like having to be forced to do what the brass wants me to do." He said.

"Then don't do it babe." She held him and looked into his eyes. "Look, we're getting to be an item and I don't want it to end. I want you and you want me, and I think that we both want more."

"You're right hon I do." he said. Then he kissed her. "All right, you mean too much to me to fuck this up. I'll tell the brass, that I'm not going thru with it." And then in an after- thought. "I'll see you as soon as I can. Claire nodded and blew him a kiss as she went back inside.

Barbara had arranged a meeting for Tony to meet with DeMarco. Actually, she couldn't do it, but she talked to Frankie who talked to DeMarco and it was agreed. The meeting place was the same restaurant where the hit on the former Columbo boss, Carmine, was gunned down. That famous picture of him appeared on the front page of the New York Post, showing him with a bullet hole on his eye and him still smoking a cigar. It was an Italian restaurant in the Bushwick section of Brooklyn, but you couldn't tell it was a restaurant because it was in the first floor of a house. Tony knocks on the door and the door opens a crack. To the right Tony and Barbara see this old time wise guy dressed in a gangster type of suit with a hat on and to the left a burly type guy with an apron on. He sees Barbara and nods.

"Hi Nicky" she said (this was Nicholas "Big Nicky" Cavaliere) who was the owner. "This is Tony, 'a friend of mine". Again, she said that Tony was a friend of hers, so it was okay- she was vouching for him.

He acknowledges them and opens the door wide for them to enter. He leads them past the bar area into the restaurant. There DeMarco, Frankie and Patch are already seated at a table for 4. Barbara introduces Tony to DeMarco." This is Tony Philadelphia."

DeMarco tells Barbara, "Thank you Barbara, why don't you seat by the bar." Barbara nods as DeMarco points to the open seat that Tony should sit in.

A Matre di stops by the table, "Can I get you anything to drink?"

"I'll have a beer on tap." Tony tells him.

DeMarco says to the Maitre Di " Bring him a beer on tap and bring us some calamari."

The Matre Di nods and leaves to fetch the items.

DeMarco looks straight at Tony."So detective, Frankie tells me that you are willing to help us."

"Yes." Tony answers," provided I get credit for bringing in some of the cops who's on your payroll."

"Detective", DeMarco talks to Tony," we can always help you with that as long as you bring us the same type of information that they have always done for us."

"Mr. DeMarco, I can bring you a lot of information, but you have to help me first. I want to become a Detective First Grade and the only way that I can do that is to make a very big arrest by bringing in all of the cops that are on your payroll." Tony tells him.

"Detective that is what we want to, to help you rise higher up on the NYPD ladder. But what else do you want- a nice place to live, women?" DeMarco asks him.

"No, that's not me." Tony answers. "But one thing that you can do for me is to tell me who is supplying K2, that is the pot that is laced with some crazy shit that is making a lot of homeless guys crazy."

"Detective." DeMarco says. "That's not us. The Mexicans, Dominicans and the niggers are selling that and not giving us our share. But we can help you get them too, as long as you're willing to become part of our family. I hear that you and Barbara are serious and considering getting married."

"News travels fast, Mr. DeMarco." Tony tells him. "We haven't set a definite date yet, but it's getting there."

"Great. I love a big wedding."DeMarco says grinning.

"Mr. DeMarco, get me the names of the cops and I'll do whatever I have to for you." Tony tells him.

"Good. Frankie will get them for you and we'll let you know what you can do for us." DeMarco says.

"Agreed." Tony says, standing up.

"You're not going to stay for the calamari? It's the best in Brooklyn."

"No. I have to get back to work." Tony says and extends his hand to DeMarco.

"Welcome to our family." DeMarco says and embraces Tony.

Tony shakes hands with Frankie and Patch and leaves to get Barbara from the bar area.

Tony takes Barbara outside and immediately asks her." You told your family that we're getting married?"

"Well, sort of. I mean you and I are going to have to, now that I'm pregnant." She says.

"Barbara, you're pushing me." Tony told her sternly." I haven't decided anything yet."

Just as he made a turn onto Bushwick Avenue to get to the Brooklyn-Queens expressway so he could get back to Barbara's house, Tony saw another typical NYC scene. A car was double parked, because there were no available vacant spots to park in. There never is enough available parking spots, so most people double park to run into get something or are waiting for someone. An officer on patrol sees this and wants to make tickets, starts to give the driver a ticket for double parking. The driver apparently starts to mouth off to the officer (which you should never do), and the officer pissed, opens the car door and pulls the driver onto the ground.

Meanwhile, other officers also on ticket patrol (they just love giving out tickets), see this and join the original officer in punching the skel.

The skel screams out " Ya'll is punching me in the face. What did I do to deserve this!"

Tony pulls over and doesn't get out of the car, but watches as another officer throws something on the street, near the skel. It's a bag of marijuana. The driver is now going to be charged with resisting arrest and possession of marijuana.

Tony shakes his head and pulls back onto traffic. "See what happens when you double park." He tells her.

"That's not right." Barbara says and shakes her head too on disgust. "Another criminal resisting arrest. They're emboldened now thanks to all of the other criminals who support them .This thug deserved it for his disrespect of our laws."

Tony turned to her amazed at what she said." What!" he yelled." And you don't think that your brother-in-laws shouldn't get the same treatment?"

"No." she answers him. "They're just trying to make a living."

"Not an honest buck." Tony says to her.

"Tony, nobody from the public is getting hurt." She says.

"And you don't think that drugs and robbery and how many other things that your family is into is not harming the public?" Tony asks her.

"Well not in the way that you say." She responds.

Tony shakes his head again in disgust." I guess that you Mafia types have this in your blood and that you don't think that it's a crime."

"Tony," she tells him." I don't want to argue with you about this."

"Fine!" he says disgusted. He thought how did he get himself involved with her and the mob.

Tony finally delivers Barbara to her house in Bay Ridge.

"Do you want to come in for a little bit?" she asks him demurely.

"No, I have to get back to work." He tells her. "But I want the tape that you just made of us and DeMarco."

She reaches into her purse and gives it to him.

"Thanks." He said." When is your doctor's appointment?" he asks her.

"Tomorrow – do you want to come?" She asks.

"No, but let me know" he answers.

"Okay, I will." She tells him, leaning over and kissing him on the cheek.

Tony waits until she walks up the 5 steps and goes inside. He shakes his head again and goes back to the squad room.

At the squad room, Tony tells Loo about the meeting with DeMarco." I'm in." he says showing the tape to him.

"Great." Loo says." Let's get IAD and Organized Crime Unit on this as soon as possible." Then thinking a minute, asks Tony." How are your other cases coming along?"

"Loo." Tony tells him." I've been concentrating on this major case, so I haven't been able to work on any other case."

"Philadelphia." Loo tells Tony," you still have to do your other cases, they are starting to back up."

"Loo c'mon. I'll try. " Tony says." But this case is so big, I'm going to have to work more OT."

"I'll ask Cap if that's okay."

Tony nods, but wonders how is he going to get to these other cases.

"Loo, one more thing." Tony says to him. "What should I do; go thru with this "fake" wedding and keep finding out about the mob?"

"Well I talked to the FBI and they are all in favor of it." Loo told him.

"I still don't know Loo." Tony said." I'll have to think more about this. A lot more."

"Philadelphia, it's up to you, but if you go thru with it, I can guarantee that you'll make Dick 1."

Tony nodded and went back to his desk.

All Italians in Brooklyn know "somebody" in the Mafia. Maybe not personally, but they know of somebody who knows somebody to help them. It's inbred, but that's the way it is. Say for instance that your father or grandfather worked on the docks. You could get your son or grandson into the union there to work on the docks also; it's common knowledge.

Part of the 9th precinct's jurisdiction is Alphabet City, so called because there is Avenue A,B,C and D that's the area south of 14th Street and near the East River. One of the cases that Tony is also given by Loo now is to go see, is that of a homeless woman who was gang raped and murdered and left by the housing projects there.

He goes to the crime scene that is cordoned off. There are 5 cops plus a SGT and Ed Longo is also there. You never just see one cop at a crime scene, you see dozens. And the reason for that is very simple; every cop gets an assist on his record for backing up another cop, or just patrolling the crime scene for crowd control. And they don't do anything, they just stand there, relaxing.

And again, at a crime scene, even if there is a SGT. there or a Detective, they never talk about the case-it's just small talk about anything. Most of the time it's all about other cops who bagged a piece of ass or broke the law.

"Hey did you hear about Robustelli?" Officer Andy Farmer, asks the crew standing there." He was busted for the 10th time for domestic abuse; and he got away with it."

"Of course "Sgt. Fallon says," but 10 times, c'mon he has to be a psycho."

"This is his girlfriend, right?" Officer Gene Nelson asks.

"Yeah," Office Farmer says." He threatened her and threw a kitchen knife at her. He also punched her and violated an order of protection 4 times. And the DA told the woman stop making false statements or you'll be arrested. Well, at least they have our backs."

"Yeah, I remember now." SGT. Fallon says." He was a SGT. but he was ousted because he tested positive for steroids."

Another cop, Officer Dell Quintana, says." And I hear that he was also arrested for stealing like $76,000 worth of IPADS and IPhones while he was working part time as a security guard. And the DA never charged him. Remember- it's the blue laws."

"I could see that." SGT. Fallon says. The others nod in agreement. Ed Longo doesn't say anything. He's waiting for Philadelphia to come and help him inspect the crime scene.

And not to be outdone, Officer Nelson tells the others, "Listen to this, when I was in the One Oh Five(105th pct in Queens), I got a call of a domestic disturbance. So I knocked on the door and this little girl opens it. I say to her, Is your mommy home? She's in the shower. Can you go get her? I say to her. So this woman comes to the door with just a towel wrapped around her."

"I was in the shower! What is wrong with you?" she yells at me.

"So I tell her," Ma'am don't take an attitude with me."

"This is my house!" again she screams at me.

So I tell her," Ma'am don't take an attitude with cops, because we don't play. When a cop shows up, you're not the one in charge. I don't care if this is your house." I tell her.

So she runs to get a cell phone to video this. And she takes 5 steps and I tell her' Stop or I'll arrest you!" I grab her, the towel drops, nice tits and ass, and I handcuff her. Then I told her that she's under arrest.

"Stop touching me!" she screams. So maybe I took a feel, so what.

My partner arrives and says, maybe we should release her. She may press charges. So I nod and take off her cuffs. But she never pressed charges."

"I guess that maybe she wanted it." Officer Quintana says.

"Right." Officer Nelson says.

The victim, 39 year old Pamela Woods, was lying face up with her Capri pants pulled down , and her blouse pulled up to her neck; her bra was nowhere to be found. From the relaxed look on her face, no one could tell that she was dead. No one, not even the police had tried to cover her up with a sheet or anything. Even in death, you are not supposed to disturb the scene. The five cops, Sgt. and Ed Longo were maybe 5 or 6 feet away from the body in a semi-circle, just looking at each other and not even looking at the victim.

"Longo" Tony said as he approached the scene. "Has CSU been here yet?"

"Not yet." He responded. "This was just called in maybe 2 hours ago."

"Were there any witnesses?" Tony asked.

"Dunno." Longo mentioned. "I just got here a few minutes ago myself." he lied.

There was a crowd gathering already and Tony looked right into their faces. Sometimes, you can tell from a face in the crowd that somebody saw something. He went over to the crowd.

"Did anybody see anything?" he asked. "Does anybody recognize this woman?"

One guy near the back raised his hand. "I saw it. I was the one who called." A light skinned black about 5'-10" immediately was given the clearance by the crowd to come closer.

"HI." Tony said to him. "I'm Detective Philadelphia. What did you see?"

"This woman was going crazy, screaming like she was on something, and these guys, must have been about 6 of them, started to touch her. Then they started to fuck her, front and back and in her mouth and she seemed to be enjoying it. I had wanted to join in too, but I was afraid. They shouldn't be doing this right in front of everybody. And then one of them hits her real hard and she falls to the ground. "the witness Eugene Damon told him.

"Do you know any of them who did this to her?" Tony asked.

"I see them all of the time. They're always drunk. They're always drinking. They're always down there." He said, pointing to a staircase that went down to the cellar. "I called the cops, but these cops there" he pointed to the crew surrounding the body," never asked me anything."

"Longo." Tony called to him," didn't you start canvassing the crime scene?"

"No." Longo lied again. "Like I told you I just got here."

Tony shook his head." Get this guy's information. I'm going to look in the cellar." He turned to Sgt. Fallon. "Sgt. Please have some of your guys accompany me down the stairs."

Tony drew his gun and two of the other cops did too and followed him into the cellar. He opened the door which led to a corridor. There were several storage rooms and they looked at all of them. Near the end of the corridor Tony heard some voices coming from a room. He opened the door and there were the 6 skels who were still drinking.

"Okay guys. Party's over. Get your hands up." Tony said, pointing his gun at them.

"What do you mean?" one of the skels replied."We didn't do nuthin'- just sitting here drinking."

"Oh yeah." Tony said."You didn't do nothing? How about that woman outside that you fucked and killed."

"We didn't kill her, she just wanted to play and we partied with her."One of the other skels who wasn't as drunk as the others said.

Tony called into his intercom." Sgt. Fallon. Call for back-up. We've got the fucks down here."

"Okay guys. Get up and stand against the wall." Tony said pointing the gun at them.

"Longo get down here!" Tony yelled into his radio. Tony started to read them all their rights and told them that they were all under arrest.

The witness, Eugene Damon was able to identify all of them. It seems that they were all high on K2, even the dead woman, that's the marijuana that's spiked with something else. The skels are taken back to the 9th pct and booked on rape and murder.

CHAPTER 13

After Tony and Ed Longo finish their paperwork on this new murder case, they go on stake-out by the coffin cops hideout. Tony photographs Rossi go in and several other of the cops from different pcts. They then listened to what they were saying.

"Okay guys." Rossi tells the other cops." I'm going to be running things from now on. So let's see if we can get some K2 from these drug dealers. Let's start with Luis Santos crew. He's always good for a few thousand."

In detective work, waiting is a big part of the job. You wait on stakeouts, you wait on witnesses, nothing ever runs on time.

Tony and Ed Longo decided to follow Rossi to see where he went. Also of interest to them was the goofy looking cop, Bobby O'Mara, since he led them to the "coffin cops" hideout, he could probably be invaluable in getting the goods on the rest of the bad cops.

Rossi was good for a couple of hundred a night from the drug dealers. All of them knew who he was and that he wanted the money; keep the drugs he told them, I just want the take from today, and I'll leave you alone. Most of the big drug dealers like Rodriguez and Santos did just that- leave him alone. But some of the others got either a gun shoved up their chin with the safety off and the glare that Rossi would give them. The Dominicans, the Columbians, they all knew that Rossi was one bad ass mother fucker, and would kill them as look at them. They knew that Griffin would beat them up, but Rossi would kill them. They would rather give him their take for the day then taste a bullet on its way from their chin to the back of their head.

"Here comes the fucking po- lice" they would say to each other as they saw him approach.

Luis Santos has an employee network. If you close down one of his dealers, he'll set up shop in another location. K2 was just the latest drugs that he pedaled. K2 is a synthetic marijuana and not only was he a dealer, he was a user as well.

"It's a zero to 60 high." He told his crew. "I've done plenty of drugs in my life and it only compares to dust (PCP). But it doesn't last as long, but it's cheaper, cheaper than china white or coke. So let's start pushing this a lot."

Rossi's arrests were up, way up, since Griffin died. He concentrated on specific blocks, making dozens of arrests, then moving onto another part of the precinct. Midtown North is so big that it's split into two sub- precincts; the main one on West 54th Street and the sub-precinct on West 42nd Street. Hell's Kitchen (along 10th Avenue) was where most of the activity took place.

"He's doing it solo." Ed Longo said. "So he knows who the drug dealers are and they know him."

"But why wouldn't he bring back-up?" Tony asked.

"Because he wants all of the unassisted arrests on his record, and he doesn't want to share the money he's taking with them."

"You're right." Tony responded. "Who are the skels going to complain to –the judge?"

"But shouldn't narcotics be watching this?" Longo asked.

"I agree." Tony answered. "But do you see any narcs here? I don't."

In one bodega, Rossi opened a door to a cabinet, revealing scales, empty crack vials packaged with cardboard wrappers, multi-colored plastic tops, different colored plastic heroin bags, laxatives to cut the cocaine and heroin with, even an order book for supplies.

"Looks like you guys are doing very well here." He said to the owner, who muttered under his breath," fuckin po-lice."

Rossi would come in every few days with an arrest. Eighteen misdemeanors, crack vials, 6 felony arrests for sale of narcotics, 24 arrests for possession of narcotics, nine arrests for criminal trespass. All bullshit arrests, but they count. And the cops take all of the money from the sale of the drugs.

Skels cluster in front of bodegas, playgrounds catering marijuana, heroin, cocaine and crack to customers from all over New York, New Jersey and the surrounding areas.

Tony and Longo decided to go back to the squad room and fill out their reports on what they had seen Rossi do. However coming back they were amazed at what they saw going thru the 17th PCT. A throng of at least 14 officers detained a man with one leg by sitting on his prosthetic limb after they mistook his crutches for weapons. The man Patrick leBouvier, told the officers," These are my crutches. I use these to walk." Then the officers wrestled him to the ground.

"What the fuck is wrong with you? Is this what you do? "The cops did not listen and just threw him in a police van.

"I'm not touching this." Ed Longo said.

"Neither am I." Tony added. "Each day gets crazier and crazier."

Back at the squad room, Tony had a message from Roseanne DiMuccii of CSU to call him.

"Hey, Mr. Big Dick." The message said. "This is Roseanne from CSU. I found some interesting stuff from Griffin's condo vault. Give me a call when you get this."

Tony called her immediately when he got the message.

"Hi, Miss DiMuccii, what do you got for me." Tony said.

"Mr. Philadelphia." Roseanne said, being formal." I got a lot of information for you. Names, telephone numbers and the best one is that we traced one of the guns found in Griffin's condo, the one that Detective Longo found under the toilet, to the murder of Joseph Marino, you know the former head of the Columbo family."

"Wow! That's interesting." Tony told her. "Can you catalog it and send it to me? Don't e-mail it- this is really important. Have them send a messenger."

"It's already cataloged." She told him. "You'll have it in a little while."

"Great!" Tony told her. "Thanks for your help."

All unsolved murders are put in a data base, including autopsy reports, etc. and the shell fragments from the guns that killed the victim. All they have to do when the gun is recovered is examine the gun by firing it, and seeing if the shell fragments match those of the victim's. They

take a picture of the shell fragment from the victim and the shell fragments from the recently fired gun and compare them side by side. In this case it did, as well as the shell fragments from Barbara's husband Tony. Griffin's gun had killed them both. Now the question was, is Griffin the hitman? It sounded logical, since Griffin was on the payroll of the Columbo family to do their bidding and also whack people that the mob didn't want to dirty their hands on. And were DeMarco and Barbara's brother-in-laws anywhere near the scene when Barbara's father and husband were killed; like when the Gambino family head was murdered. For a crime family head to be killed, it had to be approved by the other crime families or else they would be whacked themselves. Tony doubted if Barbara knew about this information and he didn't know if he should even tell her.

Roseanne DiMuccii was true to her word. Within an hour a large envelope was delivered to Tony by a rookie 3rd grader, Terrance O'Neil. Typically, a 3rd grader is assigned to the night and weekend task force for about a year, and then to a district robbery squad or as a precinct detective. But O'Neil had maybe 46 arrests in a three week period, so they promoted him to CSU as a gofer. Go for this and go for that. Do all of the dirty work like bagging and cataloging stuff. But he was learning- arrest everybody that you see- legal or not, it counts on your arrest quota.

"Mr. Philadelphia?" O'Neil came in to the squad room. "This is for you from Detective DiMuccii."

"Thanks." Tony said acknowledging him. "How's it going in CSU?"

"Okay, I'm learning." O'Neil said.

"Good. Tell Roseanne thanks a lot." Tony added. O'Neil nodded and left.

Tony greedily opened the large 11" x17" manila envelope and pulled out its contents onto his desk.

"Hey Longo. Come see this!" he shouted across the desk to his partner.

"What do you got?" Ed Longo asked.

"This is the stuff from CSU that they cataloged." He told him. "And Roseanne DiMucci told me over the phone a little bit ago that Griffin's gun that you found under the toilet was the one that killed both 'Joey Pitts' Marino and Barbara Marino's husband Tony."

"Wow!" he said coming over to Tony's desk. "Everything seems to be falling into place."

Tony nodded in agreement. "Just look at all this stuff."

CSU was very organized also. You had to be to present evidence to the DA.

The list of telephone numbers that they had found in the vault was an assortment of cops, lawyers, escorts, and Columbo gang members. And Griffin was very organized. He had sub-headers for "cops", "mob", and "lawyers".

There was also other sub-headers for "escorts" and an asterisk next to the names. 2 or 3 asterisks next to an escorts name means that they must have been really good in bed. The cops were listed by Precinct and by name with "PO(such and such)" or "SGT(so and so) ", so it seemed from this list that Griffin was the head of the cop organization. With this list alone, they could get several of these bad cops to squeal. They had to have a team of IAD guys interrogate them to see which one would talk first to save their own necks.

The only thing that CSU couldn't pinpoint was the key, probably a safe deposit box key. So Tony will have to get a court order to go to all of the banks in Manhattan and Brooklyn or Queens to find out if Griffin had an account there. And if he didn't, did he have a safe deposit box there. Typically, you didn't need a court order for a bank account; all you needed was an official NYPD letter asking if they had an account there. But for a safe deposit box, you needed a court order.

Judge Daniel Sawyer of the New York State Superior Court was a regular at an Italian restaurant on Baxter Street, near Chinatown. He would eventually get a plaque above his favorite booth because of the many times he ate lunch and dinner there (free of course to judges and cops).

The police usually have specific court orders already made out except for the person's name and address and what they are looking for, say to search a vault or a house. Then they just fill in whatever it is and the judge signs it. Very rarely will a judge not sign a search warrant.

However, when Tony went to Judge Sawyer with the search warrant filled out for a safe deposit box, the judge asked.

"And do we know what is in this safe deposit box?"

"No Judge" Tony answered." But it must be important stuff because all of his other valuables were in a vault in his apartment."

"Ok Detective." He told Tony," I'll sign it because this is a cop and probably a dirty cop, and who knows what he has hidden in this safe deposit box."

"Thanks Your Honor." Tony said, and took the court order back to the precinct.

When Tony got back to the precinct he went directly to Loo to ask for more help in going through the banks. There are literally hundreds of bank branches in the 5 Boroughs of New York City and it is a very slow process to go bank by bank to first try to see if Griffin had an account there and if he did, did he also have a safe deposit box there.

"Loo," Tony said," I got the Judge to sign the court order, but Longo and me are going to need help in going through all of the banks to find out where Griffin had his account there."

"OK Philadelphia you got it." Loo stated. " he went outside his office and yelled "Granite! I need to see you." And then in an afterthought," NOW!"

Jack Granite is Tony Philadelphia's other partner when Ed Longo is off, either on a sick day or on a vacation day. Because Ed Longo has a lot of years in, he has accrued a lot of sick days and vacation days. Civil Service has this crazy rule that if you don't use sick leave and accrue it, by the time that you retire, you can get cash for half the amount of the total sick leave accrued. This rule makes you want to come into work sick or not, because it is money owed to you when you retire.

Jack Granite is also a Detective 2nd grade and is the same age as Tony. He also has about 12 years on the job and is a go getter. That means he has a sharp picture of crime, he takes collars away from patrol cops to add to his arrest record. He says to anybody who will listen that he wants to make Detective 1st Grade before Tony.

"Granite." Loo tells him," I want you to help out Philadelphia and Longo in searching out these banks."

"But Loo," Granite says to him," I've got my own cases that are piling up fast. Can't one of the other guys help out with this."

"No." Loo said." I want you to do it."

"And my other cases?" Granite asks."

"You'll have to do them also." Loo tells him.

Granite looks at Tony and says." Why can't you do this shit work."

"Because it's a lot of work." Tony tells him.

Tony, Longo and Granite, split the major banks and start calling each banks branch, because a bank can have maybe 40 or 50 branches in the city or in the other boroughs. And some of the branches do not have safe deposit boxes, only several of them.

And it's always the same spiel,

"Hi, this is Detective Philadelphia of the 9th precinct, badge number 4589. I'm looking to see if a Charles Griffin has an account there. I have a court order signed by Judge Sawyer. And also, if he has an account there, would he also have a safe deposit box there?"

The problem is that even if a customer has an account there, the safe deposit box information is on another database, so they have to look for that too. Again, a very time consuming process.

There are maybe 500 bank branches in the city's 5 boroughs (or at least it seemed to be to Tony) since all they were doing for days was call bank branches to find if Griffin had an account there. First they tried bank branches near where he lived by Mercer Street, then they tried bank branches near the 9th precinct, then they went to the rest of the bank branches in Manhattan, Brooklyn, Queens, Staten Island and the Bronx. And all came up empty.

"This can't be." Longo said. "Maybe he had a bank in Long Island or Upstate New York or even in New Jersey."

"And he did not have a direct deposit from his paycheck into a bank." Tony said. "That was the first thing I looked at. He got his check. We will have to find out where he cashed it,"

"I did that already Philadelphia." Granite said." He cashed his paycheck at the NYPD's bank; took it all in cash."

"Maybe he kept it in his vault in his condo, after all there was $50,000 in there." Longo added.

"But that was all in 100-dollar bills." Tony said.

"This is strange, very strange indeed." Granite added. "What would a cop do with his paycheck money, or even the money that he took, and not put it in a bank."

"And another thing." Longo added." How does he pay his bills- he doesn't have a checking account. Does he go buy money orders all of the time?"

"We're overlooking something guys, where else would you do with your money?" Granite said.

"The only other things that I can think of is either Credit Unions" Tony said "after all the PBA has one, or Federal credit unions. Let's see if he was in the Army or Navy. Or else some of the Wall Street stock trading companies have their own banks."

"And you're right Philadelphia," Longo said. "Griffin had a bunch of stock certificates in his condo vault."

"Yeah, but you just can't walk into a stock trading company on Wall Street and plunk $10,000 down in cash to buy a stock." Granite said.

"Why not?" Longo asked.

"Because for one thing the feds want to know where you got $10,000, everyplace like banks, etc. has to report it ;was it drug money, and secondly, these Wall Street trading companies are afraid of the feds, they want to be able to show back-up, in case they are audited." Granite told him.

"Ok," Tony said. "Let's try credit unions first and next the Wall Street Trading companies to see if he had an account there."

"I'll take the PBA credit union. I have money in there too." Ed Longo said.

"I'll do the Wall Street Trading companies." Granite said.

"I'll start on the rest of the credit unions." Tony added.

Cops behaving badly are throughout the city and it was no different on this day. Jack Granite also lived in Brooklyn when he spotted four cops trying to take down a black man by the name of Frederic Diminue. He pulled over to the curb to see if he could get the collar.

"What's going on?" Granite asked them showing his shield.

"This guy was trespassing and trying to burglarize the place." Officer Monroe of the 7-5 told him.

"I LIVE HERE!!" said the 29 year old Diminue.

One of the other cops was putting a banned chokehold on him. Another cop punched him "viciously".

Diminue's parents who also lived in the building came out of the house and pleaded that their son lived there and wasn't trespassing or trying to rob it.

"If he lives here". Granite said," why are you arresting him?"

Officer Monroe came over to him and whispered in Granite's ear." I need the collar for my arrest record."

Granite nodded. "Call a sergeant." He said to him and left without the collar.

A sergeant was called and told Diminue that he'll know the reason for why he was being arrested when he got to the precinct. But he was never told when he got to the precinct. Diminue was charged with resisting arrest, trespassing, burglary and obstruction of government administration.

Even if you live somewhere, when a cop wants a collar for his arrest record, you still are not safe.

Because of the Knapp commission only narcotics officers could make narcotics arrests. However, that was 30 years ago and different Police commissioners make different rules. Now any detective or cop can make a narcotics arrest, but they still have a narcotics division primarily for a buy and bust type of operation. Cops were also told to stay out of stores and bodegas but they won't because of all of the free stuff that cops get from stores or bodegas.

Crooked cops are drawn to each other, because they have a siege mentality- them or us. And there are still "pods" of entire precincts that have been paid off to overlook gambling or prostitution.

The next day the detectives hit pay dirt.

"I found him!" Longo proclaimed." He has an account in the PBA credit union. I guess that they pay better interest than the banks do."

"I traced his stock certificates to a brokerage house." Granite said. "Listen to this. He has a portfolio that's worth over $5 million dollars."

"Wow! Where did he get the money for that?" Tony asked. "he even can't get that much money from stealing from drug dealers."

"It's got to be mob money." Ed Longo said.

"What mob money?" Jack Granite asked.

Tony and Ed Longo started to fill him in on what Griffin did for the Columbo gang.

"That's some nice racket he had going." Granite said.

"But we still don't have where that safe deposit box is from." Tony said dejected.

"You know that a lot of banks have merged lately" Granite added. "Do you think that it bypassed us because the bank changed its name and the records haven't caught up with it yet?"

"That could be." Tony answered." What we should do is look thru those banks again that have recently merged,"

"But you know." Longo added. "We may be overlooking something else."

"What?" Granite asked.

"You know all of these storage places that have sprung up. Do you think that the key is for that?" Longo stated.

"That could be too. It looks like we have some more work to do." Tony said. "However, I still feel that it's for a safe deposit box someplace and not a storage facility."

"I'll still try the storage facilities." Longo said. "You never can tell."

"I'll make a list of the merged banks and start calling." Granite added.

"Then I'll just sit here and try to think of what other places could have a key."Tony laughed.

"That's good Philadelphia." Granite added. "We do the work and you just "think'?"

"Well, I'll think of what's inside that safe deposit box that is so valuable." Tony added.

A few minutes later, Tony gets a call on his phone. "Homicide, Detective Philadelphia." He answered.

"Detective, this is Mary Stark from Crown Bank. We used to be called Sovereign Bank."

"Yes." Tony answered.

"We rechecked our records and a Charles Griffin does have a safe deposit box here." She told him.

"That's great. Where are you located?" he asked her.

"Third Avenue and East 4th street." She said.

"That's right here." Tony said amazed. The 9th Precinct was on East 5th Street between 2nd and 3rd Avenue. "Can we come over?"

"We are closing in 5 minutes." She told him.

"Miss, this is a police matter and we have a court order to open this safe deposit box." Tony told her.

"Well I guess that will be all right. Please bring the court order with you." She said.

"On our way." Tony said putting down the phone.

"Guys" he yelled to Longo and Granite." We have the bank and it's a block away. Let's go."

Tony, Longo and Granite got up and raced down the steps of the precinct to the bank.

When they got to the bank, Tony asked for Mary Stark who was the chief teller.

"Miss Stark, Hi, I'm Detective Philadelphia, this is Detectives Longo and Granite." He introduced them to her. "This is the court order signed by Judge Sawyer." He showed it to her.

Mary Stark, had to go to the branch manager and show him the court order. When he nodded okay to her. Mary got the main key to the box and took the key from Tony and went into the vault area, which contained maybe 100 safe deposit boxes.

"Detectives." Mary handed the court order back to Tony."I'm going to open the box numbered 123 belonging to Charles Griffin." She told them. "Would you want a separate room to examine the contents?"

"Yes." Tony responded.

She opened the 8" X 11" box and brought the box to a small private room and left the detectives there with the box. "After you remove the contents please return it back to me.

"Yes, ma'am." Ed Longo said.

Picture this ,3 detectives looking at this box and just staring at it. Finally, Granite says to Tony , "Okay, how about opening it."

Tony lifts up the cover of the box and it's empty. He looks further inside and finds a little receipt inside which he takes out and stares at it. It's from an Italian bank and it's got a lot of numbers on it, and a lot of Italian words, but one thing that Tony made out was" $5million dollar CD- 3 OF THEM!"

"Holy shit!" Tony exclaimed. "This is a receipt for 3 $5 million dollar CD's!"

"Whaat?' Granite says astounded. "This is definitely mob money."

"But how did he get it?" Longo asked.

"Remember," Tony said." Griffin had a passport and it was stamped for Italy. He did something for the mafia and it has something to do with this money."

"It could be money laundering to Italy or Switzerland. Who knows." Granite said.

"We got to talk to Loo." Tony added. "Hey guys want to take a trip to Italy?"

All major banks in New York have offshore accounts in the Cayman Islands and they transfer $5 million dollar CD's there each day. That's legal. But because of money laundering, the Mafia has the same offshore accounts in Switzerland, but they have to do a 3rd party transfer of a large amount like a $5million dollar CD. So places like Italy (Mafia headquarters)are transfer points from CD's to go to Swiss numbered accounts. Since all of the Columbo bosses would be followed, they chose the most trusted person, a cop, Charles Griffin, to go to Italy and transfer their $5million dollar CD's to Switzerland via an Italian bank.

He went there on the guise of buying Italian wine for the family. But in reality,he was taking several $5million dollar CD's with him to transfer to Switzerland. The Italian bank owned by the Mafia in

Italy would oblige for a small fee, which the Columbo family gladly paid.

Later that day, Tony went to Barbara's house to tell her what he had found out. But before he could even get a chance to tell her, she blurts out ,"Sweetie, I went to the doctor and yes I am pregnant- with twins!" she embraces him.

"That's great, Barbara." Tony tells her emotionless, and pushes her away.

"Listen Barbara," Tony told her."I found something out about the murder of your father and your husband. One of the dirty cops that is on DeMarco's payroll is the one who killed your father and your husband. DeMarco and your brother-in-laws must have ordered the hit on them, but this cop Griffin was the actual triggerman. We traced a gun found in his apartment to the bullets that killed them."

"Well it doesn't surprise me." She said matter of factly." These pieces of shit don't want to get their hands dirty, so they hire zips or cops to do their dirty work for them. I'll bet that they waited outside to make sure that they were dead. That's how these other killings happen."

"Well", Tony said." I know it doesn't bring you any comfort, but at least you know who did it."

"Thanks for telling me baby." she told him. "I missed you, you've got to come over each day sweetie." She kissed him and then reached for his crotch. "For some of this." And then she unzipped his fly and started to stroke his cock. "Barbara," he told her, but it was too late. She had started to suck his cock and it was erect in seconds. "BARBARA!" He yelled, and he tried to push her away.

"C'mon babe you want it, I can see that you do." she told him and continued to stroke his cock."I want to fuck you." She said.

He was so erect by now that he couldn't hold it any longer.

"Ok, I give up." he said. They went into her bedroom and he started to kiss her and play with her breasts. Her nipples were erect in seconds. Then he pulled off her pants and started to go down on her. He let her get up again to suck his cock and then he entered her again and again.

After a few minutes, he came in her. He didn't want to, but it felt so good that he let his load come into her.

"Honey." he told her." I can't keep doing this. I enjoy the sex, but I need some time for me."

"But I want you to be with me Tony." She told him. "As my husband."

"Barbara, I know that you miss your husband, but I'm not him. I'm me! And I don't know if I can go through with this, just to get some wise guys on tape, so that we can put them away."he told her. He got up and got dressed. "I'll have to think about this." He left and got in his car to go back to the squad room.

As he went through Brooklyn going back to the squad room, again he came across cops behaving badly. There was block party going on when all of a sudden he sees what was a man on crutches being attacked by about 5 cops who jumped on the man and started punching and kicking him, and some even used their batons.

"Leave me alone, I didn't do anything!" he shouted at them.

They finally handcuffed him, and one cop struck the man with a metal baton on his leg, shouting,

"I don't give a fuck about your foot. You're under arrest for resisting arrest." And then he slapped him in the face."Don't give me any dirty looks, you fucking piece of shit!"

Tony didn't want to get involved, and shook his head in disgust, but it brought to mind the old cop adage. If you can't make arrests, the next best thing for a cop to do is to write summonses. So you would write about 25 summonses that were false, when the legit ones were only 2. Nobody checked, and you were on the precincts list of best summons givers.

Frankie Marino tells Rossi that Tony is going to be joining them.

"You mean that goodie two shoes?" he asks." Why would you do that?"

"Because he's going to become part of the family." Frankie tells him," by marrying my sister-in-law.So whatever you think of him, you will have to work with him."

"But he may tip off Internal Affairs." Rossi said.

"I doubt that, because we made him an offer." Frankie says. " And we'll give you the same deal that Griffin had- his condo, the broads- all of the benies."

"OK, it's a deal." Rossi answers.

They didn't tell him that he was on the list of bad cops to get taken down.

CHAPTER 14

Tony and Longo were on the way to Easy's, when they passed by the Grand Hyatt hotel on East 42nd Street and Lexington Avenue ,when they saw another outrageous cop thing that they had to pull over to the curb. A plainclothes police officer in shorts ran up to a light skinned black just standing near the hotel and texting and grabbed him and threw him to the ground, turned him over and put the handcuffs on him. He then picked him up and brought him over to 4 other plainclothes officers.

The officer never said a word nor identified himself. The victim, said to the officers," I'm going to do whatever you say. I'm going to cooperate, but do you mind if I ask what this is about?"

One officer replied." We'll tell you. You are in safe hands."

The victim said,"I don't feel very safe."

Tony and Ed Longo ran over to the scene and flashed their gold shields." What's this about?"

Officer James Francis said," This guy was id in a credit card scam."

Tony looked at the victim and said," This is Blake Edwards, the tennis star, you idiots."

Mr. Edwards said," Check my license, in ,my left front pocket and my USTA Open credential, in my back pocket."

"No, detective, it can't be. He was positively id by a witness." Officer Francis said.

"Take the cuffs off of him, officer, NOW! This is Blake Edwards." Ed Longo ordered him.

"OK." Officer Francis said. "But I need the collar?" The cop removed the cuffs from the victim.

Tony said to the tennis star."Mr. Edwards. On behalf of the NYPD we apologize."

"Detective," Mr. Edwards said. "This is not going to be the end of it. The officer never said a word, never identified himself and just rushed me."

"I understand completely." Tony said.

Midtown North is still in the jurisdiction of this hotel. Across the street and below 42nd street is the jurisdiction of now Midtown South, what used to be the old 14th precinct.

As Tony and Ed Longo went back into their car, the same Officer Francis rushed another light skinned black and did the same thing to him.

"I guess he still needs that collar." Ed Longo said to Tony.

PBA President said in a statement," The apprehension was made under fluid circumstances where the subject might have fled and the officer did a professional job of bringing the individual to the ground to prevent that occurrence." This is still called protecting a cops 'blue law' rights, in other words, never rat on a fellow cop, no matter if the cop was wrong. He then wrote an editorial in the newspapers:

"If you have never struggled with someone who is resisting arrest or who pulled a gun or knife when you approached them for breaking the law, then you are not qualified to judge the actions of police officers putting themselves in harm's way for the public good. Let all of the facts lead where they will, but police officers have earned the benefit of the doubt because of the dangers that we routinely face. Again, this officer has a distinguished record and should be applauded for bringing down what could have been a vicious criminal instead of a tennis star."

When Tony read this in the newspapers the following day, he told Ed Longo, "I'm seeing the same things wrong that most of what the public sees."

And Longo told Tony," You know for almost 20 years…"

And Tony corrected him," What happened to 18 years, 8 months and…"

"Okay Philadelphia" Longo said annoyed, "I'm trying to say something here. For almost 20 years I treated the public who makes it possible for me to collect a pay check with respect. I never rushed to judgement that a suspect was guilty of a crime and could be abused and used because they held some sort of less than human or even less than animal status."

"You're absolutely right Longo." Tony said to him." We treat people and act like civilized human beings instead of a gang of goons and thugs." He then went on to say," Apparently our brethren police officers are thugging unarmed people with enough manpower and militarized armaments to start a revolution in some small countries."

"They have to change the police entrance requirements." Longo added.

"Right." Tony stated.

It used to be all that you needed to become a cop was to be 18 years old and pass a civil service test like Tony and Ed Longo did. Nowadays, you have to be 21 years old, have 2 years of college and pass a civil service test. But you still have to undergo a thorough background check and most minorities can't pass that portion, because they're involved in a bunch of petty crimes.

The Police Commissioner tried to change the rules by relaxing the rules to allow for minorities to become cops if they only had" petty crimes." But you can't change generational differences- a thief is still a thief and that's why so many cops are arrested for stealing from drug dealers or others. They are supposed to protect the law, instead they break the law.

Contrary to what most police department officials will tell you, cops do have a minimum quota system. In the NYPD it's as follows:

25 summons per month

3 arrests

15 stop, question and frisk

If you do not get these minimum per month, you either get transferred to traffic duty or fired.

Ed Longo and Tony go to Easy's, but Claire and Angela were off duty. Kathy with a K served them.

"What'll it be boys?" she said, placing a napkin by each.

"Beer on tap." Longo said.

"Me too." Tony added.

Ed Longo started to ogle the dancers running their lithe bodies up and down the pole. He took a sip of the beer, smacked his lips and asked Tony.

"So what are you going to tell Claire, that you're going to marry Barbara Marino?"

"I'm not." Tony said. I told Claire some of it, but not all of it. First, I won't go there with it, even if it means getting the goods on the Mafia. And second, I don't love Barbara; I like fucking her, but that's it."

"So are you going to tell Barbara?" Ed Longo asked him.

"No. I'll just go long enough with it for awhile." Tony answered him.

"But she's going to want a ring, the wedding plans, the whole nine yards." Longo told him.

"I'll play it for a little while longer." Tony tells him.

"Yeah, just long enough to get into her pussy twice a day more." Longo mentioned.

"Well she's not bad." Tony told him." I mean she does really suck like a water pump, takes it in the ass, and everywhere."

"NICE!!" Longo adds.

"But it's still not enough for me." Tony mentioned to him." If it was Claire, I would marry her in a second."

"Did you tell her that?" Longo asked him.

"No," Tony said." I just want to get this cop and Mafia thing over with, and get back to my life, and then I'll get serious with Claire."

"But what are you going to do about this baby thing with Barbara?" Longo questioned him.

"I'm just a surrogate Longo." Tony replied." She told me that I have no responsibility to her or the babies, and besides, once this is all over with, she is going into the witness protection program and I'll never see her again."

"What do you mean babies? Philadelphia do you mean she is having twins?" Longo asked astonished.

"Yes. Twin boys." Tony said.

"Congratulations." Longo said raising up his glass of beer.

"Fuck you Longo." Tony said disgusted. "I would probably never see them if she went into witness protection."

"True" Ed Longo said and motioned to Kathy with a K for another round for him and Tony.

Tony looked at his watch and said to Longo." After this round let's go over to Cherry Street and see what "our" boys are up to."

"Sounds good." Longo answered.

When Tony and Ed Longo got to the warehouse where the coffin cops were at, a patrol car from Midtown North pulls up and Officer James Francis gets out and goes inside.

"Look who's here." Tony says, "The cop who tackled the tennis star."

"Yeah," Longo said," I figured that he would be one of them."

They start to listen to the tape. They hear Officer Francis tell Rossi." Those 2 detectives interrupted my collar at the Hyatt. I need another collar soon."

Rossi tells him." Why don't you troll for skels."(trolling is like a fishing term to throw a line out and see what you can catch)

"Good idea." Officer Francis says." Maybe I'll pick up something."

When Officer Francis left the coffin cops hideout, he immediately spotted something to collar.

Warren Hines was riding his bike on the sidewalk, Officer Francis immediately pulled his car over and grabbed Hines, pinning him to the driveway. Soon after, Natasha Diggs, his girlfriend was sitting near the sidewalk, and asked him to identify himself. Officer Francis flatly refused. She moved Hines's bike into the house. Meanwhile, Officer Francis had handcuffed Hines to his patrol car and went into the front door of her house and said that she was tampering with evidence by taking the bike. Office Francis then grabbed her and pulled her out of the house.

He arrested both of them with resisting arrest, riding a bike on the side walk, tampering with evidence and he threw a bag of pot that he had for such circumstances, and also drug possession.

On the way back to Midtown North to process these collars, Officer Francis pulled over another driver, Stefon Cline. He asked him why was he being pulled over for.

"License and registration." Officer Francis told him.

When he gave it to him, Officer Francis gave him three straight shots to the mouth and called for back-up to arrest Cline for disrespect to an officer. Now Officer Francis had 3 collars for the day, and he was satisfied.

Most of the police who are cited for excessive force live in Staten Island, Long Island or upstate New York. For some reason these rural cops just don't take anybody's guff.

Officer Francis, was completely exhonorated for all of these incidents, a tribute to the NYPD's blue law of not prosecuting a bad cop.

Tony and Ed Longo decided to tail John Rossi went he left the coffin cops hideout. Rossi drove straight up West Street to the usual places in Hell's Kitchen where he knew that he would find some skels selling drugs. And he did.

"We've got to record what we're seeing Longo." Tony said.

"Got ya partner." Ed Longo answered.

Their entry said:" 1220 hours: Detectives Longo and Philadelphia see Detective Rossi remove numerous bags of heroin from unidentified youths near West 42nd street and 10th avenue."

They watched Rossi for a number of hours and kept writing down what they saw.

"1320 hours: Detectives Longo and Philadelphia see Detective Rossi steal cash and vials of crack from George on West 44th Street and 10th Avenue".

"1400 hours: Detectives Longo and Philadelphia see Detective Rossi and two male P.O.s beat and robbed Jefferson, a drug dealer on West 48th Street and 10th Avenue"

"How much is he going to do in a day?" Tony asked Longo after this last entry.

"He wants to get rich I suppose." Longo answered him.

But obviously Rossi had had enough for the day and went back to Midtown North on West 54th Street to record his haul.

The next day Tony calls Claire," Hey, do you want to go to a concert in Central Park? And the best part is that it's free and it features all of the groups from the 80's and 90's."

"Great!" Claire tells him "When?"

"Saturday night. I'll pick you up for lunch. We'll eat in the park and get a good seat and then watch the show. They're expecting like half a million people there." Tony told her.

"That sounds fantastic." She told him. "I love that music."

"Okay. I'll probably see you at the bar before then." Tony said. "But seriously Claire, I'd like to see you more than just that."

"Okay," Claire said." Who's stopping you? Not me"

"That's great." Tony said. "Can I come over now? I know it's getting close to your bedtime, but I'd like to see you."

"C'mon over now Tony. I'd like to see more of you too." Claire added

"I'm on my way." Tony replied. He knew and so did she that he was going to fuck her. He put on his red and blue flashing lights and broke all speeding laws to get to her place.

When he got to her place, they immediately went at it, sucking and fucking for hours.

"I take it that you're staying until I have to go to work?" she asked him.

"You know it honey." Tony replied and started to kiss her again."Claire," he told her," I feel something for you and I think that you feel the same way towards me."

"Sweetie," Claire told him." There's definitely chemistry between us, and I'd like for you to keep seeing me."

"That's what I plan to do honey." Tony told her. "You're beautiful, sexy, smart and you turn me on all of the time."

"Well, you're one handsome, sexy man sweetie." Claire told him."and I love the way that you fuck."

"It's only you that can turn me on to do it to you like that." Tony added caressing her breasts." And I love your body."

"It's all for you babe."she told him. They looked into each other's eyes and kept kissing each other and holding each other until they fell asleep. Tony spent the rest of the day with Claire. He felt her snuggle up to him and then, all of a sudden, Tony felt her sucking his cock. He looked at her and she met his gaze.

"I saw this big cock just standing up, so I just had to suck it" .She told him.

"That feels great!" he told her. "Will you do that to me every night?" he asked her.

"Every night, every day, every minute that you're here." She told him and kissed him and went back to sucking his cock.

"You know honey, if you do that to me, I'm going to be here every single day." Tony mentioned to her.

"That's what I want Tony. I'm falling for you." She answered.

"That's the way I feel about you too." Tony told her and lifted her back up and started to kiss her passionately. They embraced and started to feel each other up and before long he was fucking her again and again.

"You are one sexy man." Claire told him after they had both came.

"And you are one sexy woman." Tony tells her, "And you keep turning me on every minute." She kept stroking his chest and he kept caressing her body and kissing every part of her.

"Sweetie, I have to go to work." She told him since it was almost 11PM and she had to be at Easy's at 12AM. "Will I see you later?"

"You know it honey." he answered her. "Let's take a shower together."

"That's great sweetie, but you can spend the night here if you want." She tells him.

"No, I'll drive you there and then I'll head back to my place." he kissed her again. She nodded. "But I'll pick you up after work and we'll have dinner together."

"That sounds good." Claire added. "I really want to be with you sweetie."

"Claire," Tony told her." That's the way I feel about you."

After Tony dropped Claire off at Easy's , he really felt good about himself, but began to wonder what to tell Barbara. Should he continue to fuck her for the sake of getting the goods on the Mafia or the dirty cops. He liked fucking her, but he really enjoyed fucking Claire. He's beginning to think that he's falling in love with her.

On his way back to Brooklyn he sees a black NYPD cop from Highway 1 giving a ticket to a driver. Tony knows of one black cop in Highway 1 who is blowing the whistle on the NYPD Highway Division. Racism is routine in the elite unit and there is a quota system to write a minimum of 70 summons a month. Any officer not making his quota can be given inconvenient tours of duty, a bad car or motorcycle to work with and even an involuntary transfer out of Highway, something which bodes badly for the officer's career.

He didn't go to Barbara's house that night and heard it from her the next morning at breakfast.

"Tony why didn't you come over last night after work?" she asked him.

"Barbara I had to work overtime on another case." he said. Starting to get undressed in order to fuck her again, he noticed that she was starting to show a baby bump." Wow, you are starting to show the baby already."

"Babies!" she told him"We're going to have twins, sweetie."

"What?" Tony exclaimed.

"Yes babe I told you that already, don't you remember? I came from the Doctor today, and he confirmed that we're going to have twin boys. Isn't that wonderful" she said kissing him.

"Great, just great." Tony said, not knowing what else to say. He kissed her back and she started to suck his cock, and in no time he was erect and started to mount her.

On one of the tapes that Barbara gave Tony, was DeMarco giving Frankie Marino orders to kill a prosecutor who he thought had been disrespectful to him. It is the kind of Mafia hit that according to the lore of La Costra Nostra is forbidden.

"I want you to kill that mother fucker Williams." DeMarco tells Frankie in the tape. "That son of a bitch disrespected me." Disrespecting a Mafia chief by anyone, even a judge, cop or prosecutor is a crime punishable by death.

Frankie, who as underboss, is a wannabe boss, is very ambitious and wants that top spot someday, tells DeMarco.

"Don't worry boss, it's as good as done. He's a dead man walking."

Demarco then tells Frankie," Give it to the Rico brothers and also Santamarita. Three of them should make sure he's dead, dead, dead!"

"Boss, I will personally scout the Williams office in Manhattan, and give the order to kill him." Frankie answers DeMarco.

"Frankie, that's why you'll be boss one day." DeMarco tells him. "You pay attention to detail."

"You know that you can trust me boss." Frankie says. "I'll even ask Barbara's cop boyfriend, Philadelphia to help."

"That's good too Frankie." DeMarco tells Frankie." Get him involved too, so that we know he's one of ours."

When Tony and Longo hear this, their eyes almost bulge out of their heads.

"Now what am I supposed to do Longo? Tony asks him. "Kill a federal prosecutor?"

"No way, Philadelphia." Ed Longo responds." We'll go to Loo or Cap and see what they want us to do. But you're not going to help them kill a federal prosecutor. You'll be an accessory to murder."

"That's for sure, even in a back handed way." Tony tells Longo."like if I give them information about him."

Gerald Williams was the top organized crime federal prosecutor in Manhattan. He had convictions on most of the 5 New York Mafia families, including "Dapper Don", Sam 'the Plumber', and the 'Snake' among others. Mr. Williams also shared a law office with his father George Williams. The senior Mr. Williams also worked as an administrative law judge for the city, ruling on challenges to parking tickets.

On another tape, Frankie tells Barbara that he wants to see Tony alone. "I need to see your boyfriend."

"Fiance." Barbara corrects him.

"Whatever. Tell him to come to my place tonight." Frankie instructs her.

When Tony and Longo tell Loo about this Loo tells them," Great. Now we'll get him on an attempted murder charge."

"You mean that you want me to go thru with this Loo and give them information?"

"No, we'll have your ass covered and then we'll arrest the lot of them. Good work Philadelphia." Loo tells Tony who looks at Longo like he's being suckered into a trap.

That night, Tony goes to Frankie's house.

"Detective." Frankie greets Tony." I need some help that will cement your role with us and I'll give you the names of all of the cop's who's working for us."

"I'm listening Frankie" Tony says.

"There's this prosecutor, Gerald Williams, who's giving shit to DeMarco, and we want to get rid of him." Frankie tells him. "all we need from you is to find out where his office is, where he lives, and we'll do the rest."

"You mean that you're going to kill him." Tony says.

"No, we just want to rough him up a little so he leaves DeMarco alone." Frankie lied. "Once you get us this information, I'll give you a list of crooked cops."

"When do you need this information by?" Tony asks.

"As soon as you can get it for me. " Frankie says. "Tomorrow will be okay."

"I'll see what I can do." Tony responds.

Tony goes back to the squad room and tells Loo what the Columbo's want him to do.

"Philadelphia, this is what we'll do. Tell them what office he works in and we'll be waiting for them with half the police in this city.

"Okay, Loo, but I don't like it. Something can still go wrong." Tony tells him.

"You worry too much. We'll have the prosecutor covered all of the way." Loo tells him.

Tony reluctantly agrees and goes back to Frankie Marino's house with the information that they want.

"Frankie," Tony said giving him a slip of paper with all of the information on it." Here's what you wanted. Now where's my information."

"That was fast Tony." Frankie says." I can see that you're going to be an asset to our family. I'll have the information that you wanted tomorrow."

"Okay." Tony says.

"Also, Tony, DeMarco would like to invite you to his son's wedding. Barbara knows all of the details."

"Okay." Tony says.

But even before Frankie can give the hitmen this information, in a mistake of biblical proportions, the 3 hit men found and tracked not Gerald Williams, the intended victim, but his father, George Williams, 78.They shot him to death in a laundry near his home in Queens.

When DeMarco found out about this botched assignment, on tape he is yelling to Frankie,

"What kind of assholes did you get to do this! This was a very simple thing to do Frankie!"

"I'm sorry boss." Frankie explains." I'll kill him myself."

"And you got Barbara's cop to help you?" DeMarco asks.

"Yes" Frankie tells him." But I didn't have time to give the information from Barbara's cop to them."

"See what happens when you rush?" DeMarco tells Frankie. "Get this job done Frankie."

"I will boss." Frankie tells him.

But Frankie didn't want to dirty his hands with killing and also not to leave any witnesses, so he hired two new hitmen to kill the first three hitmen that had botched up the killing. Then he hired 2 more hitmen to kill the 2 hitmen who had killed the original hitmen.

But there was a sub-plot. After the Rico brothers were killed, Frankie took up a sexual relationship with one of the Rico brothers wives, Kim,28. But this didn't last too long and he dumped her. Kim then married a cop, named Henry Dole. He would be killed later on by Frankie when Frankie wanted to fuck Kim again.

As Tony and Ed Longo were headed back to the squad room, they came across another police incident. They just happened to pass a department store on Broadway and then saw 4 officers pinning a squirming Orlando Holland to the floor and punching him in the back several times.

"Stop fucking hitting him!" one woman yelled as a crowd gathered. The woman was shooed away as more cops headed toward there to control the situation.

As the cops held down Holland, the officer who had punched him repeatedly, used his knee to pin his head to the ground. And then 15 to 20 cops headed the call for assistance and walked into the area. That same woman said," 1 person, 50 cops. That's what happens in this area."

"Kick him in the balls." One officer yelled.

Holland was finally subdued and arrested on charges of disorderly conduct, trespassing on city property(the sidewalk),obstructing governmental administration, and resisting arrest, all of this for not having ID on him, which he had left home.

"They treat newly arrived immigrants better than this." Tony said to Longo, not wanting to stop and see what caused this.

"Just a normal day on the streets." Ed Longo stated. And Tony nodded in disgust.

"I have to go see Barbara Marino later." Tony said to Longo.

"Why for more pussy?" Ed Longo smirked.

"That too." Tony said. "But listen to this. I just got invited to DeMarco's son's wedding. Can you believe this?"

"No shit!" Longo exclaimed." Are you going to go?"

"Probably." Tony said." I'll ask Loo and the FBI first, but can you imagine being on the inside with all of the 5 Mafia families. I can get enough on tape to put all of them away."

"That'll be great Philadelphia." Longo mentioned." How come you get all of the luck –the pussy and the limelight."

Tony smiled." I'll make Dick 1 after this." He said.

"No doubt." Longo mentioned. "But which one would you rather have- the pussy or the promotion or the Dick 1 badge?"

"Both." Tony told him.

"How come you didn't tell me?" Tony asked Barbara.

"About what sweetie." Barbara said kissing him.

"About being invited to DeMarco's son's wedding?" Tony tells her.

"Oh that." She answers. "Frankie wanted to tell you himself. And it's an honor to be invited. All of the families will be there as well as some movie stars, like the one who played in "Pulp Fiction"and the famous director and actor who played in "Goodfellas"."

"So where is it being held?" Tony asks her."And when is it for?"

"It's at the "Castle" on Long Island this Friday." She tells him. "and it's black tie."

"But I don't own a tuxedo." He tells her.

"So you'll rent one sweetie. And the gift is $5000."

"WHAT!" Tony yells at her. "I don't have $5000 laying around to give to some Mafiosa's son".

"Sweetie, don't worry about it. Frankie is taking care of it for us." She tells him. "And we'll all be at the same table – isn't that great."

"Great. Just great!" Tony responds "Just make sure that you bring that wire."

"I will. I told you that I'll do anything for you sweetie." She said and immediately unzips his fly and grabs his cock. She kisses him and then starts to get on her knees and takes his cock in her mouth.

He let's her and this time he came in her mouth and she swallowed it. She wipes off her mouth and kisses him again. "See what I do for you baby. Anything that you want." She said.

"I know that you do Barbara." Tony responds and kisses her back.

CHAPTER 15

The lavish wedding of Paul DeMarco's son, John, guests were shaken down for a minimum gift of $5000 and the gangsters had to stagger their appearance to avoid unlawful contact with fellow criminals. Well -wishers arrived at John DeMarco's wedding and deposited their envelopes in an "elegant birdcage" by the door. With about 500 people attending the event at the posh "Castle" on Long Island, the same place that politically connected owner, Peter Maloni was shot in the face during a still-unsolved ambush last year. The groom and bride, Lisa Manuto, raked in about $2.5 million. DeMarco's round the clock wedding began at 5PM on Friday and lasted until 1PM on Saturday and included a multi-course meal at midnight and breakfast at 7AM.

All of the 5 NYC crime families were there- the Gambino's, Lucesse, Bonanno, Columbo and even DeCavalcante from New Jersey. But felons can't consort together, and they had to stagger the felons, much like an annual Oscar party. That's standard mob procedure. There was enough security to guard an army with all of the Mafiosa there.

Tony was introduced to many criminals, who were aghast that a cop was invited.

"He's going to be family now." Paul DeMarco told them. "He's a friend of ours." They nodded that he was vouching for Tony.

DeMarco's daughter Trish had been married to a made man, Angelo "the Bull" Tratoria, who showed up with two law enforcement officers who stood guard at the doors. "The Bull " had to get a judge's approval to travel from Cleveland, where he's awaiting trial on racketeering charges in an alleged $3 million stolen car scheme to weigh down junked cars with sand and dirt before selling them for scrap metal.

DeMarco later regretted his choice of "the Bull" to be her husband describing him, as an "imbecile" devoid of any common sense.

"Does he get in the back seat of the car and think someone has stolen the steering wheel?" DeMarco had once asked his daughter during a prison visit.

Trish had divorced the philandering dumbfella years ago after he was convicted of racketeering for the same crime that he's on trial now, along with giving racehorses drugs to enhance their performance,and exposed for cheating on her with his Queens secretary.

"That's all part of being a mob princess". Barbara told him. " you're married to the mob."

A team of feds also kept watch outside the gates. "We want to gather some intel on which mobsters are still hanging around." One of them told Tony later. And true to the mob code of conduct the wedding was listed under the brides name and that staffers at the Castle had to sign confidentiality agreements "or else".

Even if you're not a skel, there is a common police practice called "driving while black". They figure that if you're black that you must have done something wrong and that's why nine times out of ten a police car will stop a driver who is black in order to make arrests.

One Highway 1 cop pulled over a black female who was driving a BMW on the Upper East Side, near Sutton Place. So apparently according to the cops you can't be black, you can't be driving a nice car like a BMW on the Upper East Side at 11AM in the morning.

The woman, Tamika Torrence James, (yes, that Tamika Torrence ,who was the dispatcher when Tony did the shootout at Penn Station years ago) is now the wife of a New York Jets football player, Antonio James, said to the officer." Why have you pulled me over?"

Officer Timothy Robbins, said to her ," Roll your window down."

"Officer, you're asking me to roll my window down, which is almost all the way down in my car?"Mrs. James told him.

"For safety reasons." Officer Robbins said.

"For safety reasons?" she asked." I'm not authorized to do that officer."

"You don't have to, which I explained to you." Officer Robbins said.

"So now I have to tell you why I'm even on Sutton Place?" she asked him.

"You don't have to." Officer Robbins said.

"But why are you asking me why I'm on Sutton Place?" she responded.

"Just curious." He said.

"You don't have to be curious about why I'm on Sutton Place." She told him.

"Ok, all right. Just hang tight ma'am for a minute. I'll be right back, all right?" he said and returned to his vehicle. He found out that she lived on Sutton Place. Obviously you can't drive a nice car or live on Sutton Place if you're black.

Back at the 9th precinct there is roll call at each shift. Each patrol officer is given his beat and when his meal break is by the desk Sgt. and what to look for if anything is special. This particular desk Sgt. Kyle Brendan, started deriding Dominicans as "stupid and crazy."

He was upset about a minor car accident involving a man he presumed to be Dominican by the way that he was acting. So he started asking all of the Hispanic patrol cops there where they were from. Whoever said that they were Dominican, he would say," Well I can tell."

Then one of the patrol cops, Officer Roberto Ramirez, said, " I was born and raised in the D.R.", and Sgt. Brendan turns around and says, "What are you doing here? Why don't you go back?"

"Sgt., because I live here now," Ramirez says." I'm an American just like you are."

"No. Not like ME!"Sgt. Brendan said.

As the officer's left roll call, another officer, who is not Dominican, who was friendly with Tony said,

"We were shocked. How can somebody say that at roll call? Brendan's tirade took everybody by surprise. We couldn't believe that this just happened." He said." As the guys were walking out some had their heads down."

Tony told him that he would ask the Captain about taking Brendan off of roll call. But that didn't happen. A Sgt. is still a Sgt. and above the rank of ordinary patrol cops.

On the way back from watching the coffin cops hideout, Tony and Longo passed by the 10th pct. on the way up to Easy's for a brew and a chance to see Claire.

A 40 year old woman, one Hannah Nicks, was leaving a birthday party with her children, ages 7 and 11, and just walking on the street back to her place. She passed by a patrol car, their cruiser lights flashing next to a car blasting an alarm.

The office, John Maloney, from the 10th pct, asks her,

"Is this your car?"

She said," No sir, it's not."

Then Officer Maloney says to her," Then mind your own fucking business!"

"Officer, I'm just responding to your question if this car is mine, and I said it wasn't." she tells him.

Then his partner, Officer Peter Kelly says to her," I don't like your attitude. You're disrespecting an officer of the law."

"Officer, no I'm not." She replied.

Officer Maloney then says, " I'm arresting you for disturbing the peace and disrespecting an officer of the law."

"But I didn't do anything except to tell you that it's not my car that's going off." She tells him.

With that Officer Kelly punches her in the face in front of her children. She falls to the floor as both cops struggle to pin her to the sidewalk. Her kids started crying and she says to a passerby

,"Please help me!."

But no one comes to help her and they arrested her for resisting arrest, and battery of a police officer.(struggling with them).They took her in their patrol car and left the kids on the street screaming,

"Mommy!!"

Lucky that the birthday party parents took the kids into their house. The cops did not even look back to see what happened to the kids. They were just concerned with the arrest.

Tony and Ed Longo refused to stop after seeing this,

"I'm not touching this with a ten foot pole." Longo said.

"Yeah," Tony said. "We'll just get into trouble for interfering with a lawful arrest."

Rossi was at Easy's already when Tony and Ed Longo came in.

"Well look who's here. It's the big Dicks." He said.

"Fuck you Rossi!" Tony said.

"That's all you can say, Philadelphia." Rossi stared at him. "Mr. Goody two shoes himself."

"Well at least my shoes ain't dirty." Tony replied.

"And what's that supposed to mean?" Rossi inched closer to Tony.

"Take it how you want Rossi." Tony told him.

"You know something Philadelphia, you're a phony fuck." Rossi glared at him" You come in here thinking that you're better than everybody else. Somebody needs to knock you right on your ass."

Tony wouldn't back down. There was too much history and bad blood between them.

"Let me know when you feel up to it." Tony told him.

Rossi lunged toward Tony but Ed Longo stepped in-between. The three of them jammed against the bar, Longo's big body blocking everything.

"Let's not be stupid Rossi." Longo told him. "We're all on the same job."

"No, we ain't! "Rossi said, eyeing Ed Longo's big muscles and then stared at Tony. "You know where to find me Philadelphia."

"Anytime, Anyplace Rossi!" Tony wasn't going to back down for this dirty cop.

Rossi wobbled out of the bar from the several drinks that he had just had.

Tony had gotten the name 'Goody Two Shoes' because he wasn't a bully. He never had a complaint against him for excessive force, and he treated even skels, with respect. But a lot of cops, and even skels, thought him an easy mark to be taken advantage of. They soon learned that he was no pushover and would teach whomever started with him a lesson that they would always remember.

Claire saw what had happened.

"What was that about sweetie?" She asked Tony and leaned over the bar to kiss him.

"Oh he's just thinking that he's now Mr. Big shot and wants to throw his weight around." Tony told her.

"Try to steer clear of him babe." She told him." He's like Griffin was, only meaner."

"I'm not worried about him Claire. He's all mouth." Tony said to her.

"OK." She said." But I've got a stake in your well- being."

"I know." Tony smiled at her.

"What can I get you boys." She said placing a cocktail napkin by each of them.

"Beer on tap." Longo told her, "and keep them coming."

"Me too." Tony added." It's been a rough morning."

She winked at him and leaned closer to the bar."I bet that I can make you feel better later." She flashed those come hither eyes at him.

"I bet that you can." Tony said." And I will see you later."

"Promise?" she asked coyly.

"Promise." He said.

When she left to get the beer, Longo told him.

"You've got some sweet deal here Philadelphia. Every female wants your cock."

Tony laughed. "What can I say Longo. It pleases them."

Later that afternoon, Tony went to Claire's place and soon was doing things to her that was just downright horny. She was down on her knees sucking his cock, when he couldn't stand it any more.

"Swallow it, Swallow it!" Tony ordered her. He felt that he was going to come in her mouth and he did. She felt the sperm squirt into her mouth, it was warm and a lot. She stopped for a second and realized that he had come in her mouth, but continued to suck him dry, and as he told her, she swallowed it.

"Like that sweetie." Claire asked looking up at him from her kneeling position, still holding his cock.

"I love it!" he told her, gently holding her head near his cock. He pressed her mouth closer on his cock.

She continued to lick the oozing sperm off of his cock and then sucked it again. She was good Tony thought. Too bad I can't keep her doing this all of the time without having to promise to marry her. But he did feel something for Claire, he didn't know if it was love or just lust.

"I'll do that every day for you sweetie." She said looking up at him.

"I know that you will honey and that's why I want you all of the time." He said.

"You can do anything that you want to me sweetie." She told him," and I'll take it all in."

He knew that she meant taking it in the ass.

"That sounds very good to me honey." He said and lifted her up and kissed her.

He led her back to her bed and just lay down with her. He rubbed his cock near her pussy from behind and she loved the way that he made her feel.

"You know sweetie, that I want to be with you like this forever." she murmered to him.

"I do too honey." He told her and nuzzled her again.

Tony was seeing Claire almost every day now and fucking her incessantly. They both couldn't get enough of each other. This had an effect on him doing Barbara as well and she noticed it.

"What's going on sweetie"? she asked him" You don't like me anymore?"

"No, of course I do Barbara." He told her." It's just that I'm on a number of cases that's taking a lot of time and the brass doesn't want to know about all of the cases that I'm working on."

"You tell them for me that you're only one person and how do they expect you to do everything." She said.

"Yeah, right." He answered her sarcastically." I'm sure that the brass doesn't want to know how many cases that you're working on. Even if I tell them that you said. They think that you're superman."

"Well you are to me." She smiled at him and grabbed his crotch.

"Barbara, please." He pushed her hand away." I just need the tapes."

"OK babe." She said giving it to him." Will I see you later?"

"I'll try." He said and turned around and went back to his car.

"What, no nookie?" Ed Longo asked him as he got back in the car.

"It's getting too much." Tony said.

"I never thought that I'd hear you say that Philadelphia." Longo mentioned it to him." I thought that you were the stud of the century, fucking three women all of the time."

"Well it's not as it's cracked up to be, Longo." Tony said. "And it's only two –Claire and Barbara. I haven't been with Angela in awhile."

"Yeah, but it's non-stop with both of them. What a way to go." Longo told him. "I only wish that I had half of the pussy that you get. No, I stand corrected; I'll take even a quarter of what you get each day."

Tony laughed." Hey, Longo. I hear that you were quite the stud in your day. Picking up every eligible female that so much as looked at you, and arresting them for indecent exposure until they gave it to you for free."

"That was long ago Philadelphia." Longo told him." Now I'm lucky if I get it 3 times a week."

"That's better than most married guys get it." Tony said to him." And how would you handle it now?"

"I'd die a happy man." Longo told him. "Wow, fucking three, no correction, two women at once every day. I'd do anything to do that now."

"So tell me Longo, professionally speaking, how did you get them to do that?" Tony asked.

"I just told them that it was indecent for them to be that sexy and beautiful and if they didn't stop, then I would have to arrest them for indecent exposure." Longo said.

"And it worked?" Tony asked.

"Every time." Longo told him." Because if they didn't agree to give it to me, then I was going to arrest them for real."

"And none of them pressed charges?" Tony asked.

"No, I guess that I chose them correctly- the way that they looked at me- I could tell that they wanted it."he said.

Later that day at the coffin cops hideout Tony and Ed Longo hear Rossi say that he had stolen a kilo of coke from a drug dealer and sold it for $15,000. And then they hear that he tells the other cops that he's working on a plan to get the drug dealers to pay them for protection.

"I mean, if they want to keep operating, they should pay us." Rossi says. "Otherwise, we're going to keep coming after them; it's just a business expense, I told them."

"That's right" Sgt. Fallon says. "If they don't pay us, then not only are they going to get hit, but they'll have to pay the mob many more times for protection from us."

"And the mob is on our side." Rossi says. "So it's a no win situation for them, and a win-win situation for us. The mob pays us, they should pay us too."

"You can't beat that." Sgt. Fallon says laughing.

"So which ones are going to pay and which ones are not going to pay." Bobby O'Mara asks.

"I'll make a list of the known dealers, but the problem is that there is always the lone wolf who's dealing that we don't know." Rossi say." But we'll find them too. It's just a matter of time."

Friend is a code word for made member of the Mafia. One of Barbara's tapes has Frankie Marino venting to Patch Marino,

"I'm a fucking friend. 37 fucking years a wiseguy." Frankie says." Cocksuckers never did shit. Never did shit what I done in my life. They never stole a fucking napkin."

"You're right Frankie." Patch Marino says. "You deserve everything."

"You know, I remember the $1,000 dollar a hand poker games at Dapper Dons social club." Frankie says." Yeah, you could go into the Copacabana night club and they would make up a table just for you."he goes on to say." And you don't have to dress like a movie star. I'm talking a night when you go out to a club, you look nice. You don't look like crap, because guys think that you're a fucking brokster." Frankie says.

Frankie's father and grandfather were also Mafia members. A company man, even if the company's business was murder and extortion. He has a tattoo on his arm that says" Death before dishonor." Never rat on another member of the mob.

But Frankie Marino is a relic from another mob era, a has been, the guy who doesn't get respect from his son Jerome, who is also a capo. Jerome refused to lend Frankie money and put him on a "pay me no mind list."

"He wouldn't help me out, even after I got him inducted in the crime family." Frankie says." My son's a real son of a bitch. He wouldn't lend me a dollar, not a fuckin dime. He broke my heart."

Frankie is also trying to think up ways to make money while reminiscing about the old days.

In the big Lufthansa robbery at JFK, Frankie complains that he didn't get a big enough cut.

"We never got enough money, not what we were supposed to get, we got fucked all around." Frankie says, then again," We got fucked all around, that fucking Jimmy Burke kept everything. He kept the money from the other guys and then he whacked all of them."

But Frankie found the money to buy a speedboat and a specially designed Lincoln.

Years ago Frankie was an enforcer, a mob killer like Sammy the Bull. He once strangled a suspected snitch with a dog chain. Once when a guy wouldn't come up with protection money, Frankie hollered at him," When I'm done with you, your own Mother wouldn't recognize you if you don't pay me."

Most mobsters go after business's to pay protection money. They use intimidation methods including arson, systematically extorting money from local construction companies, supermarkets, furniture and clothing stores, produce and fish vendors and cafes.

One businessman was forced to give up his construction company and sell his house after paying tens of thousands of dollars to them . Most of the extortion money went to supply families of imprisoned mobsters. When you're a Don or a capo you never have to worry about money if you go to jail.

CHAPTER 16

Back at the squad room, Loo realized that the "coffin cops" case was getting too much, too involved, to have just Tony and Longo on it. Especially to look up the minutia involved in a case as big as this one was. One of the other detectives in the 9th precinct was also assigned. Detective 2nd grade, Jim Caulfield was a big man, 6'-4", 240 lbs. He liked to wear a grey/black sports jacket with a black dickie shirt, and a big, very big gold cross. He felt that it scared the skels away and it was very impressive looking.

But Loo was a stickler for the Detective code: suits, suits, suits.

"Caulfield- get a suit!" he shouted.

"But Loo, this sport jacket is fine for our work." He said.'Not in this squad." Loo told him.

"OK, but the skels are scared shitless when I approach them like this." Caulfield says.

"I don't care- get a suit!." Loo shouted at him.

"Oh, ok." Jim said and looked to Tony for some help.

Tony stopped off at Claire's place later in the day and when she was getting up to go to work. He leaned her near the bed and knocked off a piece while she was still in her nightgown.

"You keep doing this to me sweetie every day and I'll never go to work." Claire mentioned to him.

"That's my plan honey" Tony told her." I need to be with you every day."

"Wow." She said to him. "So we're an item."

"Definitely!" he said as he kissed her again and again.

Loo tells Jack Granite.

"Granite, you're going to Italy."

"Why me Loo." He said." This is Philadelphia's case."

"Yeah, but he and Longo are too involved to let them go."

"And what am I supposed to do when I get there?" Jack asked Loo.

"Well." Loo told him." We have the CD receipts for 3-5 million dollar CD's. This is mob money taken from everybody, so it's ours and we want it back."

"Who do I see Loo? Granite asks.

"I'll get you all of the details." Loo told him. "See my secretary and she'll get you the airplane tickets." And then in an afterthought. "You do have a passport, don't you?"

"Of course I do." Jack Granite told him.

"Come see me tomorrow and I'll give you everything." Loo told him.

The next day Loo tells Granite," Okay, we got permission from the Commissioner for you to go to Sicily to get our money back. Here is your plane ticket to Palermo, a letter from the Commissioner saying that Griffin is dead and you are to bring this money back to us."

Granite looks at the NYPD official letter signed by the Police Commissioner.

"Also here is the address of the bank and the police station address." Loo tells Granite." You are to meet an Italian police Detective named Nicky Prezzama when you get there. He will help with getting anything that you need from the bank. You leave this afternoon."

"Wow!" Granite says." That soon. They must really want this money."

"It's mob money." Loo says, "and we want it."

"OK" he says. " I'll go home and pack."

"You won't need much," Loo tells him," You'll probably be back in a day or two."

That afternoon, Jack Granite boards an Alitalia flight from JFK to Palermo Sicily. The almost 6 hour flight gets him there just before the bank opens, the next morning. He gets into a cab and gives him a piece of paper with the address of the police station,

"Centile san Giovanni Degli Brometi 2" The taxi driver looks at it and says to Granite" Poliza?"

"Yes." Granite says.

It's about a 30 minute drive from the airport to the police station in Palermo.

Granite did not have time to change money, so he gives him 2-$20 bills" Is that enough?"

The driver nods his head.

"Give me a receipt." Granite tells him.

He goes into the police station, flashes his gold shield and says," Nicky Prezzama?"

The desk officer motions to the stairs and with his finger motions" UP".

Granite nods. It seems that all police detectives are on the 2nd floor, no matter what country they are in.

Granite goes up to the second floor and yells out," Nicky Prezzama!"

Detective Prezzama looks up from his breakfast of coffee, prijole and melon, and waves him over.

"Detective Granite I presume?" using a napkin to clean his hand and extends it to him.

"yes." Granite says and extends his hand to shake it.

"Your New York Lt. spoke to me about this thing that you have to do." Prezzama tells him." Let me finish my breakfast and we'll go to the bank."

"Great." Granite responds.

"You know" Prezzama continues," that this money is probably mafia money."

"I know." Granite tells him." The cop who died was transporting it to the bank here."

"They may try to prevent you from taking the money." Detective Prezzama says.

"I know. I brought a letter from the NYPD Commissioner to say that the cop is dead and we want his stuff."Granite says.

"Just so you know, if it's Mafia money, as soon as you leave here, the bank will get on the phone telling them that their money was taken." Prezzama tells him.

"I know but we have an undercover cop on the inside to warn us of it."

"Good to hear." Prezzama says. He gulps the last drop of coffee and wipes his hands and says," Let's go."

The bank is Banco di Sicilian Palermo(the bank of Sicily) located on Via Generale Magliocco 1, about a 10 minute drive. When they arrived there, Granite realized that Prezzama was right, the bank was reluctant to give him the CD's.

"He has the required receipts for the money." Prezzama tells the Vice-President of the bank, Guliermo Conte, in Italian.

"But it's not the guy who signed for it." Conte tells the Detective.

Granite figures that was what they were talking about and tells the Vice-President" Look, that guy is dead, and since he has no living relatives, it is NYPD property."

Conte looks at him and takes the paperwork to the President who looks at the paperwork and then looks at Granite and Prezzama and nods to him.

Conte then goes to the vault that had the CD's, opens it and brings the 3- 5 million dollar CD's to Jack Granite and the Italian cop.

"You have to sign for these." Conte says.

"Okay." Granite says and signs the paper that he took the CD's. Granite and the cop leave the bank.

"That was easy." Granite tells Pezzama as they get into the police car.

"Too easy." Prezzama says." I'd watch my back while you're here in Sicily."

"Thanks." Granite says." Well my flight back to New York is later this afternoon."

"Well you can stay at the police station, until your flight and I'll drive you back to the airport." Prezzama tells him.

"Great." Granite says." If you're ever in New York, I'll do the same for you."

"Cop to cop." Prezzama says," We watch out for each other."

"That's right." Granite says smiling.

Unknown to them, the President of the bank calls the Columbo family in Brooklyn and tells them that the cops have taken their money.

DeMarco tells Frankie to tell Barbara to ask Tony about it and how to get their money back.

Tony says he knows nothing about it but will try to find out about it.

Tony and Ed Longo are leaving Barbara Marino's house in Bay Ridge when another "cops behaving badly" situation occurs. A "presumed skel" Shakim Davis, was walking to his home when a car with two cops inside drove up to the curb in front of him. The cops, PO George T. George, and PO Vanesa Grimes got out and frisked him without informing him why. They needed an arrest for their monthly quota and Davis was it. After asking him what he was doing in the middle of the day walking in the sidewalk, Davis said," I'm walking to my house over there." And pointed to a row brick house." They both nod and walk back to their vehicle, but Davis takes out his cell phone and starts to take a photo of their license plate. PO Grimes, incensed that they might have to explain a stop and frisk, drives their car directly into him. As he lay on the ground they begin to frisk him, and go thru his pockets.

When Tony and Longo saw this, they pulled up to the curb and got out, flashing their gold shields.

"Hey guys, what's going on here?" Tony asked.

"This skel was getting rambunctious with us and he didn't show us the proper respect." PO George said.

"What?" Ed Longo said in disbelief.

"And look at this Detective." PO Grimes said taking out a glass lined bag of marijuana that she had conveniently planted on Davis.

"That's not mine!" Davis screamed.

"Shut up!" PO George said. "We're arresting you for possession, jaywalking and lack of respect."

"That's a good one." Longo said in disbelief "Lack of respect."

"Do you want the collar?" PO Grimes asked.

"No." Tony said, waving his hand in a downward motion. "This is all yours."

Tony motioned to Longo to get the hell out of there. Longo nodded.

As they got back in their car, they had not even gone maybe two or three blocks, another case of rogue cops happened in front of their eyes. A white MTA engineer was pulling into his driveway and his wife was in the passenger seat. A patrol officer was standing there watching them. The car pulled into their driveway at a snail's pace and when the car stopped, PO John Diego issued the driver Henry Djiverchic a summons for reckless driving. PO Diego told him that he pulled into his driveway at a "high rate of speed" causing the cop to "jump out of the way."

Tony and Longo pulled over and asked the officer what happened.

"He tried to run me over!" PO Diego said.

"He did not!" Said Djiverchicks wife.

"Are you sure of this officer?" Tony asked him. "We were watching and it didn't look like he drove onto his driveway that fast."

"Why, do you want the collar?" PO Diego asked.

"No." Longo said." But you better be sure officer, because you can be held accountable for making a false statement."

"Detective," PO Diego said to Longo." Who are you going to believe- them or me?"

"You." Tony said." But just be sure."

With that PO Diego called for back-up and placed the man and his wife under arrest to take them to jail.

Tony shook his head. "Let's get out of here before we're called as witnesses."

"Gotcha partner." Longo said.

The follow-up to this was that the city had to pay $175,000 to the man and his wife for false arrest.

Tony was at Claire's place each day, fucking her incessantly in every position possible. He did it to her non-stop, without even giving her a chance to rest between coming. She was screaming her head off, but wanted him so much, she let him take her in every position, even her ass. After several hours of fucking her, he finally came in her, almost collapsing on top of her.

"WOW!!" she yelled. "You are something else. Nobody has ever fucked me like that before." She exclaimed as they both breathed deeply.

"Honey, you just turn me on every second, that I can't seem to stop." He said." I love your body and that you let me take you in everywhere."

"I'm for you sweetie, anytime, anyway," she told him.

"Well if that's the case, then maybe, just maybe, we should think about moving in together." He said and kissed her.

"You sure about this?" she asked.

"Yup." He answered her. "You're place or mine."

Unknown to Tony, Claire had stopped taking the birth control pill. She figured that he was the man that she was going to live with, and if she got pregnant, so much the better. She knew that he wanted to be with her and live with her, so if a baby came along, he would have no choice but to marry her. And she really loved sex with him, better than any man that she had been with. Tony felt the same for her, and resolved himself to live with her, and probably marry her.

He would text her," You are going to be so fucked so many times tomorrow."

She replied," You have fantasies."

He replied." You turn me on all of the time, and you're going to oblige me in my fantasies.

She replied. "YES!!"

But all this time in seeing Claire every few moments he had (and even on duty) was taking its toll, not only on the coffin cops case, but on all his other cases. Ed Longo noticed it, even Loo noticed it.

"Hey partner." Longo said. "You're going to have to keep your cock in your pants because I can't be on this case alone and even some of your other cases are getting looked at."

"I know." Tony said." But Claire is so good in bed that I can't stop being with her."

"Well," Longo said." You're going to have to bite the bullet and pay attention to your job."

"This coming from the original cocksmaster." Tony said.

Longo chuckled." I agree." He said. "It's hard to stay focused with somebody's mouth around your cock."

"I'll say." Tony added. "But not only me, but you also have so many cases dropped on us that even with OT it's hard to close out a case."

"I agree Philadelphia," Longo said." The brass probably doesn't give a shit how many cases we have. Just get them done. Let's talk to Loo about getting more help. A bunch of the other Dicks don't do anything and we do it all."

"Right!" Tony agreed with him.

A lot of times, if one detective takes too long on one case, another detective will tell him,

"Don't worry about this one dead guy, another one will be along tomorrow."

There just isn't enough hours in the day. Detectives field former "Grounders", old fashioned domestic disputes, ugly but easily solved, and instead finding themselves fielding more crimes that take in all sorts of bad guys: robbery –murders without a witness and without any coherent motive."He disrespected me." There are also drug murders by gangs(the Blood and Crips) who are willing to kill anyone. Killers today are more clever, more vicious, and they just don't give a shit taking a human life. Detectives are like commercial fisherman, some killers are pulled into their nets, some don't. So "ordinary" detective work." – discovering a crime, identifying and locating the criminals, and assembling the evidence for use in prosecuting, takes a lot of time, time that detectives aren't given the time or proper help in solving it.

Tony was very anal for a detective; he would follow something to the end, nothing would stop him. If he decided on something that he wanted or needed, no one or nothing would deter him. But that was the way he was with a case, and he wanted to devote all of his time to that one case and not be overloaded with as many cases as the brass threw at him.

That's why so many cases go unsolved, there is no time to delve into solving a case. Except for emergencies, if a case isn't solved in

4 days, it becomes a cold case. But a lot of detectives, say so what, if I can't solve in 4 days, no matter, 10 or 20 cases will come along. There is a spread sheet in the squad room to say which detective is assigned to which cases, and when the "due date" for it to be solved. Then, if it becomes overdue, and then after a couple of weeks, it becomes cold and taken off of the board spread sheet. Because skels who murder don't stay in the area too long to be caught. That's why you have to move fast in collecting all of the facts and depose any witnesses that may have seen something.

But Tony could spot a killer by the way he walked, by the way he talked, even by the way he carried himself. Most killers, except for crimes of passion, have no feelings. No compassion, they are just cold blooded bully's, who would kill somebody just to see how it feels. And they did not feel anything; they were sociopaths.

Tony would do the same with a woman as he did with a case. When he decided to fuck somebody, he would keep coming after them and would not let them deter him or stop him from getting into their pants. If he could not get to them one way, he would devise a way to get to them another way, but he kept coming after them and was going to get into that piece of ass. Probably, if he would have devoted more time to his cases then getting laid, he would be a Dick 1 by now. But Tony wasn't as ambitious as say, Jack Granite was. Tony was just methodical, maybe too methodical, and maybe he was a little naïve to think that there wasn't office politics in the NYPD. There is and as rampant as in any other profession, and maybe more so in the NYPD.

But Tony was good at fucking women, because he made them feel special. Pleasing them was his way of getting them to do things that he wanted.

"Do you like the way I fuck you honey?" he would ask each and every woman if they did.

Or "Do you like the way my cock feels inside of you?" or

"Does it feel good, honey?" Or

"Do you like it this way?"(from the rear)or" Do you like it this way?" (riding him)or "Do you like it this way?"(in the ass)

Any way he would take them, he would wear them down with a lot of foreplay, then licking their pussy or sucking their nipples.

"Do you enjoy that honey?" Only then, after they told him yes, that he would enter them in every position imaginable. He would work at this like working a case, deliberately teasing them with his cock, until they screamed enjoyment to his satisfaction. He would continue non-stop until they came again and again.

"You are too much for me." Most of them would say. "He doesn't get off of me." They would say to a female friend. He was like their master and they were like his slave. Once he got to them, they obeyed him in whatever he desired, because he got inside their head, inside their karma, not only inside their pussy. He owned them totally and they knew it. He overwhelmed them with his desire, with his love of fucking women. He was addicted to sex, not only because it made him feel good, but he saw that it made the women feel good, very good. Maybe that's why he liked Claire so much, she gladly obliged him every time, instantly and with as much passion as he had for her. She loved his cock and he knew it. More than Barbara did, more than Angela did, even more than any woman he had been with. She would text him and flirt with him, as he did her, and it pleased him. She was going to be the fuck of his life and was going to be his mistress and possibly even his wife. He couldn't think of anybody else, which for him was unusual. He loved the way he felt when he was inside her, his cock was extended to the maximum and he enjoyed watching her facial expressions as he pounded it in her. There's nothing better than this, he thought.

As soon as Claire knew that Tony was coming over, she knew that he wanted sex and that he was going to fuck her as soon as he came in. She prepared for this by not even putting on clothes, just a bathrobe, not even panties or a bra. She knew that he wanted to take her immediately, whether from the front or the rear. And she readily obliged him. Right on cue, he came in and he was all over her. She didn't even have time to breathe. He was kissing her mouth, her neck, then first caressing her breasts and then sucking on those pert nipples.

"WOW!" Right on time." She managed to say to him. "I know what you want." She said smiling at him.

"You!" he said and then continued kissing her stomach and started to lick her genitals. This time when he came in her, he came the most of any time and he stayed longer in her to make her feel the moment. Unknown to both of them, he had impregnated her, and she was going to have identical twins.

On one of the tapes that Barbara gave Tony, Emilio Marino admitted to killing a friend of his. Augie Marino asked him.

"How long had you and this guy been friends?"

"Thirteen years." Emillio said.

"So how did you do it?" Augie asked.

"There was me and this big guy, Guiseppe Dragna, and he grabbed him and put the rope on him. And then me and another guy pulled it from one end and the other." He laughed.

"So he's looking at you, he knows what's going on- did he say anything?" Augie asked.

"No" Emillio said." He couldn't talk, because we were choking him, and his eyes were bulging out. Later we buried him in a vacant lot in Canarsie. We buried several people there like those wise guys from Murder Inc did."

"So Emillio," Augie asked. "How did you feel about having to kill someone who was a friend? Did it feel like when we had our brother Tony killed."

Emillio smiled and then said," Nothing that you can do about it. I had a job to do and I did it, you know what I mean? Nothing I can do."

"So Emillio," Augie asked again," What's the secret?"

"I proved myself, that's why the bosses promoted me. I could do a lot of things that other people couldn't do. I could set people up. I could kill them. I was a good money maker; The bosses picked me when they had something tough to do." Emillio answered.

There are two types of dirty cops, "the meat-eaters" and the "grass-eaters."Meat eaters are police officers who "aggressively" misuse their police powers for personal gain, while the "grass-eaters" simply accept the pay-offs that happens to be thrown their way. Some cops "ate grass" to prove their allegiance to the dirty cops. Others just enjoyed their spoils and eventually became "meat-eaters." Ten percent of cops in New York are absolutely corrupt. Ten percent are absolutely honest, and the other 80 percent – they wish that they were honest. Patrol officers even pay bribes to be assigned a patrol car, because having a patrol car means that you can make rounds to collect bribes, shake down drug dealers and make deals with bar owners and businesses by looking the other way. In nearly every precinct are set up monthly " pads" or payments to protect gamblers, pimps, or other members of organized crime. The "coffin cops" were all " aggressive meat-eaters" and they routinely looked for more and more stuff to feed their habit.

Tony and Ed Longo were driving back to the squad room, when they saw a crime being committed against some fellow cops. One Eugene Cortlandt, was limping up to a car and used it as a rest to shoot down two cops walking their tour across the street. The shooter brought down one cop, catching his target in the buttocks, and putting a bullet through the hand of another cop. The skel was an easy catch . He could only travel so fast on his foot as he relied on a cane. Longo was driving and he pulled up alongside him, enough for Tony to get out and yell" Freeze!" aiming his gun at him. The skel turned around and started to shoot Tony , but Tony quickly squeezed off one shot hitting him between the eyes.

"Damn why did you do that for." Tony said as he came up to and straddled the dead skel. Meanwhile Longo lumbered over, out of breath.

"I'll go check on the cops." He said. Tony then then back to their squad car and had radioed for back-up and an ambulance for the other two cops.

"You okay Philadelphia?" he said.

"Yeah, I guess." Tony said, and waited for the crime scene unit to arrive. They checked on both the other cops who had non -life threatening injuries.

Another thing that cops on the beat do is to steal money from the dead. And it doesn't mean if it's a murder, it can be just a heart attack or a car crash, to cops, this is easy money. And who's going to complain- the dead guy? They also pilfer crime scenes for anything left behind by burglars, and some even fucked recently dead women corpses, in addition to confiscating cash from drug busts. And when the takes from crime scenes weren't enough, they created crime scenes of their own.

The "coffin cops" used to radio their own and gather all parties interested in going on a raid which included anything from breaking into a business after hours to busting down the doors of gambling and drug dealers solely to steal any cash on hand.

Detective Rossi's talents for lawlessness are a legend in the police forces. He built an empire by protecting drug lords to the tune of $10,000 a week. At the same time that he was stealing cocaine from drug dealers, and then selling it. The profits were huge and Rossi made no efforts to conceal them. He said he was just getting rid of the skels operating cash.

CHAPTER 17

Meanwhile, back at the squad room Tony is getting pushed by Lt. Mark Murphy, to "clear" more cases.

"Loo," Tony tells him." How can I even work on these other cases when I'm working almost full time plus overtime on these "coffin cops"?

"Philadelphia," Loo says to him," I know that you're doing your best, but the brass, and this is coming straight from the top, that all Detectives have to clear more cases. I know that this is just B.S., but we have to do it."

"Why so they'll look good on paper?" Tony tells him. "I'll try Loo, but you know that we get new cases every day; it's like trying to plug a hole in a dike."

"Try your best Philadelphia." Loo tells him.

Tony shakes his head and walks away to tell Longo.

"Do you hear this shit Longo." Tony says to him. " Loo wants us to clear more cases."

"And how are we supposed to do that? Pick up some skel on the street and arrest him for nothing?" Longo says.

"I bet that's what the brass wants." Tony tells him. "Just numbers for the record."

One of the things that the brass in the NYPD wants is to "clear a case." That's the police term for a case closed by a suspect's arrest or death. The clearance national average across the US is 59 per cent of homicide cases cleared. In NYC, the clearance rate is an anemic 44 percent. Clearing 6 out of 10 killings is not the same as making as 6 out of 10 killers pay for their crimes. 10-15 per cent of those arrested for murder are never indicted, and more than 15 percent of those who are indicted end up in dismissal or acquitted. In NYC ½ of all killers are getting away with murder. Nobody gives a damn about clearing a lot more homicides because you would need 3 times as many detectives working a lot of OT because it is a necessary part of homicide investigation. But still 3 things solve cases- eyewitnesses, physical evidence and motive. If you don't have any of these, forget about it.

The precinct that Tony and Ed Longo are working in, the 9th precinct, has a reputation called the "Notorius Ninth", because it was overrun with unsolved murders and crime. The principal mission of a patrol cop is to present a visable presence in the area to reassure the lawful and deter the lawless. Of the 38,000 police officers in the NYPD only 7,000 are detectives and 12,000 are patrol officers. The reason that there is more patrol officers is that the police commissioner wants publicity for resolving petty crimes such as people evading the fare by jumping over the turnstiles. A friend of Tony's at the 9th precinct, PO Tanner saw that most fare beaters were white women and not black and Hispanic teens. The then Captain told him," You describe to me who's committing the crime, and that's not who we're supposed to be getting off of the street."

PO Tanner told him" If these people are not committing the crimes, then what am I supposed to do?"

"You just hide and arrest the "right people" whether they're guilty or not. We need numbers to prove that we are getting the "right" people arrested."

Most of the time on patrol is spent in a slow prowl around a sector of the precinct, engaging in amicable conversation, punctuated by containers of coffee.

Ed Longo said to Tony," Feel like taking a ride?"

"Why" Tony answered him.

"C'mon, the streets are jumping Philadelphia, I need a collar." Longo mentioned to him.

"But you have so many Longo, what's the big deal?" Tony asked.

"Philadelphia, from my almost 20 years, okay 18 years plus, I can feel that there is action out there in our precinct today and I want a collar." He said" and I need the overtime."

"Okay Longo." Tony said. "You're the best."

After they went in their old beat up unmarked police car, they went out for several hours of slow canvasing the worst places in the precinct. Up and down Alphabet city, all of the people in the street, recognized an unmarked cop car at once. They were staring and staring at them.

But like Longo said, he could 'smell' a collar. Both he and Tony observed a blue and silver pick- up truck, towing a hitch trailer. The car circled the same block several times, and did not stop, but kept circling.

"Hey Philadelphia, this car is dirty." Longo told him.

"How can you tell?' Tony asked.

"I don't know, it's just a hunch." Longo said. "Let's stop it on the next go round and see what we can find."

"Ok" Tony mentioned. "You're the guy with the nose here." A Detective's nose is what gets arrests, and it is developed over time.

They put on their flashing lights and pulled the car over.

Longo and Tony approached the vehicle and identified themselves.

"License and registration please." Longo told the occupants in the car. Omar Garcia and Jose Romero were both here on a travel visa from Guatemala. They had driven here all the way with one thing in mind. Sell drugs.

They both looked at each other and gave Longo their driver's license from Guatemala and their passports. Their car was unregistered to operate in the US.

"Okay guys, get out of the car." Longo ordered them.

"What is this about officer?" Garcia asked.

"Well for one you're operating an unregistered vehicle, and for another, I think that you've got drugs in this car." Longo told them.

Jose laughed." Why because we from Central America?"

"No" Longo said. "Because you've been driving around the block six times like you're looking for your buyer."

They both got out of their cars. "Watch them Philadelphia, while I take a look see."

"OK." Tony said.

Longo started to search the pick-up truck and then the trailer. He took out a pocket screwdriver and started to remove the rocker arms on the pick-up truck.

"Bingo! Look what I found," he said, pulling out several bags of heroin.

Tony drew his gun and said. "Put your hands up! You're under arrest."

Omar shook his head. They called for back-up and the pair was taken into custody. Upon a further search of the vehicle, heroin was also found hidden within a car axle casing that was in the bed of the vehicle.

"I told you Philadelphia, the nose knows." Longo said.

"You're my hero Longo." Tony said." How did you know that there was drugs hidden in the rocker arms?"

"I saw it in an old movie, The French Connection." He said." You can learn a lot by watching old cop movies."

On one of the tapes that Tony and Longo listened in on, they hear Rossi talking about a cop that was running a prostitution ring.

"Yeah, this guy from the 6-9, Carl Edwards, is a pimp off duty and is running a hooker ring." Rossi said.

"How do you know that?" Sgt. Fallon asks him.

"He also supplied Griffin with some hookers." Rossi answers him." This guy would transport them to motels on Long Island, New Jersey, Staten Island, and the Bronx in a patrol car no less."

"How could he get away with this?" Fallon asks.

"Simple. He was also supplying the brass with hookers also." Rossi said." Let's say some Loo wants a woman, he would call up Edwards and in a short while, he had his pick of maybe 10 girls."

"Wow!" How can I get some of that action?" Fallon asks him.

"Well, you've got to split the fee with him and he'll do it. He wants to keep our blue brothers happy." Rossi says.

Longo looked at Tony. "We're doing something wrong Philadelphia."

"I'll say." Tony said looking back at Longo." I want a piece of that action also."

"I figured that you would say that." Longo said. "You're just a horn dog and you'll do anything for pussy."

"You are absolutely right Longo." Tony responded. "Almost anything for that,"

Later, Tony and Ed Longo were sitting in their car listening to the coffin cops talk. Rossi was bragging about getting other money from karoke bars.

"Yeah," Rossi said," We are also getting some bucks from those Chinese karoke bars in Chinatown" He told Sgt. Fallon. Rossi is one of 6 cops (a Lt., a Sgt.,Rossi, and 3 other cops) in different Pcts. that are getting paid.

"I want in on that." Sgt. Fallon told Rossi.

"Well," Rossi explained" Detective Jang is getting $2000 a month from the owners of 2 clubs. We use a messenger app called WECHAT to warn them of raids before they happen."

"Sweet!" Sgt. Fallon said.

"And what's better" Rossi continued "We don't do an inspection there, but we transfer the inspection over the police band radio. We are able to give several clubs a heads up about impending state police raids too. So everybody gets paid money, the cops and the clubs."

Tony and Ed Longo looked at each other in amazement.

"Don't look surprised Longo," Tony said." These dirty cops are everywhere."

"I see." Longo nodded and said.

Again, trying to pass the time at the coffin cops stakeout, the subject between Ed Longo and Tony turns to women and sex.

" I hear that 2 cops in Manhattan South keep picking up women on duty and fucking them in their patrol cars." Tony said.

"Who were they?" Longo asked.

"PO Nick Valenzuela and PO James Louis would arrest them for no reason ,like loitering, or doing drugs. These women were young like 19,24,25, and one was even 34 and each would take turns having sex with them in the back seat, many times, so they wouldn't be arrested."

"I hear a lot of talk about that but I didn't think it was happening on a regular basis." Longo said. News travels fast when sex is concerned throughout the NYPD and it's a common practice to have sex with any women they arrest. Most women are attracted to cops, their blue uniform or that they have power with a badge and a gun, but most cops will take advantage over any women when they can and they do get away with it.

Unless a cop works OT, he/she does not stay a second more. When they clock out, they are off duty. That's the rule.

Ed Longo was telling Tony about this Captain in the 7-3 in Brooklyn who was stripped of his gun and his badge after he clocked out when 2 cops were shot in Brooklyn.

"Are you shitting me Longo?" Tony asked in disbelief." A Captain didn't go check on what happened?"

"Yeah, it seems that he just passed the Captains test and he was probationary when people told him what was going on and he said." I'm off duty in a few minutes." And then he left before his tour ended and he had a Loo sign him out." Longo told Tony.

"Wow!" Tony exclaimed." I bet the Chief went ape shit."

"That's for sure and everyone up the brass's ladder did too." Longo said. "What he should've done is just show up and even fall asleep and no one would have said anything. But he didn't. Philadelphia, he had to have rocks in his head not to go, and you may remember him- Jack Scott, he was a weightlifter off duty."

"I know who you're talking about." Tony said." I used to see him sometimes at the range."(the shooting range up at Pelham Park)

"But listen to this Philadelphia." Ed Longo continued," But this Cap was in deeper shit not only from going home, because several of the other brass called his cell phone wondering where he was, but he didn't even answer."

"No shit." Tony remarked.

"Yeah, but it gets better Philadelphia," Longo kept talking." The next day the DI(Deputy Inspector) called him into his office to explain why he wasn't at the hospital for the cops who were shot, and he called in sick, claiming he was suffering from stomach pains and diahreaah."

"Unreal!" Tony exclaimed.

"Yeah, and get this." Longo continued." By the time that the Mayor and the Commissioner showed up, there were more brass and stars in the hospital than there is in the Milky Way Galaxy. Everyone was there and knew that Scott fucked up."

"So what was the end result Longo?" Tony asked.

"Well the Captains Endowment Association (their union) said that the union is still examining it."

"What a shithead." Tony added.

"Amen to that brother." Longo said.

They were still listening to Rossi and Fallon talking about their heists.

"I know that Griffin and Rossi were into a lot of drug stuff, but this blows my mind." Tony said to Longo.

"Not only that Philadelphia, but if you connect the dots, not only are they getting the dealers who peddle cocaine and heroin to pay them, but they are also getting gun dealers to give them money." Longo added.

"How do you figure that Longo?" Tony asked him.

"Very simple." Longo said." The dealers take the money and not only can they sell that, but they sell the drugs for money too. What they do is sell the drugs and they resell them for 4 times what they paid for them and then they buy guns."

"So do you think that we ought to tell ATF and DEA?" Tony said.

"Why?" Longo said." They are the ones that will get the collar, not us. What we should do is wait until all the coffin cops are taken down, and then we go tell our guys about it, so we can get credit for it."

"That sounds like a good idea, Longo." Tony answered.

"Hey, Philadelphia," Longo said," I'm here almost 20 years- you learn how the system works."

"You're right as always Longo." Tony said.

"You know that I am." Longo mentioned.

CHAPTER 18

In another coffin cops car crash, Rossi and Sgt. Fallon had just left Easy's bar after a night of drinking when one of their fellow coffin cops crashed his vehicle into a beauty salon near the bar. The cops drove off and waited more than 3 hours to report the incident after making a series of calls to union officials to see what they could get away with.

The only other problem with this, was that a Loo, Lt. Matthew Vincent, had been drinking with them (even though he supposedly wasn't a coffin cop) and he had been promoted to commanding officer of Rossi's detective unit in NYPD's high-profile force investigation division. Rossi and Sgt. Fallon was attempting to suck up to him and try to keep their coffin cops capers under wraps.

Upon the brass hearing about this crash, Vincent was suspended without pay along with the driver of the car that crashed into the beauty salon and two other detectives there. But Rossi and Sgt. Fallon were not. Under the rank of Lieutenant, there are two special designations, which bring more pay. Vincent, who was making more than $175K, was already receiving special assignment pay equivalent to a Captains salary. The promotion to commanding officer of the detective squad would have gotten him more money.

Longo and Tony overheard Rossi talking about this while on stakeout.

"Yeah," Rossi said," Loo had started making the money the day of the crash, but now he has lost that bump in salary."

Sgt. Fallon is saying to Rossi," I heard that Detective Frank Bratton, the driver of the car was also suspended."

"So what." Rossi answered him." The union is on our side and they'll get off."

Fallon agrees, "I know the head of the Lieutenants Benevolent Association which represents Vincent and they told me, it's a whitewash that the Commissioner wanted somebody to pay for this publicity."

Longo tells Tony, "You know Philadelphia, this thing of theirs gets deeper and deeper, and I don't know where it will end."

"You're right Longo," Tony says," It may go up all the way to the top brass."

The crash caused about $100,000 worth of damage to the hair salon.

There is also widespread cheating on promotion exams. Ed Longo and Tony hear Sgt. Fallon talking to Rossi at the Coffin cops hideout.

"Yeah, I passed the Lieutenant's exam."

"Great." Says Rossi.

"Yeah, but it was real easy." Fallon says. "I had all of the answers."

Tony and Longo look at each other.

Rossi asks Fallon," Where did you get the answers?"

"Well, there was several ways and I used all of them. There is a photo on the message board of the test and then one of our guys said that if you need the exact wording of a specific question, message him the question and he will send it to you. And another guy said he can send me 2 questions undated so it's good for everything." Fallon told him.

"Neat." Rossi said." But didn't they search you guys when you went in for the exam?"

"No." Fallon said." Test takers were not supervised."

"But how many guys passed." Rossi asked.

"Out of 2400 test takers almost ½." Fallon said.

"Wow. Almost ½ passed." Rossi said."Didn't the brass think that it was strange that so many passed?"

"No problem." Fallon told him." Everybody knows that over the years it has become a right of passage. But the only problem that I can see is that I would be transferred to the Bronx and that I wouldn't have this spare change to have."

"True." Rossi said. "There's something for staying in grade."

Tony and Ed Longo are also picking up more information about crooked cops then they want to know, and it's not only about the coffin cops. It's also running rampant thru the top brass.

Every cop takes gifts, whether it's a free meal, or a gift and even paid vacations for some of the upper brass. The probe into illicit favor trading was sparked by a comment caught on a not only an FBI wiretap, but also on Tony's and Longo's coffin cops hideout.

Rossi was heard telling some Detective 2nd Grade from the 6-6 precinct in Brooklyn to keep his mouth shut and plead the 5th to the grand jury. The Dick, one Martin Millwick, would provide two local businessmen, including police escorts for funerals, and as a form of payment, he was given one or two diamonds to give to his wife. It just wasn't this dick that was involved, it went all the way up the brass ladder and included a lot of brass. One NYPD Deputy Inspector was heard accepting hundreds of dollars said,

"I'm fucked! I can't go to jail."

It would eventually go all the way up to the Chief of Department, who recently resigned.

"Holy shit!" Longo said." This really gets more and more involved."

"You're right Longo." Tony added." If this goes much higher, the PC will be involved."

"If he's not involved already." Longo added.

Still Tony and Ed Longo had to continue on their other cases. In one "grounder" case, one that was typical of a former child movie star who killed his "grifter" wife. Tony was in charge of the investigation and he said that the case against the husband (former child movie star Donny Adams) wasn't perfect- but it was solid.

"It's not your CSI case," Tony said to Ed Longo, referring to the TV show about forensic investigations." But I thought that we had a very good circumstantial case."

Ed Longo agreed." You always wish that we had an eyewitness. We all wish that we had DNA. We always wish that we had fingerprints or a murder weapon. But that's Hollywood's made of. Don't worry Philadelphia." Longo continued," You can't always get these things."

Tony added." We don't get witnesses who are upstanding citizens either. We don't get these kind of people. We also don't get to pick our victims and we surely don't get to pick our suspects. We don't even get to pick our witnesses."

The prosecutor's one witness will testify that the tiny amount of gunshot residue on the husband's hand, didn't definitely link him to the gun that was recovered. Even the prosecutor told Tony that he found the evidence " flimsy".

Ed Longo mentioned," I don't think that the public at large understands how difficult it is to win a celebrity case."

"I know." Tony added." Every part of the case is different from anything that you've ever done before and that makes the job that much more difficult."

CHAPTER 19

Tony was reminiscing about all of his other girlfriends, one in particular because she was a former cop in the 2-0 PCT, Nancy Menza. She was a bleached blonde who called herself, the Marilyn Monroe of the NYPD. They had gone hot and heavy when they had dated, fucking every day, in every position in every place- patrol cars, bathrooms, kitchens, even in bedrooms.But some years have past since Tony dated her.

"I hear one of your old flames, the Marilyn Monroe of the NYPD tried to get her husband whacked. Ed Longo said.

"You mean Nancy Menza?" Tony asked.

"Yup. That's her"

"I haven't seen her in years, since she got married, But she was one good lay, I'll tell you that Longo. And she could give head- she would suck your cock like a water pump, taking it all in her mouth. And she would scream when you were fucking her to wake the dead. And then she married a cop from the 10th, Mark Davis. And I heard from the grapevine that she got divorced." Tony said. "Who did she get to kill her husband- a Mafioso?"

Longo answered. "I don't know. All I know is that he's a convicted killer and she was seeing him for about six months.She was probably giving him such good head that she told him to "take care" of her ex -husband. She gave him a picture of her ex and his address."

"Wow!" Tony said. "But did he do the deed?"

"No. This guy said that he took it with a grain of salt. He didn't know how serious it would turn out." Longo mentioned.

"Well that's what you get for going with a cop." Tony added. "He should have dated girls who were gangsters or worse."

"That's true." Longo said. "Never trust a female cop."

"Amen to that brother." Tony added. "I mean, she was a very good lay and all, but she was very possessive. And she wanted a ring right after me getting into her box. I didn't mind fucking her, but what do these women want, to get married just because you fuck them a couple of times. "

"All women want that Philadelphia." Longo added.

"That's true enough." Tony said.

Another cop that Ed Longo knew was related by marriage to the Gambino crime family.

"I hear that Michael Muccini, a cop from the 6-9 in Canarsie, got busted for running a prostitution ring." Longo told Tony.

"You're kidding me." Tony said. "You mean an active duty cop was running an escort service?"

"Yup." Longo said. "He's a 9 year veteran of the NYPD and his hookers billed well-healed clients up to $2,000 per lay, and he split the money 50/50 with them. That's some nice sum to compliment his cop's pay."

"Tony asked." Who's his wife related to in the Gambino family?"

"She's the niece of Gambino Capo Sonny Persico and her father is a Gambino soldier"Big Dick" Gagante."Longo answered him.

"That's some family tree." Tony said.

"I heard that he had 58 web-sites to attract John's and it showed these hookers in lingerie outfits or topless with a price listing next to their names." Longo said. " And not only that, he would interview the women in person at the hotels, fuck them to see if they were really good and boasted to them that his clients were the wealthiest people in the world. And one of the hookers wrote on her application," I love sex and if I can get paid for it, why not."

"Why can't I meet a girl like that ." Tony added.

Ed Longo ate and slept the job and often looked it. He not only was a big man ("put more butter on it," give me more beer') but he always looked like he was busting out of his clothes. He was also street smart and he wasn't afraid to speak his mind or take a stand about something if he felt it was justified.

The Homicide division is a very close knit "family" of Detectives and word-of-mouth recommendations are the quickest form of acceptance. Like" I know him" gets you a pass just like in the

Mafia. But in this unit, where your partner is often responsible for your life, you just don't accept people all that readily; you have to know them. If nothing is known about your background or past performance, your fellow Dicks will adopt a wait-and-see, time will tell attitude. Because there are so many cases that Tony and Ed Longo couldn't possibly handle them, the Chief of Detectives, assigned a newbie patrolman that was just promoted to 3rd Grade Detective to the unit

Patrick Roberts was an over-achieving cop who was so ambitious to make detective, he was writing 50-75 summons a month in the 7-2 precinct in Sunset Park Brooklyn. Roberts was lauded by the Commanding Officer as someone the other officers should follow (and making his fellow officers look bad.)The other officers turned his locker upside down and backward and threw it in the shower to show their grievance at this hot-shot. They just want to do their jobs and be left alone. Pranks among rank and file officers are nothing new, but they aren't dismissed as easily as they once were years ago. The brass doesn't tolerate this stuff anymore and they made it a point of find out who did it.

But rather than keep him in the Pct., the Commanding officer pressured the brass to make him a detective and get him out of his precinct. Roberts had a rep as someone who " rats out" othe officers according to the grapevine. So he came into the 9th Pct. homicide squad as someone to watch out for.

So when Loo told Tony and Ed Longo that Roberts was going to help them out with their case load, Longo told Loo" We don't need any more help Loo" he said," All we need is more OT."

Loo responded. "This is what you get Longo, more help, not more OT. So just show him what he can do."

"Ok Loo." Longo said.

Longo looked at Roberts, then to Tony, and said," C'mere kid, you see those files stacked on my desk." Start going thru them."

Roberts nodded.

Part of the 9th Pct. jurisdiction is called Alphabet city,again, so named because the streets are named A,B,C, etc. It was always a bad neighborhood and now at any street corner there is one of the worst spots in the City for synthetic marijuana, with users lighting up in broad daylight, passing out on sidewalks and stumbling into traffic.

Synthetic marijuana, also called K2 is now as illegal as the real MJ, but a lot of people said that the area around Avenue A and East 5th Street was the best place to find K2 in the city.

Tony and Ed Longo were going back to the station house when they saw a lot of people just standing around at the corner, looking like zombies. One man drifted into traffic and almost walked into a tractor-trailer.

"Look at the people at the corner." Tony said. "There must be at least 50 people lit up."

"And they don't care." Longo said." And it's becoming a major concern for teens. One teenager I know described K2 as a "Big Blackout" he said." That you don't know what's happening. All you know is that your heart is beating very fast." And furthermore" Longo continued," Your future family is bringing that shit in."

"Not my family." Tony said. He knew that Longo was referring to the Columbo's.

Everyone knew now about Tony and Barbara. Stuff like this travels fast, that a NYPD Detective was seeing a "Mafia Princess." The organized task force called Tony to say that a Columbo gang member was released on bail, and to see what Tony could find out from Barbara.

"Nicky Clams"was a Columbo Captain who had been released on bail after 3 years for a variety of crimes- gambling, loan sharking, extortion and even Viagra peddling. This latter crime brought laughs from the prosecutor and Judge. For all of this was called "enterprise corruption."

When Tony talked to Barbara later that day Barbara told him "He's a hot head, but he wants to get the prosecutor "burned to death" and see him "burned alive" for the crack about selling Viagra.

"It's a good money-maker" Nicky Clams had said." All of the old folks need that to get it up."

Nicky Clams had also spent the last couple of years in jail for Jury tampering.

Every cop and every Detective has to do quotas. Whether it's monthly summons or investigations or traffic stops, it is an unwritten law amongst cops. And if they don't fulfill their quotas, they are either given a low monthly evaluation or transferred to foot duty. One cop, Walter Dane, was told by his superior,

"Yeah, it's shitty thing, but you see a skel with his pants down walking across the street, he's probably up to no good. Now you write him up for a bullshit a ticket, like he's going to spit or urinate on the sidewalk or whatever, and the next time that he see's you, he'll walk around and go the other way."

Cops love to drink, especially when they are coming off of the midnight shift- 12AM to 8AM, or even while they are on duty. There are so many cops that are drunk while on duty, that it is amazing that not more cops are suspended for being "unfit for duty."

But who's going to complain, not other cops that's for sure. The "blue wall" of cops not ratting on other cops exist at every level, from plain patrolmen to detectives, to sargents, to lieutenants and above.

But one time, a civilian, by the name of George T. George, reported that officers Evan Rogers and his rookie partner, Richie DeJesus, both drunk, while responding to a call near the precinct.

Now normally, this complaint would be just ignored (which most are), but this civilian just happened to be a member of the Civilian Review Board. So they couldn't just ignore it. A patrol supervisor for the precinct, Lt. John Slattery, arrived at the scene and said,"I don't smell any booze."

The civilian then said, "Are you crazy! These guys reek of alcohol, and I bet if you search their patrol car, you'll probably find a bottle of liquor."

Evan Rogers joined the NYPD in 2001, and if he was caught drinking, his supervisor could be hit for disciplinary action for failure to supervise, depending on when Rogers started drinking. Since Lt. Slattery didn't want to be hit with a failure to supervise, he vehamantly defended Rogers.

"Sir, I don't smell liquor, nor was there any liquor in his patrol car. I'll write it up on this report and in three days, you can pick up this report, and if you disagree, you can take it further."

"Fine!" Mr. George said.

Detective Rossi is a muscle-bound ape and he flaunted his ripped body whenever he was off-duty or even when he's on duty, whenever he gets the chance. Angela told Tony that Rossi would take off his jacket at the bar and open his shirt to her, flexing his muscles and saying "Like that baby?"

Because Rossi was directly involved in hitting on drug dealers, most of them gave him a wide berth. They paid his "protection" money, and took their lumps when he got annoyed at them and hit them. However 4 drug dealers that did not know about his anger problem, had arranged a cocaine deal with him and the Columbo's, that went south. They had arranged for 5 kilos of cocaine to be sold thru him to the Columbo's.

He was just supposed to be the go-between, get the cocaine, which would be made into smaller packets, and he would give them the money. They all agreed to meet at a Columbo bar in Brooklyn, called "The Watering Hole" and make the switch outside in a van. Instead, when the 4 said that they wanted more money than what was agreed to, Rossi became enraged and shot all 4 of them, killing them. He had no compulsion in killing them since he had no emotion to speak of except anger. He kept the money for himself and then called the Columbo's who took the van and buried them in an upstate farm in Orange county, also called "The Farm."

Unbeknownst to the Columbo's ,"The Farm" was an FBI training facility. When the FBI's cadaver dogs smelled the dead bodies, the FBI dug them up. The Mafia can't think beyond carrying out an order and doing it. But the organized task force did not want to ruin their case against the Columbo's by taking them in. However Tony found out about it because not only did Barbara tell him that she overheard it from the crew that did it, but the NYPD also told him about it. However, Rossi was not implicated.

There is a common problem in the NYPD of sexual harassment. Upper level brass always assume that they can get away with fucking any female cop and they get what's called" white shirt immunity", because the brass wear white shirts. One female cop, a divorced mother of 3, Betsy Foster, had a 7 year relationship with the Assistant Chief of Patrol Brooklyn North. He had trysts in his office, in patrol cars, and once even in the hospital.

Ed Longo knew them both."Yeah, he still would have continued fucking her, anytime of the night and day. He would just sign out that he was on patrol and disappear for a few hours to get a piece of ass."

"Wow!" Tony said." So what happened?"

"One day the chief got her ex-husband fired which stopped her child support payments. Then she went on an outrage all over social media."Longo stated."When she was in the hospital, he had the audacity to come over for a piece of her ass with an IV stuck in her arm. He was so greedy for ass that she had to get out of the hospital bed and go over to the bathroom to give this greedy ass some more ass."

"Wow!" Tony exclaimed." So what was the end result?

"So she wrote in another rant" Somebody needs to stop chasing pregnant married girls around the department. What is wrong with this guy?" She ended up suing the city for $54 million dollars.

There isn't a day that goes by, that "good cops" see stuff happening in the NYPD that shouldn't be. Some cops let it pass because "a cop can do no wrong', is their mentality, but sometimes they can't look away.

Tony and Ed Longo were going up to Easy's (Tony to see Claire, and Longo to get free booze) when they saw a group of officers punching the face in of a 50 year old man that was pinned to the ground. They pulled over and showed their gold shields.

"GUYS!" Tony said," Why are you beating him? His face is bloodied."

Officer John Nunez told them," He was lashing out at us for giving him a parking ticket."

"So for that you punch him senseless?" Ed Longo asked.

"Then," another officer by the name of Brett Thomas said," he was resisting arrest when we tried to cuff him."

"OK", Tony said," But after you had the cuffs on him, you don't keep bashing his head in."

Another officer, by the name of Brian Lynch, who had just come out of the police van that they were in said," He had to be taught a lesson that you don't give cops lip service."

Ed Longo grabbed Tony by the arm and told him, "He's right-people can't give cops lip service by doing their job."

Tony shot him a look of disbelief," Ok, I give up Longo." He said." Let's go. I need Easy's after this."

"Now you're talking." Longo said, tasting the free booze.

As they left the area, the man would be charged with resisting arrest, disorderly conduct, and obstructing governmental administration. But he would be released without bail, because, the Loo on desk duty, did not want to get Internal Affairs involved.

When Tony and Longo got to Easy's, Claire served them both. She planted a big sensuous kiss on Tony and winked at Longo.

"Beer on tap guys?" She questioned them, putting a cocktail napkin by each one, but knew the answer.

"Absolutely." Longo said.

"Me too hon." Tony said to her" And keep them coming."

She looked at him in disbelief. "But aren't you still on duty?"

"Sshh." Longo told her putting a finger next to his mouth." Most everybody here is."

As Tony and Longo settled into their bar stools, they looked around at the dancers and of course, noticed that there was a cop on every bar stool. But one cop stood out; he was still in uniform, nursing a glass of 12 year old Scotch.

Longo, insensed, walked right up to him and said," You can't be here in uniform!"

PO Evan Richards took another swig of his drink, stared right back at Longo and said," So what?"

Tony, sensing that Longo was going to go ape-shit over this cop, runs over between them, and says to Richards, "Get out! Come back when you're off duty!"

"Yeah, well you're here." He turns to Tony and says with a smirk.

"We are on a case." Tony says.

"Yeah, I'll bet- what case? A case full of beer?" Richards said laughing.

Just then Richards NYPD phone goes off." See the man, neighbors fighting on 207 West 54th Street."

"Four" Richards replies to the dispatcher."I've got to go." He says to Longo and Tony, taking one last gulp of scotch. "Later." He tells them and walks out.

Tony and Longo watch him weave his way out of Easy's, going to the site he was told to go to.

Tony says to Longo," Do you think that we should call him in?"

Longo goes back to his bar stool." No way- let his supervisor report him drunk and unfit for duty."

Showing up drunk for duty is official misconduct, a misdemeanor punishable by a year behind bars.

Richards, a 16 year veteran of the NYPD, went to the site and someone at the scene complained that Richards appeared to be drunk. A supervisor was called and declared Richards unfit for duty and suspended him, with pay of course.

Most ADA's do not pursue criminal charges of the NYPD for drinking on the job since almost every cop does that. The NYPD also usually disciplines such cases rarely.

Longo is on his 3rd beer, when he tells Tony," You know how I know that a neighborhood is drug infested?

"No, how". Tony says.

Longo smiles." By the number of pit bulls that someone is walkng".

"What?" Tony asks astounded.

"No seriously" Longo tells him matter-of factly,"If you see a person walking a pit bull it's bad, but not too bad. But if it's two pit bulls it's real bad. And if it's three pit bulls it's very bad. Three pit bulls, it's a drug lord."

"Wow!" Tony says. "I never heard it explained that way. I had thought about it, but too much shit by the skels were happening to think about it."

"Well think about it Philadelphia." Longo stated."

After gulping down several brews, they left to go see what was happening at the coffin cops place.

New York City has the toughest gun control laws in the country, but for a price, you can get any gun, legally. Tony and Longo were watching the coffin cops when they picked up on some new connections Rossi is talking about to Sgt. Fallon that another scheme that somebody hatched in the gun licensing division.

"Yeah, they some nice thing going." Rossi tells Fallon." We should try to get some of that action."

Fallon tells Rossi," Yeah, there's this DI(Deputy Inspector) that set this up. All you have to do to get a gun license is to pay, "the price." No background check, no questions as to why the applicant needed a gun, no follow up on a job application."

"NICE!!" Rossi said." And I heard that a famous Brooklyn person set himself up as a expediter so they don't have to for a background check."

"Sweet"! Fallon says," and I heard that it's not only cash, it's jewelry, paid vacations, visits to strip clubs and freebie hookers."

"I like that." Rossi said.

Tony and Longo listening in on the conversation cannot believe their ears.

"It's not only druggies," Longo says," It's everywhere."

"You can keep the cash and the other stuff," Tony says, " just give me the free hookers."

"I figured that you'd say that" Longo said. "Can't you keep that cock of your in your pants for a second?"

"NO!!" Tony says. "I love pussy."

CHAPTER 20

Pete Ryan has come off the critical list. Once he was well enough to talk IAD was there to talk to him.

"Officer Ryan" Sgt. James Burke showed his shield to him." To get right to the point, we know that you Griffin, Rossi, and a whole bunch of other officers are involved in ripping off drug dealers."

"I don't know what you are talking about." Ryan told him.

"Officer Ryan," Sgt. Burke again said." We have proof that you are one of the "Coffin Cops" and we have recorded conversations at your place of business, on Cherry Street."

"Again," Ryan said," I don't know what you are talking about."

"Officer Ryan," Burke said," You can deny it or look at me like you don't know what's going on, but if you are willing to work with us, you won't get what your fellow "coffin cops" are going to get."

Ryan, obviously not trying to give it away said, "Are you going to charge me with something?"

"First off, you will be suspended without pay, then you'll be charged and arrested for a number of charges including falsifying arrests, conspiracy, beating up druggies, and also how the hell can you afford a $5 million dollar condo, without working for the mob." Sgt. Burke told him.

"I want to speak to the police union rep." Ryan told him.

"Sure, you can do that, and you are entitled to that as a cop, but let me tell you, I mean as of right now you are a former cop." Burke said.

"I want to see a lawyer." Ryan said.

"Again, Officer Ryan, you have every right to see a lawyer, but by the time you see a lawyer, it will be too late." Burke told him.

"What do you want?" Ryan asked.

"We want you to tell us the whole story and give a statement against your fellow "coffin cops".Burke said.

"And if I did, will I get off?" Ryan asked.

"If you cooperate with us, we will tell the DA that you helped us, which will go a long way in getting a reduced sentence or even going into the witness protection program." Burke told him.

"Well let me think about this Sgt. and I'll let you know." Ryan said.

"Ok, but don't wait too long, because some of your former "coffin cops" are also ready to spill the beans on you." Burke told him.

Ryan stared at him, and then thought about Rossi and Fallon, and all of the other coffin cops. Who would be the one to rat them out.

Tony tells Frankie that he's complied with every request that the Columbo family has made, but still wants their list of cops who are on their payroll.

"Sure, sure" Frankie tells him." I'll get them for you tomorrow and I'll give it to Barbara to give to you."

"Thank you Frankie." Tony tells him and shakes hands with him.

The next day, true to Frankie's word, Barbara gives Tony the list of cops and there are almost 200 cops in almost every precinct in the city.

"IAD is going to go ape-shit." Longo tells Tony." It's all the way from PO's, SGT's. Loo's, even Caps and DI's"

Pete Ryan agrees to tell IAD about the coffin cops and the Columbo mob. With all of his testimony and the list of the cops that Tony got from Frankie, they are prepared to go to the DA and arrest everybody.

CHAPTER 21

Claire finds out about Barbara and also that she is pregnant. She goes ballistic when she sees him.

"Tony, I just found out that you are seeing a Mafia princess and that you got her pregnant!"

She screamed at him.

"Claire," Tony said," I wanted to tell you that I was undercover trying to get info on some dirty cops and I knew this woman from, the old neighborhood who was married to a Mafioso that was killed."

"And you fucked her many times!" she screamed at him.

"Hold on, hold on," Tony tried to explain. "She wanted me to be a surrogate since her husband was dead, and if I would, she would get me the info on the dirty cops."

"But you fucked her repeatedly!!" Claire kept screaming at him," and now she is pregnant."

"Yes, that's what I told you, it was the only way that she'd help us get these dirty cops." Tony tried to explain.

"And how many times did you fuck her?" Claire screamed at him.

"Well," Tony said," it was a few times , because we didn't know if she got pregnant."

"You're a piece of shit!" Claire told him." Get out! I can't believe that you did this."

"Honey wait," Tony told her," I couldn't tell you because I knew that this was the way that you'd be acting."

"Well guess what Tony, I'm pregnant now too. I was going to tell you, but not after this." She said.

"Well try to calm down. I know that you're upset, but I did it in the line of duty." He told her.

"Yeah," Claire said sarcastically, "you didn't enjoy it either, huh?"

"No, I see that whatever I say that you're not going to listen to me." He said. "I'll call you late when you've calmed down."

"Don't bother." She said.

Tony left her apartment wondering how she found out about Barbara. Probably one of the coffin cops told her. Tony calls Angela and says that he has to see her.

He tells her about what happened and asks her what he can do.

"I don't know babe," Angela tells him,"but Claire is really hot about this."

Tony says to her," You've got to intercede for me in my behalf."

He embraces her, and kisses her and all of a sudden she's caressing his cock and he's touching her breasts. In a minute he takes her and fucks her. Unbeknownst to them, he has just impregnated her with twins also.

Afterwards, Tony is riding back to his apartment, and thinks, what is he going to do with 3 women and 6 kids. Move to Utah and become a polygamist? Nah, he has too much of Brooklyn in him. He guesses that he'll just have to pay child support and be a daddy to them all. But then, he thinks, it won't be too bad. At least he'll be able to fuck each one of them. A horn dog to the end!

THE END

Made in the USA
Middletown, DE
04 September 2017